"If we follow the course of action you suggest, Bellenzor, this world will soon be as cold and lifeless as a stone."

"I want to save the Empire, Valimagdon. I want to end the raids, and the battles, and the killing."

"So you would replace the fumbling blows of soldiers with the all-destroying stroke of magic. You would kill to end killing."

Bellenzor sat motionless, staring into the fire. Valimagdon watched but did not speak. The chamber darkened and grew chill. At last Bellenzor rose and bowed respectfully to the elder.

"You are wiser than I, Valimagdon, and your judgment in these matters is superior. I will expunge all such thoughts from my mind," he said.

Ace Science Fiction and Fantasy Books by John Morressy

THE MANSIONS OF SPACE
THE TIME OF THE ANNIHILATOR

The IRON ANGEL Trilogy

IRONBRAND
GRAYMANTLE
KINGSBANE

THE TIME OF THE ANNIHILATOR

JOHN MORRESSY

ACE FANTASY BOOKS
NEW YORK

THE TIME OF THE ANNIHILATOR

An Ace Fantasy Book/published by arrangement with
the author

PRINTING HISTORY
Ace Original/August 1985

All rights reserved.
Copyright © 1985 by John Morressy
Cover art by Kevin Eugene Johnson
This book may not be reproduced in whole or in part,
by mimeograph or any other means, without permission.
For information address: The Berkley Publishing Group,
200 Madison Avenue, New York, New York 10016.

ISBN: 0-441-81191-4

Ace Fantasy Books are published by The Berkley Publishing Group,
200 Madison Avenue, New York, New York 10016.
PRINTED IN THE UNITED STATES OF AMERICA

*For Sharon Jarvis,
who started it all*

PART ONE

1

The Runaways

They left their refuge at the setting of the moon. By the first light of morning they were near the high pass that marked the boundary of the Empire.

Mist obscured all that lay around them. The woman hesitated, and fell behind. The man turned and held out his hand.

"We're nearly there, Moarra. Don't lose courage now," he said. His breath plumed in the early chill.

She looked over her shoulder at the way they had come. The mist lay like a mantle over forest and mountainside, and she could see nothing but white wisps and dim gray forms.

"We'll be on the other side before midday, and then we'll be safe. No one will follow us beyond the pass, Moarra," he said.

She moved forward with slow reluctant steps. She took his gloved hand, but went no farther. "We may be safe from pursuers, but there are other dangers, Gariel, worse dangers. I've heard stories in the city, and they frighten me."

"They were told by frightened men and women who only repeated things they themselves had heard. It's no worse out here than elsewhere," he said confidently.

"Evil things are out there," she said.

"I can hold back the powers of wood and mountain. There's nothing to fear."

"But the raiding parties—the marauders. We know how cruel they can be."

"We know what we're told, Moarra. More stories. I've never met anyone who actually witnessed a raid by the enemy. It may all be a lie."

"But if it's true...."

"Even if it's true, we have nothing to fear. Remember, I'm a smith. If there are marauders, they'll do no harm to a smith. They'll need me to repair their weapons and their armor. And you have healing skills that are precious to such men. There's nothing for us to fear, Moarra. I wouldn't take you into danger."

She looked up at him earnestly and clutched his hand tightly in both of hers. "You're giving up everything for me. You can never go back. Are you certain, Gariel?"

He drew her to him, and as they embraced he said, "I'd gladly give up everything for you. Life itself, if it came to that. But in truth, I've given up nothing. It's you who make the sacrifice."

"You could have been one of the Thirty-three. You would have been chosen, Gariel, I know you would! Even now, if you returned...."

She felt his firm hands on her shoulders. "My brother is already twice as good a wizard as I could ever hope to be. That's the life he craves, and he's welcome to the power, and all the honor and glory that go with it—and all the loneliness." He looked down into the face he loved; Moarra's dark eyes were wide with fear, her pale cheeks reddened by the raw chill. A tendril of jet-black hair had come free from the confining hood and lay along her cheek, held there by the dampness of the morning air. He drew the glove from his big calloused hand and brushed the strand away gently with his fingertips.

"That isn't true," she protested. "Bellenzor works hard, but you could be better than any of them. You could be a great wizard."

"A wizard must foreswear all love but the love of magic. I could never do that, Moarra. I want nothing but to live my life at your side."

"And will you always feel that way?"

"I will, Moarra, always. Do you doubt me?"

"No, no," she said passionately, throwing her arms around his neck and clinging tightly to him. "I love you so much, Gariel. I can't believe such happiness will last."

"We will make it last. Before we left, I sacrificed to the Protector. Ebanor will watch over us."

She looked up with a sudden smile. "I sacrificed to the Nurturer."

"Then Ilveraine protects us, too. Forget your fears." He kissed her and held her close, then he cried, "Look! If ever there was a sign...!"

The wind was rising, chasing the mist and blowing scattered flakes before it. They both knew enough of weather signs to tell that a heavy snow would soon be falling, covering their tracks and, in all likelihood, preventing any pursuit until the spring.

"Ilveraine is our mother!" Moarra cried joyously.

"Do you believe now that our happiness will last?"

"I do, Gariel!"

"Then come," he said, starting up the mountainside to the dark wall that loomed through the rack of driven mist. "Let's be through the pass before the storm arrives. Once we're on the other side, our new life will really begin!"

Six days later, at the fall of dusk, they reached their journey's end, a nameless hamlet on the sunward slope of a wide valley. A broad, shallow river, still unfrozen, ran through the valley, with a ford just below the hamlet. By the ford stood five poles, in a quincunx. Leather pouches hung from three of the poles; one bore the skull of a bird with markings on it; the fifth pole was notched with symbols. Moarra, at the sight of them, stopped and turned to Gariel.

"What are they?" she asked fearfully.

"Protection against the things that are said to dwell in the woods," he replied.

"Are there really things in the woods?"

"They believe there are. We've seen none, so I don't share their belief, but I won't mock it."

Gariel and Moarra crossed and made their way up the gentle slope. Nine substantial, well-made houses stood before them, and a cluster of outbuildings huddled around each house. Gariel, who had been here before, knew that seven more homesteads lay beyond the rise. There was no other settlement within twelve days' travel.

"This is where we're going to live, Moarra. Do you like it?" he asked.

"It looks like a quiet place."

"The people keep to themselves. They're not unfriendly, but they like their privacy."

"I don't mind that," she said, squeezing his hand.

The rhythmic ring of metal on metal came to them from ahead. Gariel pointed to a big house of pale wood with thick black straps binding its corners, and long black hinges fixing door and window shutters. A bright glow streamed from one side of the house.

"That's Yotan's forge. He's at work still," said Gariel, leading the way to the iron-trimmed house.

They rounded the corner of the house and stopped in a little graveled courtyard, at the open doors of a forge. Light and warmth reached out to them, as if to welcome them after their long journey. Gariel shouted, and a huge figure inside peered out for a moment and then waved them in.

"I thought you'd be coming about this time, lad," said the smith. "This is your wife, is it?"

He looked at Moarra in frank appraisal. She returned his scrutiny calmly and patiently, with an air of complete self-possession. Indeed, she acted as if she were wearing royal robes and a diadem, rather than shapeless, mud-spattered, travelworn furs.

"She's as pretty as you described her," Yotan said solemnly.

"Thank you," Moarra said, smiling at him.

Yotan's expression did not change. In the same judgmental manner, he said in his deep rumbling voice, "She does not look strong."

Moarra's brow rose for an instant, but she showed no other reaction to his words. Coolly, she said, "I was strong enough to travel here."

"That is true," Yotan conceded.

"Then how much more strength is needed?"

"What I mean is . . . you are a small woman."

Moarra laughed. It was a laugh of pure delight, so patently free of malice or mockery that Gariel joined her, and even

Yotan found himself grinning, though he was not completely certain why.

"Yotan," said Moarra, "next to you, all women are small, and all men, as well."

The smith nodded slowly, as if giving his considered assent. He was in truth a gigantic man. Standing half a head over Gariel, he was twice Gariel's girth. His forearms were thicker than Moarra's waist, and his hands were like trenchers.

"That is true," he said thoughtfully.

"Sometimes it's good to be small—remember the story of Ilveraine and the bees," said Moarra.

Yotan pondered her words for a time, rubbing his white-stubbled chin with the back of his hand, and at last said, "A good story." Then, as if everything were settled, he said, "You will have the big house as your own. I will stay in the small house across the yard."

"We don't want to take your house from you," said Gariel.

"That house is too big for one. Too many memories in there. In the small house, I can look out my window and see the forge. The big house is yours."

"Thank you, Yotan," Moarra said.

"You will keep house and cook for us," said Yotan. He turned away from Moarra, and thus missed the sudden anger that flared in her eyes at his words and manner. To Gariel, he said, "You will help me at the forge, and in return, I will teach you all I know. When I think you ready, I will sell you the forge and the lands at the price we agreed on. Is this still your thinking?"

"It is, Yotan."

"Then it will be so. Go in, now. There is food in the kitchen, and you are hungry from travel."

Once inside, Moarra turned to Gariel and said angrily, "You never told me that I was to be a servant. Why did you promise that I would be housekeeper?"

"Yotan said nothing about it when I was here before. He must have assumed that you'd do it, because that's what the women do here."

"I have no idea how to cook or keep house, Gariel! I was never taught such things. I'm a councilor's daughter—I was taught to heal, not to cook!"

"You'll have to try, Moarra. I'll help you all I can. We must not do anything that might make these people suspicious of us."

"You said that they keep to themselves."

"So they do. But they can't help noticing a newcomer whose ways are different from theirs."

"That would not matter unless someone came from the city and asked about us. Tell me truthfully, Gariel—you do fear pursuit, even here, don't you?"

He took her hands in his and said earnestly, "No. I don't think anyone will find us here except by accident. But if someone from the settlement should travel to the Empire—it's not likely to happen, but it's possible—and should happen to mention a newcomer who's a trained healer but doesn't know things all the other women know... well, that might remind people of a councilor's daughter who ran away with an apprentice mage."

"With a mage," she corrected him.

Smiling, he said, "Not quite. A very minor fledgling mage, at best."

"A mage, nonetheless. And I'm very glad for it. We may need all your magic to keep us safe."

"They won't seek us for long, Moarra. Once they're certain we haven't gone over to the enemy, they'll forget about us. We'll be safe by the end of next winter."

Gariel's prediction seemed accurate. They settled down to an uneventful life in this remote hamlet, and found it a better and happier life than they had hoped to enjoy so far from their birthplace in the White City at the heart of the Empire.

They had cause to be grateful for the ancient tradition that required every man and woman of the White City, regardless of birth or rank, to master some practical skill. All those who guided the course of the Empire, and those who used their magical knowledge to shield it from the enemies who ringed it, even the Thirty-three themselves, had once stood at a forge or a carpenter's bench, or turned a potter's wheel, or helped to heal the sick, or worked with wood, stone, or glass. It was believed—and wisely so, it seemed—that one who has labored hard to create some useful or beautiful object, or to preserve the life of a fellow human being, was apt to govern more soundly than one who knew only theories.

Gariel had been a willing and capable worker at a smith's forge all during his studies under the mage Valimagdon. Now, working from first light until long after sundown at Yotan's forge, he soon matched the skill of his master and went on to surpass him. His strength increased with his skill, and while he never equaled Yotan in strength, his youthful stamina enabled him to work on at the forge when the older man became exhausted.

Moarra, out of caution, did not practice her healing skills openly. Nevertheless, she gathered herbs and simples and prepared a little stock of medications for her own household. Yotan was particularly grateful for a salve she made that healed burns in a single day, and an ointment that eased the stiffness in his aging legs and shoulders.

The snows of that first winter fell frequently and lay deep. The spring thaw, and heavy rains, left Gariel and Moarra assured that all trace of their passage had been effaced. A second and third winter passed with no visitors from outside, and they felt safe from pursuit at last.

At the end of their third summer in the little settlement, their second child was born. Yotan, whose own children had left home long ago and never returned, became like a grandfather to the son and daughter of Gariel and Moarra. The pale house with the black iron trim was a happy home, and the forge became a common meeting place for the community.

Early one autumn day visitors came: five armed men, hard-featured and weather-browned, with quick observant eyes and a taciturn manner. They purchased a supply of food and drink and warm clothing, and paid generously with gold and silver coins from distant kingdoms. Two of them came to the forge where Yotan and Gariel were working. The neighboring woodsman Strolsse and his oldest son were there, observing Gariel's work on an axe-head of unfamiliar design.

After a guarded exchange of greetings, one of the visitors, a lean red-bearded man in a dark cloak, asked, "Do you make weapons at this forge?"

Yotan looked at the two men and paused for a time before replying, "Why would I forge weapons? This is no camp of warriors."

The visitors exchanged a knowing smile. The cloaked man looked at the other settlers and said, "Do you eat no meat, then, and wear no skins? Or do the animals come from the forest and lie on your doorsteps to be butchered?"

"We make spears and arrows for hunting," Yotan said, "but those are not weapons, they are tools."

"Call them whatever you like, they're what I want. We mean to do some hunting before the snows come."

"You have weapons."

The visitor threw back his cloak and slapped the hilt of his sword. "This is meant for other use. It's no proper hunting weapon. Come, show me what you have. If it's to our liking, we'll buy it all and pay you well."

"I have no weapons to sell," said Yotan, shaking his grizzled head. Gariel, knowing of the stock of boar-spears and broad arrowheads in the loft, was surprised, but he said nothing.

The cloaked man held out a pouch of soft leather and bounced it in his hand so it clinked for all to hear. "I've paid in good coin for provisions, and I'll pay in the same for hunting weapons. Gold adraxes and double-draxes from the Kingdom of the Three Shores; mercils from the Mountain League; even jewels, if you prefer."

"You are generous, but I have no weapons to sell."

"If you're so scant of weapons, how do you protect your homes?" the second visitor demanded.

"We have no enemies," said Yotan.

"No enemies? Nothing to fear?"

"No," said the smith.

"I've heard that there are dangerous things in the wood, and in the mountains beyond."

"Weapons are useless against such beings. We propitiate them, and we fear no human enemies."

The second visitor seemed about to speak, but the cloaked man restrained him with a gesture. Smiling, he said, "Well, then, you have no need for weapons. You're fortunate, all of you, to live without enemies in such troubled times."

The visitors left, and Yotan watched until they disappeared into the forest on the far side of the river. He turned to the others, and his face was grave.

"They will attack soon. We must prepare," he said.

"How do you know this?" Gariel asked.

"Strolsse will tell you how we know."

Nodding, Strolsse said grimly, "They will attack. It is certain. In the winter without snows, a man came to us. He was badly hurt, and he died soon after reaching us, but he told his story before he died." He paused, and with lowered eyes, went on, "Strangers dressed as warriors had come to his village. They claimed to be hunters. They bought provisions, and they paid generously for them. When they offered great sums for weapons, the villagers gladly sold all they had. Two days later the strangers returned with a score of companions. They stripped the village bare, killed everyone they found, and burnt the buildings."

"Why did they kill? I thought the raiders took prisoners as slaves."

"These raiders were troops of the Empire. They claimed that the village was an outpost of the enemy," Strolsse replied.

"The men we saw were not from the Empire," Gariel said flatly.

"Does it matter? If they're soldiers of the Eastern Alliance, they may do the same to us and claim that we are an outpost of the Empire. If they want to kill and destroy, any reason will serve them. We must prepare," Yotan said.

By nightfall, every household had been alerted and was arming for defense. Yotan was their leader, by unanimous consent. He made the rounds of the settlement with Gariel at his side, and when they returned to the forge, his expression was solemn.

"When do you think they will attack?" Gariel asked.

"Pray that they do not."

"Why not? There are fifty-two of us, all armed and ready. We can stand off a score of raiders."

"Half the fifty-two are old men or boys. They've never fought for their lives before. A score of experienced soldiers will overcome us."

"Do you really think so?"

"I do, lad. Oh, we'll leave our mark on them. It will be long before they make another raid, and many will be buried here. That's why they tried to deceive us into leaving ourselves weaponless. But they will defeat us in the end," Yotan said matter-of-factly.

Gariel still possessed the power to prevent such an outcome. He had not practiced magic of any kind since his departure from the White City, but such knowledge was never lost. For the sake of Moarra and their children, he had concealed it; now, for their sakes and for their home and their neighbors, he knew that he must use his power. All that remained to be decided was the choice of means.

"I have an idea, Yotan," he said. "The night is clear, and the moon is just past full. If I can find the soldiers' camp, I may be able to learn their plan of attack. We could prepare an ambush, and take them completely by surprise. We could beat them."

The old smith was silent for a time, pondering this suggestion, and at last he said, "It would be very dangerous for you. Their camp would be well guarded."

"It's the only chance we have. I must try."

Reluctantly, Yotan said, "That is true."

"I'll go as soon as I've said goodbye to Moarra."

"Wait," said Yotan. He went to a chest in the corner of the forge and threw back the lid. He rummaged in it for a moment, then removed a bundle which he proceeded to unwrap from its covering of soft leather to reveal a short sword about the length of a man's arm from elbow to outstretched fingertips. He drew it from its dark sheath to reveal a blade as black as charcoal. "You will need a blade like this," he said, sheathing the weapon and handing it to Gariel.

"Thanks, Yotan. I'll bring it back to you."

Moarra was still awake when he entered the house. He sniffed the air and knew what she was about before he entered the kitchen, where healing salves were in preparation.

"It appears we've reached the same decision independently," he said as she looked up.

She hesitated, momentarily puzzled by his words, then said, "Your magic! You're going to use your magic against those men, aren't you?"

"Yes. If I succeed, you won't have to use your healing knowledge."

"Can you still remember, Gariel? It's been a long time."

"I'm going to use a very simple spell to confuse them and disturb their memories. I remember it well."

Moarra rose and put her arms around his neck. "You'll have to go among them to do that. Be very careful, Gariel."

He kissed her and whispered, "I will be back to you, Moarra."

• • •

THE TIME OF THE ANNIHILATOR 13

Once out of sight of the village, Gariel drew a pouch from inside his belt and took out a pinch of dark powder. Murmuring a potent phrase, he threw the powder into the air. It hung motionless for a time, then it gathered in upon itself and began to glow with a faint blue light and move into the forest. He followed.

The light led him on at a good pace for about three great-marks, and then it vanished. Faintly, far ahead, he saw the gleam of a campfire. His quarry was close at hand. He began to call out, and moved noisily toward the fire. A harsh voice gave challenge, and he came up against a man with a pike, which he leveled at Gariel's chest. Almost at the same moment he felt the prick of a spearpoint between his shoulders.

"What are you doing here?" demanded the man facing him.

"I've come from the settlement. I want to talk to the men who visited us today."

"What have you got to say to us?"

"Those men wanted to buy weapons. I have weapons to sell."

"I see no weapons."

"They're at the forge. I could not bring them with me."

"Let's take him to Omir," said the man behind Gariel.

The other guard consented. He stepped to one side. Gariel felt a sharp jab in the back and lurched ahead. A laugh came from behind him.

"Just walk straight on, and don't try to run. Head for the fire," said the unseen voice.

The fire glowed at the center of the little camp. In the firelight, Gariel could distinguish sleeping forms on the ground, rolled in their cloaks. Others stood near the fire, one of them the cloaked man who had come to the forge. Gariel counted eleven in all. Allowing for guards, and for sleepers obscured by shadow, the band would number from twenty-five to thirty.

"Stop here," his guard said, and Gariel obeyed. "Here's a man from the settlement, Omir, come to sell us weapons," the guard called out.

The cloaked man turned from his companions and stepped close to Gariel. He studied Gariel's face for a time, then pointed and said, "You were at the forge."

"I was."

"You had no weapons to sell us then. Have you discovered

some?" the man asked, and those around him laughed.

"We have weapons, but the old smith, my master, would not allow us to sell them. Some of us convinced him that he was wrong, and I was sent to find you."

"You're a good tracker, to find us in the dark."

"I know this forest well. I've often hunted here."

"You hunt here? I thought you people feared the things that live in the forest."

"There are places we never go, and other places where we can hunt in safety."

Omir nodded absently and looked closely at Gariel, as if appraising him. "Why didn't the old man want to sell us weapons?"

"He's afraid. He thinks we need them to defend ourselves."

"Against what? Your settlement doesn't look as though it's ever been attacked."

"It hasn't. He's suspicious, that's all. He thought that you . . ." Gariel fell silent, looking down at the ground as if embarrassed.

"Us? He thought we'd attack?"

"Yes."

"It would serve the old fool right if we did. We paid in good coin for what we wanted. What right does some crazy old man have to think we're marauders?" Omir said hotly.

"He's heard stories of raids. They've made him suspect all strangers."

"It's the troops of the Empire who do the killing and the looting. We serve the Eastern Alliance. We're soldiers, not brigands."

"That's what we told the old smith. Now he's willing to sell you all the weapons we can spare."

"What have you got?"

Gariel threw back his cloak and reached for the short sword Yotan had given him. At once strong hands gripped his arms, and he felt Omir's dagger at his throat.

"Don't draw a sword in my presence," Omir said. "I can be suspicious, too, stranger."

"I only wished to show you what we have. Take it yourself, and examine it."

Omir drew the sword from its sheath, and his men released Gariel. As Omir inspected the dark blade, the others drew around him and expressed their admiration.

"It's a good blade. How many have you?"

"We can sell you one for each of your men," Gariel replied.

"How many men do you think I have?"

"Oh, about... twelve or fourteen."

"A good guess, stranger, but too generous. There's hardly enough of us to attack a settlement half the size of yours," Omir said, smiling, as he handed the short sword back to Gariel. "What else can you sell us?"

"Spears for each man. Arrowheads, good iron ones, thirty score of them."

"Good. What else?"

Gariel spread his hands wide. "That's all we have. We're not soldiers."

"Be glad you don't have to be. It's a hard life. A lot harder than farming, that's certain," said Omir. He looked up and studied the stars for a moment, then said to Gariel, "We'll go back with you at first light. Get some sleep while you can. There's room here by the fire."

Gariel heaped together some of the fir branches that lay piled nearby and rolled himself in his cloak on the makeshift mattress. He closed his eyes and lay still and soon was in a deep sleep.

While his body slept, the spirit within him came forth and moved among the men of the encampment, passing silent and unperceived through their minds. He worked quickly, as a master artist, with swift strokes too subtle to be noticed except in their final effect, changes a merely pleasing picture into a living scene. When he returned to his body at last, each in the little band of men was changed in one small way. Those who slept had experienced a troubled dream; the waking had felt an instant of confusion that left them blinking and looking about like children suddenly aware of unfamiliar surroundings; all had lost their memory of the settlement and the plan to destroy it the following day—for such was the thought Gariel had found in the mind of every man.

Now, in place of their thoughts of conquest, they felt a vague threat, as of something evil lying all around them, like the mist of the forest, waiting to enfold them and do them harm. They remembered tales, and warnings, and they looked fearfully into the darkness beyond the fireglow. Each man, from

Omir to the youngest recruit in the band, wanted only the coming of light so he might hasten from this place.

Gariel opened his eyes cautiously. He was much weakened by the effort of working magic, and he lay still for a moment, sensing the fear that twittered in the air of the camp, before intoning one final brief spell to obscure him from the eyes of those around him. He was already expunged from their memories.

He rose unsteadily and passed through their midst and into the darkness. As he leaned against a tree, breathing deeply, aching in every bone and sinew, the blue light came to life before him. He trudged homeward in its wake, sometimes stumbling and falling in his utter exhaustion, and reached his home just before sunrise.

Yotan was waiting with Moarra. Gariel staggered and collapsed in the doorway, and they were at his side in an instant.

"Oh, Gariel, have they harmed you?" Moarra cried, cushioning his head while she unfastened his shirt.

"No. Just tired... exhausted," he gasped.

She knew at once that he had used his magic. The anxiety vanished from her features, and she closed her eyes and breathed a deep sigh of relief.

"He's run all the way," said Yotan, and they did not contradict him. "What news, lad? Are they coming?"

"They've gone away."

"Gone? Where did they go, lad?"

"Toward the mountains. They took the loggers' trail. They left in a great hurry."

"Did you see them?"

Gariel shook his head. "Found their camp. Fire was still burning. I followed their trail... about two greatmarks. They were moving fast."

"It sounds almost as if they were scared off. But what could have scared a band of armed men?" Yotan said, looking to Moarra in perplexity. "They'd be more than a match for anything that lives in the forest."

"Maybe there are worse things in the forest than you know about," she said.

"What things?"

"I've heard tales of moss giants stronger than thirty men. And of the whisperers. It's said that nothing can resist the whisperers... they lure men off, into the forest, and they're never seen again."

Yotan's eyes grew wide. "I've heard of such things, but I never believed. Could it be?"

"Something made them flee, Yotan," she said. "We may never know what it was, but we should be grateful."

"We are, Moarra. It saved our settlement, and all our lives."

The old smith helped Gariel to the bedroom, where he sprawled across the bed helplessly. Despite the mildness of the autumn dawn, he was shivering, and Moarra drew a coverlet over him. When Yotan, much bemused, had left to spread the news of their deliverance, she sat at Gariel's side, rubbing his cold hands.

"We're safe, Moarra," he said in a weak, weary voice. "They'll remember nothing of the settlement... and they'll always think of the forest with fear."

"Our secret is safe, too. Yotan suspects nothing."

"That's the best part of all," he said, smiling.

"But you paid a heavy price, Gariel. I never saw you so weak. I didn't know that magic demanded so much."

"I'm out of practice, that's all. But now... now I can forget about magic, Moarra. We're safe at last."

2

The Progress of Bellenzor

When word of his brother's defection reached Bellenzor, he went at once to the chambers of the wizard Valimagdon. Once admitted, he prostrated himself before his master.

"Come, Bellenzor, rise up and speak to me on your feet," said Valimagdon, helping the young man up.

"Master, I am shamed," Bellenzor said with bowed head.

"What shameful thing have you done?"

"My brother has abandoned his calling and fled from the city with a daughter of the family Venturan."

"If there is shame in this, it belongs to your brother, not to you. Gariel is a grown man, responsible for his own acts. You are neither his master nor his father."

"But he has brought shame upon me!" Bellenzor cried, looking up at the old wizard with pain in his dark eyes.

"Then you are too easily shamed," said Valimagdon.

Bellenzor was silent for a moment, then he lowered his eyes once again and softly said, "I am corrected, Master."

"Good. Now, hear me, Bellenzor. Sometimes, people close to us will do things we consider harmful, or even wicked, and we will have neither the power nor the right to stop them. This is a hard lesson to learn, but a necessary one. What Gariel

THE TIME OF THE ANNIHILATOR 19

has done, I must add, is truly neither harmful nor wicked."

Bellenzor looked up quickly, astonished by these words. The old wizard held him silent with a gesture and went on, "I foresaw that it might happen. Moarra, youngest daughter of the Venturan, is uncommonly beautiful, and of great goodness and wisdom. Your brother might make her happy, and find happiness himself with her. Is there such shame in that?"

"For a commoner, there is not. But Gariel might have been one of the Thirty-three. There is shame in denying a high destiny in order to live an ordinary life."

"You are too stern, Bellenzor. Gariel had the promise, but not all who have the promise have the dedication. I sometimes thought that he was happier at the forge than at his studies. I never had that feeling with you. You were a fine potter, but you never looked upon your pottery as anything but a duty that took you from your real work."

"True, Master. I obeyed the tradition only because I had no choice," said Bellenzor.

"Perhaps Gariel, too, had no choice. Can you understand that?"

With disarming frankness, Bellenzor replied, "I confess that I cannot, Master. But I will endeavor to understand such things."

"Do so, Bellenzor. Have you anything more you wish to say?"

"I have a question, Master."

"Ask it, then."

"What effect is my brother's action to have on me?"

"As much as you allow it to have, neither more nor less. The only shame you need fear is the shame you bring upon yourself. Remember that, Bellenzor."

"I will, Master."

"Now return to your studies, and fix your mind on them. You have much work ahead."

Bellenzor bowed, turned, and made his way from the dark chamber. Valimagdon looked at his retreating back and smiled to himself. In all his long service as Master of Apprentices, he had never seen two brothers so equally gifted with the promise of magical skill and so thoroughly different in all other ways as Bellenzor and Gariel.

Valimagdon rose, and drawing his cloak close around him he went to his balcony. There he stood for a time in thought, looking down on the imperial city whose white walls shone brightly in the light of a moon just past full. It was a lovely city, one of the great works of man, and he took satisfaction from the knowledge that he had helped keep it safe from its enemies for more than a hundred winters.

The threats were growing more severe of late, and he felt the strain of increased effort. But this was his life's work, and he had long ago dedicated himself to it without reservation. He would use his magic in the service of the Empire until he was too weak to be of use, and then another would replace him among the Thirty-three. The city would be safe; the Empire would prevail.

For some time, he had looked upon Bellenzor and Gariel as the most likely candidates to succeed him in that distant day when his powers failed. The other apprentices, even the most dedicated, could not approach their skill. Now the need to choose between them had been taken out of his hands.

Bellenzor was a cold and distant man whose chief emotion seemed to be pride; not the jostling, boasting pride of the mob, but the silent stony pride of the man to whom failure is more to be feared than death. Tall and slender of frame, he was pale from a lifetime of study, but he had resources of will that surpassed mere bodily strength. He could drive himself to the limit of endurance, and then force himself to work on when all others had fallen away.

For Bellenzor, the subtle art of magic was the only worthy pursuit, and he pursued it with all his heart. He already possessed powers that the masters looked upon with high regard and his fellow apprentices envied. He was well aware of his standing, and yet he could not rest. His pride fretted him, like a splinter that drove ever deeper under the skin and could not be removed. His younger brother's defection had come as a personal blow.

Gariel was very different from Bellenzor. At a glance, one would not imagine them to be brothers, for Gariel, though almost as tall as his brother, was twice as broad, with a smith's deep chest and burly arms. He was much less serious-minded, capable of schoolboy pranks and hearty laughter. As his most recent action showed, he was also capable of a love that quite overcame all obstacles. But in spite of the differences, anyone who saw the two brothers side by side would notice that they had the same quick eyes, Bellenzor's of a brown so deep as to be almost black, Gariel's gray as cold iron, and that they both had a born affinity for magic.

Now Gariel had abandoned the life of a wizard, with its austere and solitary rewards, to be a husband and a father in the world of men and women, where work was hard, feelings were strong, time was short, and the powers that moved in the realms beyond this life were left unmentioned except in prayer. Valimagdon was disappointed, for he had seen rare promise in the young man, but he knew that the wizard's calling could not be forced on anyone. Gariel had made his choice, and Valimagdon wished him well. He knew that Gariel and Moarra might need all his good wishes and all the magic at Gariel's command, as well as a great deal of luck, if they were to find a safe haven in which to live out their lives.

The rulers of the White City at the heart of the Empire did not permit unplanned marriages among the ranks of the councilors, nor did they allow anyone from the ruling families to leave the Empire. The fugitive couple would be pursued. If found, their punishment would be severe. Any suspicion of contact with the enemy would render them liable to death. And even if they escaped their pursuers, life in the lands beyond the Empire was hard and dangerous. The troops of the Nine Lords were savages to begin with, and had grown ever more brutal as the long war dragged on. And though he reflected on it with sadness and spoke of it to no one, Valimagdon knew that the rangers of the Empire could match their enemy in barbarity.

The thought of the ongoing war recalled Bellenzor to his mind, for he knew that Bellenzor would soon play a greater role in it. Valimagdon had recommended his early installation as a master, and he did not doubt that in time—and not a very long time—the young man would be chosen to join the elite group whose power guided the Empire and protected it against all enemies.

The Empire had long been an empire in name only. The last bearer of the royal blood, a sickly, half-mad boy, had died before Valimagdon's birth. In the absence of a claimant, his council had assumed the rule. Over the years, the council had evolved into the Thirty-three.

To be called to the Thirty-three was a great honor and an

awesome responsibility. Only the wisest, the strongest, and the best were chosen, and all power was placed in their hands; in return, they gave their lives to the Empire and served it until death.

Perhaps, thought Valimagdon with a sigh, all had worked out well, after all. Gariel, who could love one woman so deeply and enjoy such love in return, might not be able to love the faceless multitudes of the Empire with such intensity. Gariel had chosen to seek his happiness in the here and now; the Thirty-three could sacrifice the present for the future. Bellenzor, whose love was only for the perfection of his art, was surely better suited to be Master of Apprentices, chief wizard among the Thirty-three, ultimate safeguard of the Empire.

Valimagdon gazed out over the gleaming rooftops. His powers assured him that all was well tonight within the walls, in the fields and forests nearby, and in the distant mountains, even to the limits of the Empire. The enemy was far away. But the aging wizard knew that the power of the Nine Lords was on the rise, and the threat was growing.

The Nine Lords, too, were no more than a name now. The original nine warlords from the outskirts of the Empire were long dead, their names forgotten, their cause of rebellion unknown. All that survived was the enmity that had passed from generation to generation. On one side stood the Empire, the White City, the Thirty-three; against them stood the alliance of the Nine Lords, the league, the outlanders, the barbarians. Names were meaningless. To each, the other was the enemy, and the long war went on, lifetime after lifetime.

Valimagdon had come to feel that a crisis was near, but he could ascertain nothing. His spies and his magic told him nothing, yet the feeling remained, troubling him even in the calm of this night. He raised his eyes and murmured a prayer to Ebanor, the Protector, then turned and reentered his study, where he worked until the early light.

Before the first snow fell, Bellenzor wore the red cloak of a master. He became Valimagdon's close confidant, and assisted the elder wizard in the selection and training of apprentices. Three winters later, when death left a vacancy in the ranks of the Thirty-three, he was the unanimous choice to fill the position. Such a rapid rise to eminence had seldom occurred in

THE TIME OF THE ANNIHILATOR

the history of the Empire, but Bellenzor's stature, even at a young age, was such that no one begrudged his fortune; indeed, there was rejoicing in the city when the word spread.

Valimagdon was particularly glad to welcome the younger wizard to the chambers of power. The enemy was becoming bolder, the defense of the Empire placing ever greater demands upon the Thirty-three. Bellenzor's mastery of magic and his inexhaustible reserves of energy were sorely needed.

Bellenzor had not mentioned his brother's name since the time of his disappearance. Valimagdon noticed this and formed his own opinion, but he kept his words for the proper occasion. One night, when they sat late in the council chamber after the others had left, weary from their mental exertions, he judged that the time had come to speak.

"I have not heard you speak of Gariel since the night you learned of his flight. Do you never think of him?" the older wizard asked.

"He is in my thoughts from time to time," Bellenzor replied.

"So infrequently?"

"I have little leisure to think on personal matters. The strength of the Eastern Alliance is growing. I must occupy my mind with our defense."

"Of course, and so must I. But I sometimes think that Gariel still has a great influence over you."

Bellenzor looked at him sharply, then lowered his gaze. "What do you mean?" he asked.

"When Gariel was still among us, you two were the best of the apprentices, but you were far more tenacious than he. Gariel could be distracted from his study of magic. You could not."

Bellenzor did not shift his gaze. "I often thought that Gariel had the quicker mind. My knowledge is deeper than his, but I have had to work harder to gain it," he said in a distant voice.

"No apprentice was ever more diligent. But since Gariel fled, your efforts seem to have doubled."

"My responsibilities are greater now."

"True. But could it also be that you are trying to do the work of Gariel, as well as your own? You saw his flight from the Empire as an act that shamed you—do you still feel that way, and allow your feelings to drive you beyond all reasonable limits?"

"I think not," Bellenzor said slowly. After a time, he added,

"And even if that were true, so much the better for the Empire if I work harder. Why are you concerned?"

"The war is beginning to go against us. Our hardest work lies ahead, and you will be needed more and more. You must conserve your strength."

Bellenzor looked at him and smiled drily. "Defending an empire is hard work, it is true."

"But worthwhile. Our magic saves lives."

Bellenzor seemed about to speak, but he shook his head and remained silent. After a time, however, he turned to the elder wizard and in a hesitant voice asked, "Can we hope to do no more, Valimagdon?"

"What more would you do?"

"End the war forever!" said Bellenzor, and his dark eyes glowed with unaccustomed passion. "Think of the lives that would save, and the great good it would accomplish!"

"Ending wars is the work of soldiers and councilors. Our work as wizards is to defend and protect the people of the Empire, to search out the enemy's plans and thwart them, to probe for his weaknesses. Our magic is not a sword, it is a shield to safeguard the common good."

"Perhaps the shield should become a sword."

"Your words confuse me, Bellenzor. To use our magic as a weapon of aggression would be a betrayal of all we believe in, yet you speak of it as something to be desired."

"I desire to end the war and save the Empire—and the enemy, as well—from further generations of suffering. Is that not safeguarding the common good? Would not that benefit all? It seems to me, Valimagdon, that by using our magic passively and defensively, by reacting to the enemy's initiatives and not acting forcefully to seize the initiative ourselves, we do harm and not good. If we were to use our magic to strike one crippling blow against the Eastern Alliance—a drought or a flood to destroy their food supplies, or a plague to decimate their army—we could end the war before spring," Bellenzor said fervidly. "We might end it in a single night!"

"The Nine Lords have wizards in their service, too," Valimagdon pointed out. "If we turned to the destructive use of magic, do you think they would hesitate to do the same?"

"It would be too late."

"Perhaps not. They are not fools. But if they were too late

to prevent us, it might be all the worse for the Empire. Instead of seeking victory, they would seek revenge. They would know no restraint."

"We could defend against any magic they know," Bellenzor insisted.

Valimagdon shook his head decisively and said, "Once the destructive power of magic is unleashed, it feeds upon itself. If we followed the course of action you suggest, Bellenzor — and it has been suggested by others, in earlier times — this world would soon be as cold and lifeless as a stone." Seeing the frustration on the younger man's face, he went on more gently, "Those who serve the Alliance know this, too. We dare not do such a thing ourselves, and we know that they dare not, either."

"It means little to be a wizard, then. For all our vaunted power, we are helpless to bring this war to an end. We can do no real good at all," Bellenzor said in a dull, dispirited voice.

"We have done much good, and will do more."

"I want to save the Empire, Valimagdon. I want to end the raids, and the battles, and the killing. This is the real good."

"So you would replace the fumbling blows of soldiers with the all-destroying stroke of magic. You would kill to end killing."

"Better small evils than greater ones."

"For those with our power, Bellenzor, no evil action is small. I know you are moved by love of the Empire and the desire to save it, but your way would lead to annihilation."

Bellenzor sat for a long time motionless, staring into the sinking fire. Valimagdon watched him closely but did not speak. The chamber darkened and grew chill. At last Bellenzor rose and bowed respectfully to his elder.

"You are wiser than I, Valimagdon, and your judgment in these matters is superior. I will expunge all such thoughts from my mind," he said.

For a time, the war continued a stalemate. The outlanders hurled their armies against the natural barriers and deep fortifications that ringed the Empire, and the defenses held. The troops of the Empire struck deep into the territories of the Alliance, but the objective of their raids seemed always to evade them. Wizards among the Thirty-three and in the high councils of the Alliance used their powers to confuse and misguide the enemy's forces, to obscure their objectives, and to sap the will of the opposing warriors. Seasons of warfare came and went with no perceptible change in the situation. Then, slowly, the tide of war began to turn against the Empire.

At first there were only minor setbacks, and some of these were offset by small victories for the Empire. But the surrender of a fortress on the southern frontier was a serious blow that fell without a warning. A long winter and a cold, rainy spring delayed planting; the heavy rains swelled the streams and washed away the roads, turning all the lowlands into a mire and impeding communication and movement. While the Empire repaired, the enemy advanced.

The summer was fiercely hot and dry. Crops withered in the sun-baked fields, and fears of shortage grew into rumors of famine. Three short bloody battles were fought in the autumn; two were inconclusive, but one was a clear victory for the outlanders. The rangers of the Empire withdrew to winter quarters with their confidence shaken.

In the White City, the Thirty-three worked almost without rest. Valimagdon immersed himself in his duties, ferreting out the subtlest spells of his counterparts in the Alliance, blunting them and turning them back upon their masters, weaving his own protective magics ever more tightly and impenetrably. Bellenzor drove himself harder than ever to assist the elder wizard and to meet his own special responsibilities for the safety of the city. When spring arrived, the Empire faced the conflict with renewed confidence; but by the first snowfall, the rangers had been driven back in the south and east.

With each passing winter the situation grew worse. The power of the Thirty-three seemed to be weakening. Throughout the Empire, people began to offer ever more fervent prayers to the children of the One and Eternal who guarded the ways of men.

The faith of the citizens of the Empire was ancient, predating the founding of the White City by immemorial ages. They believed in the One and Eternal whose name could never be known but who was called Sower of Worlds, Lifegiver, Author of Light.

This was their creator, an ineffable being whose nature it was to fill the great emptiness with peopled worlds. It voyaged eternally through the darkness that shrank before it, and became ever more remote from the concerns of its creation. But each world it spawned it placed under the protection of guardians of immense power and goodness, the gods of that world. These guardians were inferior to the Lifegiver only in the fact that they were created by its power and not self-originated. Their task was to protect the worlds in their care from the surrounding darkness that waited jealously to reclaim its sway.

The Lifegiver, it was believed, had placed three guardians over this world. Ilveraine, the Nurturer, watched over youth and growing things. Most often Ilveraine was represented as a woman holding a child, but the symbols of the wheatfield or the fruit-laden tree were common, too. The Illuminator, Teleon, was portrayed sometimes as man and sometimes as woman, but most often as a beam of light, a lantern, or the sun. Teleon guided all who sought wisdom. The Protector, Ebanor, stood between the Empire and its enemies. Ebanor's symbol was the armed figure and sometimes the tower, the wall, or the shield.

As news of the war worsened, Ebanor became the most favored object of worship. Even the Thirty-three, who looked upon Teleon as their particular guardian, included the name of Ebanor in their prayers.

In the midst of the resurgence of the old faith of the Empire there came interest in a new cult. Its deity was a being known as the Annihilator, and it was whispered that this cult had followers in the high places of the Empire—even, said some, among the Thirty-three.

The war dragged on. Men and women prayed for deliverance, but still the grip of the enemy closed ever more tightly.

3

The Summoning of Gariel

The autumn rain was light but steady. The graveled yard before the forge was dotted with pools, and the eaves dripped in an unvarying rhythm. Within, Gariel stood by the furnace, his eyes fixed on a glowing bar thrust deep into the coals. There was no sound but the soft pattering of rain, and the sigh and occasional rustle of the fire.

Gariel looked up and gave a slight start at the sight of a tall cloaked figure standing in the opening, just out of the rain. The visitor had arrived without a sound and now stood leaning on a long staff. No features could be distinguished under the shadow of the hood.

"You're welcome to warm yourself, stranger," Gariel said.

"Thank you," the newcomer replied in a faint voice, coming forward and extending pale, thin hands to the warmth.

"It's a poor night to travel. Have you come far?"

"From the White City."

"A long journey," said Gariel. He looked closely at the man, but neither form nor voice revealed anything. "Have you far yet to go?"

"I have found what I sought. I came for you, Gariel."

Gariel's fingers tightened instinctively on the hammer in his hand, but he relaxed almost immediately. A single weak old man, weary from travel, presented no danger; and if there were others waiting in the gathering dark outside, they would not take him by surprise as this one had.

The stranger pushed back the concealing hood. Gariel stared at the gaunt, wasted face framed by long white hair, and his gaze was caught by the pale green eyes that glittered under the deep brows.

"Valimagdon!" he cried.

"It is I, Gariel. And I must rest," said the old wizard, clutching at his staff to steady himself.

"Of course, Master," Gariel said as he hurried to the old man's side to offer his support. "Come, sit here on this bench. I'll draw it closer to the fire, so you'll be warm. Take off that wet cloak, and wear mine."

He took Valimagdon's dripping cloak and spread it before the forge to dry. The old man pulled Gariel's cloak close about him and hunched forward to the heat of the coals. His head was bowed, his eyes shut. His deep slow breathing was the breathing of one in pain.

"I live in the small house just across the courtyard," said Gariel, drawing a blanket over the wizard's narrow shoulders, atop the cloak. "I'll build up the fire, and when you feel ready we can go inside. You can eat and have a good long sleep."

"There's no time."

"You've come a long way, and you've found me. Now you need rest."

Valimagdon looked up. His face was drawn, and pallid as ashes. "I'm dying, Gariel."

"But you're a wizard ... a great mage! You have power to save yourself," said Gariel, shocked by his words.

"I cannot use that power. Listen to me, Gariel. I've come far to find you, and you must hear me."

"Let me take you inside, then."

"Hear me first," the wizard commanded.

Gariel drew up a stool and sat before him, an eager listener. The old wizard spoke slowly, sometimes almost inaudibly, a dry whisper out of a shrunken whiteness. He paused often, and pain twisted his features, but he would not be interrupted. Each time Gariel attempted to speak, Valimagdon silenced him with an impatient word and a fierce look.

The wizard's narrative took Gariel back to the life he had left nearly twenty winters past. But the White City of Valimagdon's account was not the place that Gariel remembered; it was a vipers' nest of plot and counterplot, of fear and suspicion and betrayal. The war was going badly for the Empire, and defeat seemed inevitable. The Thirty-three were deeply divided: A few believed that the time had come to treat for peace, and a handful held out for a war to the death; but the majority had come to the view that all the power of the masters, hitherto held in check, must now be devoted to the destruction of the Eastern Alliance.

Among the people, the cult of the Annihilator had gained great strength, and its followers demanded ever more vehemently the use of magic to crush the old enemy. It was not safe to oppose this view publicly. Even those among the Thirty-three who spoke out for peace, or for restraint, were subject to taunts and denunciation from the followers of the Annihilator.

Worst of all, the outcry was so fierce and so widespread that it must by now be known in the councils of the outlanders. It seemed unlikely that they would long withhold their own power in the face of such a threat. The devastation of both sides seemed to be at hand.

When Valimagdon finished his account and rested his head in his hands, breathing deeply and with difficulty, Gariel placed a consoling hand on his old master's shoulder. "I'm grateful for your warning," he said. "You're welcome to stay here. Whatever they do to one another, we'll be safe here."

Valimagdon raised his head and looked with pained eyes at Gariel. "Do you think I came all this way to save myself? Are you foolish enough to believe that any place is safe from the unleashed forces of magic? I taught you better than that, Gariel."

"Then why did you come here?"

"To pass my power on to you before I die." When Gariel sprang to his feet, so violently that he toppled the stool and sent it rolling, Valimagdon said simply, "It must be done."

"No, it must not," said Gariel hotly. "I made my choice long ago. I did not choose to be a wizard then, and I don't want to be one now. All I wanted was to lead an ordinary life, and to be happy."

"Are you so happy?"

"I was, for a time."

"And then you lost Moarra."

Gariel nodded his head slowly. "Moarra and both our children."

"Tell me how they died, Gariel."

"Moarra fell ill with a fever. She prepared a cure for herself—you know she was a healer—but she woke in the night in great pain. I took her in my arms, to comfort her... and she died. It happened that quickly, Valimagdon, with no warning, for no reason."

"And your children?"

"I lost them the following autumn. They went into the forest with women of the settlement, to gather nuts for the winter. A band of raiders came upon them. They killed the boy outright. When they were done with the women, they cut their throats and left them for the scavengers. We found them nine days later," he said in a monotone.

"Did you ever learn who did it?"

"The war killed them, and both sides are responsible for that. So I care very little if they destroy each other, and me with them. I don't care about anything, Valimagdon. Not anything, not anybody."

"You have suffered, Gariel, and I sympathize. I knew Moarra from her childhood, and when you fled the Empire together, I wished you happiness. I saw to it that you were not pursued beyond the frontier."

Gariel smiled at the old wizard. "I sometimes wondered at the ease of our escape. Thank you, Valimagdon."

"Words are easily spoken. Show your gratitude by accepting my power. Help to save the Empire and the world."

"To me, Valimagdon, the Empire is not worth saving, and I am not vain enough to think that I can save the world. Let me speak," Gariel said sharply as the wizard made to interrupt him. "I've spent half my life in this settlement, far from the White City and its ways, and here I will stay. My work is important here, and my life has a meaning. The graves of my wife and children are here—I dug them with my own hands, and I visit them often. My neighbors are good people. They helped me when I needed help, and they let me do my work, and live my life, in my own way. I ask no more. I can never be happy again, but I find this a useful life, and I'm satisfied with it. But when the Empire or the Alliance intrude with their hatreds and rivalries and fears, they turn all life into a horror. I want nothing to do with the world, or the people, beyond this place. I left the White City because I loved a woman. Now that she's been taken from me, I have only my work. Leave me to it."

"I understand your feelings. If I could, I would honor your wish. But I am not free to do so, nor are you free to refuse me. You cannot stand back while the world is destroyed."

"If people choose to destroy themselves, perhaps they deserve destruction."

"There is no choice in this matter, Gariel. All are victims, like your wife and your children."

"Very well, then, they are all victims. I've been a victim, too, and had to survive as best I could. Let others learn the same lesson."

Valimagdon looked at him coldly. "You seem to have learned very little. The world was not made for your unending happiness, Gariel, nor for mine, nor anyone's. You have had more happiness than most men."

"And lost it."

Valimagdon, about to speak, winced as if at a sudden stab of pain. Recovering, he said, "Would you punish the world for your lost happiness? If you can do that, you're much changed from the apprentice I knew."

"I can do nothing for the world, and it can do nothing for me."

Sighing, the wizard said, "You are needed, Gariel."

"Come, Master—do you tell me that the Thirty-three are helpless, and the wizards of the Alliance cannot act?"

"I do, Gariel. There is a force moving in the world greater than any power of man. Something immensely strong is luring us to our destruction. What it is and where it comes from and why it does such a thing I do not know, but I know it exists," said Valimagdon.

Gariel's expression became thoughtful. "It sounds almost as if the one they call 'the Annihilator' is real."

"I think there is a connection. In the earliest age of the Empire, there was a similar cult. It was suppressed with great violence and cruelty, after many lives had been lost."

"I never knew of this."

"The knowledge is not easily found. I doubt that anyone else knows of it. But there is no time to speak of such things now. Gariel, you must accept my power while I can still pass it on."

"What good will that do, Valimagdon? What little magic I once knew is long forgotten. Even with all your power added to it, I would be the least of the masters."

"You have used your magic. In the third winter, you cast an obscuring spell. I sensed it."

"That was long ago," said Gariel impatiently. "I'd forgotten. I'm past the midpoint of my life."

"Of an ordinary life, perhaps. You know that a mage may live far longer than other men."

"It's too late for me to begin again. There's too much to learn."

"You must, Gariel."

In frustration at the wizard's persistence, Gariel snapped, "Why me, of all men? Bestow your power on my brother. He was loyal to you and the Empire. I abandoned you. Give your power to Bellenzor and let me be!"

Without raising his head, Valimagdon said, "I cannot. Bellenzor is chief of those who preach destruction."

The news silenced Gariel for a time. He looked out into the gloom, then turned to the wizard who sat unmoving by the fire. Taking up the overturned stool, he placed it at Valimagdon's feet and seated himself, still silent.

"It is true, Gariel," said Valimagdon.

"I believe you. But it's unlike Bellenzor. He hated the war for the death and destruction it caused. How can he advocate a worse destruction?"

"It is long since you saw him. People change, Gariel, and there is an evil influence at work." Valimagdon had barely finished speaking when he gasped and slumped over.

"I'm bringing you inside. No more talking," said Gariel, taking the old man up as if he were a child.

Valimagdon was too feeble to protest. Gariel took him to the small house across from the forge where he had lived since the death of his family. He fed the fire, then placed a pallet before the hearth and laid the unconscious man upon it, covering him with cloak and blanket. Taking some bread and cold meat, he settled in a chair where he could watch while Valimagdon slept.

Toward dawn the old wizard stirred and murmured, jolting Gariel out of a fretful doze. When he saw the green eyes looking up at him, Gariel dropped to his knees beside the pallet.

"I learned some healing from Moarra. I'll help you," he said.

Valimagdon closed his eyes and shook his head weakly. "You cannot help. The thing that eats away my life is no sickness."

"Use your magic, then!"

"It must go to you," said the old man.

Valimagdon fell into a peaceful sleep after speaking these words. His breathing was regular and his face showed no sign of discomfort. Gariel sat keeping watch, his mind much troubled by his old master's sudden appearance and his message. The wizard hinted at much but revealed little, and his single request was the thing Gariel was most loath to do.

He had left his old life behind him, and he did not wish to take it up again. Only once since leaving the White City had he used magic, and that was to save the settlement. Now he wanted only to live out his days here, where he had known happiness and peace. Here, he was Gariel the smith. He worked hard, slept the deep sleep of honest weariness, and had no need to think of anything but his trade and his memories. He asked nothing more of life than to be left alone; and now the man he most respected and trusted had reentered his life and brought all the sordid workings of the world with him.

Over and over he told himself that it meant nothing to him if the Empire and the Alliance destroyed one another. Indeed, that might be the solitary hope of safety for this hamlet and the other settlements that lay unprotected between the two domains. Soldiers from one or the other had killed those closest to him, and he could never forgive that. Both sides were equally guilty in his eyes, and he was willing to let both perish. Since they were bent on doing so—all of them, even his own brother— it seemed almost perverse to attempt to thwart their wish.

And even if he were willing to do as Valimagdon urged, how could he? He had no answer to that, and the old wizard had given no suggestion of a plan. Valimagdon's words had been vague and fragmentary: a mysterious evil force, a cult of fanatics, echoes of some ancient, long-suppressed belief. He appeared to be ill, and perhaps the illness had affected his mind. If that were the case, then Gariel need only humor him until he was well.

But the coming of his old master had turned Gariel's mind to his youthful studies. He recalled the accounts of the perils of magic when used to destroy. It fed upon itself and grew beyond the control of even the greatest mage. If Valimagdon's fears were well founded, then the danger was great, not merely to the warring powers but to all that lived on earth. His warning might be the simple truth.

Gariel sat until late in the morning pondering these matters. When at last Valimagdon awoke, seeming a bit stronger, Gariel had resolved nothing.

"Are you ready?" the wizard asked. "We must act soon, while I still have some strength."

"What's the purpose of it all? What would you have me do?"

"You must return to the White City and prevent Bellenzor and the Thirty-three from using magic to destroy the Alliance."

"How could I hope to do that?" Gariel asked wearily. "Even with your magic to help me, I'm not the equal of the wizards among the Thirty-three if they combine their powers against me. I was never the equal of Bellenzor."

"Your brother had the ambition and the dedication, but yours was the greater gift. You neglected and even abandoned it, but the gift remains."

"But I don't want to fight my brother!"

"I ask you to save him, and all the others. A terrible evil has come among them. You must help them to resist."

Still Gariel hesitated. Valimagdon saw his expression and said, "You have doubts. Accept my power and all will be clear."

Gariel sighed and nodded in surrender. He could dispute no more. "I accept," he said.

"To it, then," said Valimagdon, climbing shakily to his feet, waving off Gariel's assistance impatiently. "We must clear the floor and lay out the proper figure. No one must see."

Gariel's decision seemed to have given the dying wizard new life. Valimagdon took charred sticks from the fireplace and drew an irregular figure with seven sides on the pale wooden floor. Drawing two pouches from the recesses of his robe, he tossed one to Gariel.

"You know the symbols for Eda and Syrac. Draw them, and speak the incantation," he said, turning to trace a symbol at the juncture of the lines nearest him with dark powder from the pouch he retained. When Gariel hesitated, he said, "Surely you remember."

"I think so. It's been a long time."

"Hurry. My strength will not last."

When the figure and the symbols were almost complete, Valimagdon inspected all closely and nodded his approval. He drew two linked circles at the center of the heptagon, then closed the figure and took his place within one circle.

"Listen carefully," he said. "When my magic has passed into you, the spell my enemy has cast will overcome me. The thing you see will not be what it seems. Do not heed it, do not believe it. Fear it, Gariel. If it approaches you, defend yourself."

"I will."

"All my power will be yours, but it will take time for you to master it. Await the time, Gariel. Return to the Empire, learn all you can, make ready, but do not act in haste. Wait for your full strength and mastery."

"I will do as you say."

"Then enter. Take your place in the circle. Put your right hand on your heart, your left hand on my brow." Covering Gariel's hands with his own, the wizard began a low, mournful incantation.

Gariel felt sensations for which he had no words. He seemed at the same moment to move through blinding light and abyssal darkness; to be crushed as if under falling mountains and to float as free and unsubstantial as smoke. He sensed wisdom and time and mystery and feeling as if they were things as tangible as stones or trees. He felt like a tiny vessel set at the foot of a waterfall, receiving and retaining the awesome cataract beyond all conceivable limits.

Suddenly all was still, and Moarra stood before him in the afternoon light that flooded their bedchamber. Her hair hung loose over her bare shoulders and fell to her waist, and her dark eyes gleamed with desire.

"I've come back, Gariel. Your magic has brought me back.

Come to me, Gariel," she said, reaching out to him.

He stepped back, confused. "I didn't summon you. I can't ... I don't understand, Moarra."

"Don't question, Gariel. Don't think of how it happened. Just come to me," she said, and the hunger in her sweet voice thrilled him.

He glanced down and saw the splayed, scaly, taloned feet of the thing that stood before him, bound in the ring that Valimagdon had drawn. As he cried out in loathing, it became a shape of horror, a great eyeless maw yawning to devour him while arms like dark sails reached out to drag him in.

He threw up his hands and spoke the words that came instinctively to his lips. The thing gave an awful scream and began to shrink, ever more rapidly, until it was the size of an insect, scurrying furiously to and fro within the confines of the circle. Gariel picked it up. With a word, he flung it from him and it disappeared into a bubble of eternity.

He was in the small house; he had never left it. The room was dark behind tightly closed shutters. Valimagdon was gone. The heptagon remained. In the circle where the old wizard had stood, deep gouges had been scored in the wooden floor. Gariel shuddered at his narrow escape. Valimagdon's fears seemed much more credible.

Gariel remained in the settlement through the winter. Outwardly he lived his accustomed life. In private, he directed his energies to the assimilation of Valimagdon's magic.

Coursing within him were powers that were new, yet not completely unknown, to him. He felt sometimes like a man cured of a lifelong disability, unable to remember the limitations of his old state even as they rendered him clumsy in his new wholeness. Often he pictured himself as an infant grown to manhood in a moment, possessed of a man's strength but unable, in his inexperience, to use it properly.

At first he felt divided irreconcilably within himself. His mind was filled with knowledge that was at once new and familiar. He remembered and understood things from remote times and far places, but those very things were also strange and bewildering. Unknown words came to his lips by instinct; his hands moved in unfamiliar gestures with the ease of long habit.

Gradually he achieved an inner balance. The powers he had thought of initially as Valimagdon's he came to feel his own. His thoughts grew steadily clearer and more penetrating, and what had been a frightening chaos of fragmented memories became the orderly furniture of his own mind. He understood much that would have been beyond his comprehension a short time earlier, and recognized solutions to problems that would have baffled him. Only one region of knowledge remained closed to him, and that very obscurity suggested that all the forebodings and warnings were true: Impenetrable darkness surrounded the power that had placed the consuming demon in the old wizard's breast and was sweeping the people of two realms to mutual destruction.

When summer came, Gariel felt that he was ready. He could learn nothing more by staying in the settlement. Early one midsummer morning, he bade his neighbors farewell and set out on the long journey to the White City. It was time to seek out the enemy.

4

Reunion

Gariel took a slow, circuitous route to the White City. He stopped in every hamlet and village along the way. In some he stayed only long enough to take a meal, but in others he remained for several days. Where he found a forge, he asked for work, and stayed on sometimes for as long as ten days, listening carefully, seldom speaking.

He learned little, but what he did learn was disquieting. By the time the walls of the city rose gleaming before him, he had begun to take Valimagdon's fears more seriously. The Empire had changed greatly during his absence. Even the humblest subjects dwelling in the outermost marches showed a new bitterness against the forces of the Nine Lords, and a willingness to take cruel measures in order to assure their enemy's defeat. A spirit of destructiveness seemed to have come over the Empire, just as the old wizard had claimed. If it prevailed among the Thirty-three, a crisis was indeed near at hand.

Towards evening on a brisk autumn day, Gariel entered the city by the Carters' Gate, near the western end of the north wall. His dress and speech and the dust of travel that lay thick in every fold of his clothing gained him unquestioned admittance. He took a bed at an inn for the night, and set out next morning to find work and lodging.

Zurlen's forge, near the gate in the west wall, stood in need of a smith. It was a busy place, with a constant flow of customers, many of whom paused to talk among themselves of the day's events. Gariel found it most suitable for his purposes, and it took only a short turn at the forge to convince Zurlen that he was the right man. The pay was adequate, and Zurlen offered him a small sleeping-loft over the forge.

Zurlen was accustomed to concentrating on one thing at a time. When he worked, he spoke only in grudging monosyllables, and kept his eyes fixed on the metal under his hands. But when work was done, he enjoyed talking. He found in Gariel a man who was as good a listener as he was a worker, and they spent most evenings seated in the doorway of the forge drinking chilled ale while Zurlen, large and loud-voiced, held forth on the affairs of the Empire to Gariel and such neighbors as joined them.

Zurlen and his wife were lifelong worshipers of Ilveraine. They credited the Nurturer with saving their only son's life at a time when the dry fever took the lives of many of his playmates. Ilveraine's symbol, a tree laden with ripe fruit, was carved into the doors of the forge, and a wooden image of a woman holding a child stood at the turn of the stair.

The wife, Umra, was a taciturn woman, but her devotion to the Nurturer was obvious in a score of ways each day. Zurlen was more outspoken, both in his belief in Ilveraine and his dislike of the new cult, the Followers of the Fourth Child, which was spreading so rapidly and gaining so many adherents in the city. His antipathy was strong and unconcealed, but his actual stock of information was small, and Gariel found himself far better informed about Zurlen's feelings than about their object. He listened patiently, with fading hopes; then, one evening when Zurlen and Umra had gone to see a cousin in the market district to the south of the city, he found himself sitting with Brugo, the son whose life was credited to the Nurturer. Brugo was a muscular youth, quite pleased with himself, and he appeared content to have this chance of a man-to-man talk with the newcomer, with no parents to overhear.

"People think well of you. You haven't been here long, but you've already got a good reputation. The father says you're the best man he's ever had working here," said Brugo, with the air of one imparting select knowledge.

"I've had a lot of experience. Used to have my own forge," Gariel said. He finished the contents of his mug, and setting it down he refilled both his and the young man's.

"Where was that, Gariel?"

"A little settlement far to the north. It's so small it doesn't even have a name."

"It must have been a dull life."

"I was always too busy to notice."

"Why did you come to the city, then?"

Gariel paused, looked upward vacantly, and said, "My family died. I didn't want to stay there after that."

"I'm sorry, Gariel," Brugo said awkwardly.

"It wasn't your doing. It was the war."

"A lot of people have suffered. The soldiers of the Alliance are like wild animals. But they'll be done with soon enough. We're going to wipe them out, the army and the people, every one of them," said the youth vehemently.

"I'll cheer when that day comes, you may be sure. But to be honest with you, Brugo, I don't see any sign of people getting ready to do it. I hear plenty of talk, but talk isn't going to wipe out the Alliance."

"We'll do it. And soon, too," Brugo assured him.

"It takes men and weapons to win a war. I came here expecting to spend most of my time making weapons, and I haven't worked on anything but tools."

"Wars can be won with other things than weapons, Gariel," said Brugo with a significant look.

"That's not something I know about. I say if we're going to destroy the Alliance, we should be making the weapons to do it."

Gariel hoped that he had opened a line that would lead them somewhere, but the conversation turned almost at once to other topics. He wondered if Brugo was being cautious, or sounding him out, or merely hinting at knowledge he did not possess. He refilled the mugs whenever their contents fell, and let the young man talk on uninterrupted. Eventually Brugo, almost furtively, asked a promising question.

"Do you follow any guardian, Gariel?"

Gariel frowned and said hesitantly, "I used to trust in Ebanor.

But when my family died, I just couldn't believe in a Protector anymore."

"My parents believe in the Nurturer. You can see the symbols all over the house and the forge."

"A lot of people believe in the Nurturer. My wife was faithful to Ilveraine all her life. She had me carve a tree right into our bedstead. She was proud of that." Gariel sighed a deep, melancholy sigh, and added, "I sacrificed with her a few times, but I never asked for anything. Now I just don't believe any of them can help us. We're on our own in this world, and there are no guardians to protect us."

"There's another guardian, you know. Ankaria."

Gariel turned to him, frankly curious. "I've heard people speak of Ankaria, but I never understood that they were talking about a guardian. All the same, Brugo...." Shaking his head, he fell silent.

"Ankaria's the fourth guardian, stronger and greater than the others. They've had their chance to guide the world, and they've failed. Now it's time for Ankaria to clear the way for a whole new age."

"Is Ankaria the one that people call the Annihilator?"

"Yes. He will come upon us as a great wind out of a cloud of darkness reaching from horizon to horizon, laying waste to all before it. The old guardians must be driven out, the old ways must die, before the new age comes," said Brugo, like one reciting a cherished tale known by heart.

"That sounds like a hard belief to me," Gariel said.

"The way of Ankaria is not easy."

"I don't mean that. If Ankaria wipes out everything and everybody, who's going to enjoy this new age? I'd rather be alive with what I've got—even the war is better than being destroyed."

"Ankaria is the annihilator of his enemies. His followers will be spared."

"Well, that's different. Has Ankaria many followers, Brugo?"

"Yes, many, and the number is growing. The time is right for Ankaria's coming. He will wipe out our enemies, so we can begin the new age in peace. The other guardians are powerless. Think of how long the war's dragged on, Gariel, and the suffering it's caused! Ankaria will end it in a single night."

"When will this happen?"

"Soon, very soon. The Thirty-three must be won over. Their wizards will be the channel for Ankaria's power."

Gariel frowned thoughtfully and shook his head. "You won't win them over easily. The Thirty-three believe in the old ways, and they're not quick to change their thinking."

"They've already changed, many of them," Brugo said with a knowing smile. "The rest will see reason, or be driven out to die with the enemy. Ankaria is our only hope. The one true way is the way of the Annihilator."

Gariel maintained his pose of doubt. "It won't be easy to drive out any of the Thirty-three. They're very powerful. It's the followers of the Annihilator who might be driven out."

"I understand your doubts. You know nothing of the power of Ankaria. Well... have you ever heard of the wizard Valimagdon?"

"I know that name. One of the Thirty-three, is he not?"

"He was. He spoke out brazenly against Ankaria, called him an abomination and a monster, and defied his power. Ankaria sent a demon into his body, to devour him from within. Now Valimagdon is gone."

Gariel felt with a sudden chill the urgency of his mission. If the followers of the Annihilator could boast openly of his power, then the crucial moment might be closer than he had feared. He could wait no longer. He must see Bellenzor that very night.

He rose lazily, stretched himself, and scratched his beard. "This is something to think about, Brugo. I had no idea of the power of Ankaria."

"It's better to follow the Annihilator than to oppose him. Soon the time for choosing will be past," said the youth, with ominous intonation.

"I may want to talk with you again before that time," Gariel said. He yawned, then looked down and peered closely into Brugo's face. "What's that mark on your forehead? Right there, in the center," he said, reaching out to touch his fingertips to the youth's brow and whispering a phrase at the instant of contact to efface all memory of their conversation regarding Ankaria. "Just a bit of ash, that's all."

Brugo shook his head and blinked, momentarily befuddled. He looked up and stammered, "What... where are you... where are you going, Gariel?"

"I have to see that man I was telling you about. If you're as tired as you claim to be, you'd better get some sleep."

"Yes. Yes, I'm tired," said the youth dully, surrendering to a protracted yawn.

"Close up the forge, will you, Brugo? I may be late getting back."

Brugo yawned once again and nodded, rising sluggishly. He would remember no details of this conversation, merely some vague fragments of an evening's boasting before a taciturn worker at his father's forge. Gariel left him to his task and set out for the high-walled sanctuary at the heart of the White City where dwelt the Thirty-three.

Bellenzor was sceptical when he received the message, but he had the man admitted out of curiosity. At sight of his visitor, all his doubts vanished. It was indeed his brother.

Gariel's short thick beard showed traces of gray; he was thinner now, and appeared taller, though he was still sturdy of build. The greatest change was in his manner. The boyish zest that had been so much a part of him was entirely gone, and his expression and bearing were somber. Clearly the winters of his absence had not been without their sadness. Yet with all the changes he was still unmistakably Gariel, returned at last.

"Yes, Bellenzor, it's Gariel. Truly it is," the visitor said in a familiar voice.

Bellenzor was known to all as a cold and distant man, one who thought deeply but did not permit himself to feel; but on this occasion he sprang forward and took Gariel's hand firmly in both of his.

"In all those winters, I never suspected that you were still alive. I never thought to see you again."

"And now I've returned."

"Come back to stay, I hope," said Bellenzor, leading him to a pair of high-backed chairs by the hearth.

Gariel settled in the chair and accepted a goblet of wine. With a wry smile, he said, "I may stay in a dungeon for a time. You must recall that I ran off with Moarra of the Venturan. One does not offend such a family with impunity."

"Think no more of that," said Bellenzor with a gesture of dismissal. "The Venturan will embrace you as a son if I tell them they must."

Gariel was visibly impressed. "You've attained a great deal of power."

"I've worked hard. So have you, by the look of you. Have you been happy?"

"For a time."

"But no longer?"

"Moarra died of a fever, and our children were slain by soldiers. I had no reason to stay out there after that happened. The White City is my home, and you're my brother. I have no one else. I had to return, even if I came back only to punishment."

"There will be no punishment. You are welcome here."

"And you, Bellenzor—do you forgive me?"

"There is nothing to forgive."

"I'm glad to hear that. I often feared that I might have done you harm indirectly; that some would try to make you suffer for what I did."

"Obviously I have not suffered. Quite the contrary. I am one of the Thirty-three, and Master of Apprentices, as well."

"You are Master of Apprentices? What of Valimagdon?"

"Our old master is dead."

"How did he die, Bellenzor?"

"A grave sickness came upon him suddenly, and caused him much suffering. Valimagdon was a wise and good man, as you must know, but he went his own way, obstinate to the very end. He refused to use his magic to save himself. You will find no grave for him by the Masters' Wall... only a marker. He left us, and went away to die in solitude, no one knows where."

"Could no one persuade him?"

"When the sickness came upon him, he became more determined than ever. He was convinced that it was no ordinary sickness, but the working of magic, sent upon him by an enemy."

"Such things are possible."

Scornfully, Bellenzor said, "What enemy could overcome such a wizard as Valimagdon by magic? He was the greatest of the masters. But he persisted in his belief. It took great determination to withhold his power and go off alone as he did."

"The Empire must feel his loss."

"The Empire does not stand or fall in one man," Bellenzor

said curtly. "Let us speak of him no more. He's gone from us. But you have returned, and have much to tell."

Gariel smiled and shook his head. "Not very much. I've led a simple life all these years. My worldly training was as a smith, and that's what I've been. I am still."

"Have you come to the city to be a smith?"

"It's all I can do now, Bellenzor. I don't mind."

Bellenzor's manner became authoritative. "Where are you staying? Have you been in the city long?"

"Not long. I found work at a forge near the Sunset Gate. It's owned by a man named Zurlen. He pays me well. I sleep in a loft over the forge."

"I cannot allow my brother to work at a forge and sleep in a loft, Gariel."

"I've worked at a forge for nearly half my life. There's no shame in it."

"You must do more important things now. You showed great promise as a wizard. I need someone I can trust to assist me with the apprentices."

"But it's been more than fifteen winters, Bellenzor! Every one of the apprentices would be far ahead of me."

"I will give you time to prepare yourself. You will soon regain your old skill, Gariel, never fear. The gift is never lost. You must do this," said Bellenzor, raising an imperious hand to forestall his brother's objection. "The war is not going well for us. If we are to win, everyone must be willing to do whatever must be done, and a mage is more valuable to us than a smith. You returned willing to accept punishment. I tell you there will be no punishment, only atonement. Help me, brother."

Gariel set his goblet down untasted and looked thoughtfully into the fire burning low before them. Turning to his brother, he said, "I will assist you."

"Good. Let us drink our wine to celebrate your return. You've come when I needed you most."

"I hope I don't disappoint you."

"I trust you will not. And if you need something to inspire you, remember this: Magic can end this war, and end it quickly. You cannot bring back your wife and children, but you can help spare others from such a fate."

That very night, Gariel took up residence in the Tower of the Apprentices. He disliked having to deceive his brother, but the things he had seen and heard since his return to the White City had frightened him. The belligerent spirit abroad in the outer reaches of the Empire was unsettling; but the talk here in the heart of the Empire was a promise of disaster.

Any lingering doubts of Valimagdon's story vanished. His doubt now centered on Bellenzor, whose last admonition had sounded chillingly close to the promise of the Annihilator.

5

The Touch of the Annihilator

All that autumn, and through the winter and spring, Gariel spent most of each day in the apprentices' library, relearning old knowledge and practicing old skills. The power of Valimagdon he carefully concealed; to all outward appearances, Gariel was working hard to make up for the long neglect of his studies in magic.

By the end of the following winter, he appeared to have caught up to the other apprentices; by the early part of summer, he had surpassed the most promising among them. At harvest time, following the traditional feast to thank the Nurturer for her bounty, he was placed over them, in a position subordinate only to Bellenzor, Master of Apprentices, many of whose lesser duties he now assumed. He had come to know the apprentices as a fellow student; now he became their guide and advisor, and he was pleased to find that they accepted him in this new role without resentment or question.

His age made it easy for the apprentices to confide in him. He was nine winters older than the oldest, and could have been father of the youngest ones. They all found him a willing and sympathetic listener, and no one suspected that his listening was purposeful.

THE TIME OF THE ANNIHILATOR 49

With the passing of time, he came to feel more at ease. The deeper reservoir of Valimagdon's legacy lay dormant, awaiting the proper occasion; but his own powers were at their former level, and he was reassured. His progress had been widely remarked, and he was less fearful now of giving himself away by some thoughtless display of magic.

He did not like the continued deception of his brother and benefactor, but he knew that it was necessary for him to work in secrecy, alone. A power sufficient to overcome Valimagdon would certainly be able to deceive Bellenzor, perhaps even possess his will. Gariel saw no sign of this, but he maintained his secrecy. If Bellenzor remained unaffected, they would be allies when the confrontation came; if he had been corrupted, all the more reason to keep the truth from him.

Gariel was able to learn very little. A new ferocity of spirit and a willingness to destroy the enemies of the Empire by any available means were evident on all sides, but that alone did not prove the existence of an inciting force beyond the human. It might equally be the outcome of frustration and weariness. The worship of Ankaria, the Annihilator, was widespread, but that fact, too, meant little in itself. The long war might have made people lose trust in their old guardians and seek new and more violent means of victory. For himself, Gariel found the cult of the Annihilator shallow and contemptible, but he understood the appeal it might hold for those weary in spirit and hungry for revenge.

He found no evidence of a link between the power that Valimagdon feared and the burgeoning worship of Ankaria. It seemed too great a coincidence that two such phenomena should appear at the same time, so similar in nature and yet unconnected. Brugo's words came to his mind and troubled him: "The Thirty-three must be won over. Their wizards will be the channel for Ankaria's power." As often as the words recurred to him he reproved himself for placing too much importance on the careless talk of a none-too-bright youth. But he recalled Valimagdon's words, too, warning him that the destroying power had gained sway over many of the Thirty-three, and Brugo's boasts became more credible.

Gariel was constantly aware of the undercurrent of tension and anger permeating the White City, and yet he could not come upon any single clear manifestation of it. He could not sense it in the ordinary way, but he was aware of it, and he wondered if the power of Valimagdon might be at work unbeknownst to him. In every dealing with the apprentices he was treated with respect and affection; on the occasions when he met with any of the Thirty-three, they were courteous to him; his servants were cheerful and efficient. And yet the presence of a wrongness was always suggesting itself to him, elusive but undeniable, like the scent of rank carrion on a fresh spring breeze.

The worst times of all were those moments when his body was exhausted but his mind was too excited for sleep, and he gave in to his imaginings and speculated fearfully on what might await him. Unanswerable questions gnawed at him, sapping his will and making him regret his promise to Valimagdon. Will I find out this evil power in time to stop it? How will I stop it? Will my magic be sufficient, or will I need help? Who is to help me if I can confide in no one? If Bellenzor has fallen prey to this power, can I turn my magic against him? Would he attack me, even under the influence of such a thing as Valimagdon spoke of?

And there were no answers, no resolutions, only the questions, whirling around and around in his thoughts. Most troubling of all was the question of the ultimate rightness of his action. From the information that reached the Tower of the Apprentices, Gariel could see that the war was going against the Empire on all fronts; barring a total reversal, the Alliance might win before another score of winters had passed, and might triumph even sooner than that. Their forces would overrun the Empire and converge on the White City, the great prize of the long war. After the sufferings of a protracted conflict, all the horrors of defeat would be upon his people: plundering, death, and devastation, then the long humiliation of subjection and slavery. If something could prevent this, even at great risk, had he the right to deny it to the Empire? Was it better for a living empire to fall, obliterated so that unborn generations might live?

Reason gave him one clear and inescapable answer, but his feelings fought against it. It seemed to him that he had a choice between two monstrous evils. Had Moarra and their children been alive, Gariel reflected, he could not have made his promise to Valimagdon. Right and wrong are very clear and obvious when one sits in solitary judgment remote from those who must suffer the consequences of one's choice; but it is hard to look unmoved on the faces of those one intends to sacrifice to a principle, however noble that principle might be.

In these times of doubt, he put his faith in Valimagdon. His old master had been a man of truth and honor. Even his death had attested to his goodness, for it had been inflicted on him by foul means and had claimed him only because he chose to reserve his magic for the benefit of others, rather than use it to preserve his own life. Valimagdon's death was the proof of his story. Gariel could not but believe, and trust.

He worked on, ever alert, listening, hoping to come upon the proof he sought. Another autumn passed and the armies returned to the White City, leaving a small force to guard the outposts. The news they brought home was bleak.

In all this time, Gariel saw little of his brother. The demands on the Thirty-three were great, and neither the mages nor the councilors among them had time for anything but their duties to the Empire. Gariel heard frequent mention of Bellenzor's dedication and heroic efforts, and his hopes rose that his brother had remained free from the influence of the dark power. But then, in the space of a few days, three things occurred that forced him to action.

Late one evening, on his way from the library of the apprentices to his chambers in the tower, he was hailed by Jalander and Montolors, two of the older apprentices, who sought his help in explicating an obscure passage in the Scroll of Haspindaine. It took Gariel little time to realize that their question was only a pretext to sound out his feelings about the Annihilator. He gave a noncommittal response; they took their leave with due deference. He gave the matter no thought until the second day following, when he attended while Councilor Zammarand addressed the leaders of the frontier rangers, the fighting men who bore the brunt of the war. The speech was predictably vague and hopeful, and Gariel listened dutifully but with little interest until the very end, when Zammarand's words jolted him into attentiveness.

"Despite all your courage and sacrifice, the war has gone against us in recent times," he said. "The forces of the Alliance are all around us, like a noose, and the noose grows tighter. But that will change. Before long, the armies of the Nine Lords will exist no more. The Alliance will be broken, its strongholds leveled, its people exterminated. Their very name will be forgotten. On behalf of the Thirty-three, I swear this will be so!"

His words were received respectfully, but without enthusiasm. The men before him were hardened soldiers. They had heard too many stirring speeches and high promises, and seen them end in the death of comrades and friends. Most of them bore the marks of battle, and those without scars on their flesh carried painful memories. Experience had made them wary of promises such as Zammarand's.

But the old councilor seemed to have anticipated the reception, for he went on, unperturbed, "I know that it is easier to promise great victories than to win them, but I tell you that this is no empty promise. We can devastate the enemy by the power of magic. Until now, we have withheld that power, because some among the Thirty-three were fearful of the consequences of its use. But no longer. The Empire must be preserved, regardless of the risk. You who have fought so hard and so bravely will soon see your enemies withered like leaves and swept before you. The Empire will live, and all who oppose it will be annihilated!"

Gariel was shaken by these words. Here was the danger Valimagdon had warned of, openly embraced by the Thirty-three—surely by Bellenzor, since he was the most influential among them. The crisis was at hand, and he was racked by the urgency to act and yet uncertain how to proceed. As soon as he could, he hurried to his quarters, where he could be alone to think and plan. A young servitor stood by his door, waiting.

"You are to come to the Master Bellenzor at once," said the youth.

"I have neglected you, brother," said Bellenzor as he ushered Gariel into the dark elegance of his chambers. "My duties have been pressing, and I have scarce had time to think of anything but the war."

"I haven't felt neglected. You've done much for me, Bellenzor."

"I plan to do more. You are to be appointed to the Thirty-three."

Gariel was too astonished to respond. He shook his head

dazedly and rubbed his brow. Bellenzor waved languidly to direct him to a chair.

"I did not think it would be such a surprise. Valimagdon's place has been too long unfilled, and there is no one better suited than you."

"But... so soon after my return! And surely there must be others...."

"You know that there are not. Humility must not be overdone. Besides, others will not do," Bellenzor said. "You have proven yourself, brother. The Empire needs you, and I want you among us. The work that awaits us is difficult and very dangerous, but the reward is great."

"Zammarand spoke of a magic that would devastate the Alliance and rid us of our enemies forever. Does the work you speak of have to do with this magic?"

"It does. But there is more to it than that. Far more."

"What more could there be?"

Without hesitation, Bellenzor said, "Unimaginable power. Infinite power, brother. Immortality for us and those who follow us."

Gariel was silent for a moment, taken aback by this quick response. "And how will that serve the Empire? Forgive me, brother, but I must ask," he said at last.

"I did not expect blind faith from you. The Empire will be delivered from the threat of the Nine Lords and made secure against any enemies that might arise in the future. The possibility of future enemies, I must say, is remote. The Alliance of the Nine Lords will be so utterly obliterated from the earth that its fate will serve as a warning for all time. The very foundation stones of its strongholds will be ground into dust."

"What power can work such destruction?" Gariel asked fearfully.

"The common people call it Ankaria, the Annihilator. Have you heard talk of it?"

"I have heard of Ankaria, and I confess it surprises me to hear you speak of such a thing seriously. It's worshiped by a cult of desperate, dangerous fanatics."

"The followers of the cult are as you describe them," said Bellenzor calmly. "But there is more to Ankaria than you perceive."

"Then you worship Ankaria? You believe in it?"

"Worship? Hardly that," said Bellenzor disdainfully. "You will not find me shouting and weeping and offering sacrifices with its followers. I have no patience with worship. But believing in Ankaria... ah, that is something very different. I believe that Ankaria—a being that men have given the name Ankaria, and the title Annihilator—is a real entity, long forgotten and unsummoned, pent in darkness for ages, and capable of giving great power to those who liberate it and call it forth."

"And you would call it forth."

"I will. And you will assist me."

This was the realization of Gariel's worst fears. He sat benumbed, feeling absurd and utterly helpless. While he had proceeded patiently and cautiously, waiting for the evil to reveal itself, it had been working its way into Bellenzor's will and capturing the minds of the people. It was subtle as silk and far more powerful than he had imagined. He looked helplessly at his brother, seeking some way to gain time to gather his thoughts.

"This is... it's quite unexpected. It's something of a shock. I don't know what to say."

"You need say nothing, Gariel. Leave it all to me. I know exactly what we must do."

"But you must tell me more! I've been gone for so long. The Annihilator was unknown in the city when I left."

"Not quite. No, not quite unknown," Bellenzor said thoughtfully. "Forgotten, perhaps, but the knowledge was here. It had been here for ages, and it was ancient when it came." He turned to Gariel and fixed him with an intense gaze. "The world is old, brother, far older than any of our scholars dare to imagine. Their knowledge extends back to the founding of the White City, and then their minds fail them. They speak of 'The Time without a Voice' and 'The Dark Time.' But there was life in the world before our people arose, and knowledge beyond any we possess."

"How can you know this?"

"Anyone could have known it if he had the persistence to seek it, and the courage to follow where his wits led him. Valimagdon, I think, suspected it; but he faltered. I was always the persistent one, Gariel. You had the greater gift, but I always excelled because I worked harder. And I had found something worth all my efforts."

"What had you found but the deity of some forgotten cult?"

"Again you choose the wrong word," Bellenzor said calmly, as if pointing out a careless error to a pupil. "The Followers of the Fourth Child were exterminated, their images destroyed. It was a crime punishable by a painful death even to speak the name of Ankaria. All this was done in the time when the White City was no more than a cluster of stone rings roofed with skins. And the cult of the Annihilator was already ancient."

Bellenzor paused, but Gariel offered no comment. He was as fascinated as he was horrified, and he wanted to learn more. Bellenzor gazed up into the darkness and went on dreamily, "I was curious, as you are now. Where had the belief come from, and why was it feared so? Being curious, I sought the answer; being persistent, I found it.

"You may have noticed that some of those in the city refer to Ankaria as 'the Fourth Child.' They do not understand that they are using the ancient name of the sect. In those early days of the Empire, beliefs were simple. The Sower of Worlds was pictured as a male, planting his seed in the wombs of the worlds he created. The guardians were thus his children, bound to their mother world. I cannot pretend to fathom the operations of those ancient minds, but I think they first conceived Ankaria as an explanation for all that afflicted them. Consider: Despite the Nurturer, children died and crops failed; despite the workings of the Illuminator, there was ignorance and confusion; in spite of the Protector's efforts, battles were lost. Clearly, some power was responsible for all this, and whatever it was, it must be the equal of the guardians—perhaps their superior. Hence the notion of a fourth child, an outcast, an exile, working in opposition to the others as their eternal enemy."

"A frightening belief," said Gariel.

"A serviceable one. It is even a hopeful belief: It makes our misfortunes the work of an active and powerful being, rather than our own failures, or the failures of the guardians. No, Gariel, I consider it a useful and harmless belief. And yet it was denounced as an abomination, condemned on all sides, and rooted out so thoroughly that in all the ages succeeding, only I have been able to learn of its existence. I asked myself why such a thing was done. Could it be that such a power existed? I sought an answer among the ancient scrolls and tablets, and found nothing. I had to know, Gariel, for the sake of the Empire and for myself, and so I took the only course open to me: I called upon the Annihilator, and charged it, if it truly existed, to reveal itself to me."

Gariel had sat unmoving, scarcely breathing, eyes fixed on his brother's face, as Bellenzor went on with his account. Now he could only nod, wide-eyed, and whisper, "And did it answer the summons?"

"It did. I learned that the Annihilator is real, and very powerful. Its presence nearly overwhelmed me. It was worshiped long ago, by a people who are now gone from the earth, and it was ancient when it came to them. When they passed away, it was left without worshipers on a lifeless world. It came to our people, and was rejected, walled out by spells of great potency. If I call it from its exile, it will serve us well."

"But why was it rejected and walled out?" Gariel asked.

"Because its destructive power is so truly terrible. The old mages feared it, but it is the thing we most need. By the power of the Annihilator we will sweep away the enemy, and with its power working in us, we will live as long as world and life survive, and grow ever stronger," Bellenzor said, like a man hypnotized by his own words.

"Destruction is not life."

"A fire grows as it destroys. We will be like a flame covering the face of the world."

"And why us, brother?"

"I, because I dare to do what others shrink from. You, because I choose you."

Gariel felt his heart pounding. "You choose nothing. This malevolent being that our ancestors drove from the Empire is using you for its own ends, as you would use me, and all the Empire. Come to your senses, Bellenzor!"

"I had hoped you would come to yours," said Bellenzor, softly and politely. "Is it so wicked to destroy one's enemies? If I allow a superior being to give me power and immortality, am I being duped? You speak like a fool."

"You know the power of magic, Bellenzor. You admit that the mere presence of this thing is overwhelming. Do you dare to think that it can be controlled? That you can command it to go just so far, and no farther; to do your bidding, and not its own will?"

"We are at one," said Bellenzor.

Gariel could not give way now. He knew that he must stop Bellenzor, whatever the cost, and he made a final attempt to dissuade him. "And what of the mages who serve the Alliance? Will they do nothing to save themselves? Will they seek no revenge?"

"You speak as Valimagdon spoke," Bellenzor said, and there was an ominous edge in his voice.

"Did Valimagdon say that this thing had been justly cursed and driven from the Empire?" Gariel cried, rising. "Did he warn you that it would destroy everything once some hungry, foolish man unleashed it?"

Bellenzor rose and turned to confront him. As Gariel readied himself for the clash, he saw an appalling change come over his brother. Another being seemed to superimpose itself upon him, and for an instant Bellenzor's features flickered, as if seen in the glare of lightning, though the chamber remained dim. He raised his hand, pointed at Gariel, and said, "You have chosen to be my enemy." The voice was Bellenzor's, but subtly changed, with a timbre that seemed to resonate through great stony distances.

In a reaction as instinctive as the prickling of his skin, Gariel drew on all of Valimagdon's magic to armor himself against the onslaught of the enemy, for he knew that Bellenzor was himself no longer. The Annihilator had chosen Bellenzor as the channel of his power, and that withering power was to be turned against Gariel.

Gariel knew that he could not overcome such a thing, but he might be able to protect himself against its blast. When it struck, he felt as if all the tides of all the seas had crashed over him, and all the mountains of the world fallen upon him. He staggered, gasping and choking under the terrible heat and pressure that bore upon him from all sides. He fell to the stone floor of the chamber and looked up at the cold impassive face that was at once Bellenzor's and the other's, and something inside him stretched and drew him away, out of himself, to somewhere free and safe.

He looked down and saw a body lying withered and shrunken as an effigy made of dry husks. Even the red cloak covering it seemed dimmed and faded by the shriveling blast of the Annihilator.

Bellenzor spoke a phrase, and then stepped back from the

mummified thing at his feet. The stone wall trembled. A human shape stepped forth from it, moving with slow, heavy strides. At a command from the wizard, the man-like thing of stone took up the remains and left the chamber with them. Gariel felt himself drawn after the creature and its burden, down into silence and oblivion.

6

A New Alliance

When the gray giant of animated stone had completed its mission, it returned to Bellenzor's chamber, where the wizard awaited it. Bellenzor dismissed his creature with a word and a gesture. It turned and moved with ponderous tread to the wall, where it blended into the stones without a trace.

Bellenzor stood by the fire, his features fixed in deep concentration. He remained thus for a long time, then he went to the door of the chamber, where a pair of servitors waited.

"Bring the apprentice Jalander to me," he ordered one, and to the other, he said, "The Master of Apprentices has left the city. Take two junior servitors, go to his quarters, and bring all his belongings to me."

The servitors bowed and departed on their commissions. In a very short time, a confused and sleepy senior apprentice begged entrance to Bellenzor's chamber and was admitted by the wizard himself.

"You are welcome, Jalander," said Bellenzor, guiding the apprentice to a chair. "The hour is late, I know, but my message is urgent. My brother Gariel has left the city on a mission of great importance. His absence will be long, and a replacement must be found. I have chosen you to be my new assistant and oversee the apprentices."

Jalander looked up, startled into wakefulness by this unexpected news. He attempted to stammer a response, but Bellenzor stilled him with a gentle gesture.

"I have been watching you, Jalander. You are skilled and hard-working. Most important, your loyalty is unimpeachable. You deserve advancement," said the wizard.

"I am grateful, Master."

"I speak of loyalty to the Empire, and to Ankaria."

"They are inseparable. Only Ankaria can save the Empire from her enemies, and only we of the Empire worship Ankaria as befits the power of the Annihilator. To be loyal to one is to be loyal to the other," said Jalander.

"True, and well said, Jalander. But you must go farther in your loyalty. You must also be loyal to me, for I serve Ankaria and the Empire."

Jalander rose from his chair and fell to his knees before Bellenzor. With bowed head, he said, "You have my loyalty, Master."

"I did not doubt it. There are still some, even among the Thirty-three, who fear the Annihilator, and would shrink from calling upon its power," said Bellenzor, raising Jalander to his feet. "They look upon me as the chief advocate of Ankaria, and direct all their opposition toward me. I must be surrounded by those I can trust, if I am to preserve the Empire."

"I will be loyal to you, to the Empire, and to Ankaria as long as I have life in me," Jalander said fervidly.

Bellenzor nodded in approval and gestured for the other to resume his chair. Seating himself opposite Jalander, he said, "Your duties begin at once. You are aware, I am sure, of most of the duties my brother performed, and I will instruct you in any matters of doubt. Information will be exchanged between us in confidence, so it might be well to choose an assistant for you whom we can trust. I have been observing the apprentices carefully, but I would like to hear of anyone you recommend."

Pausing only briefly, Jalander said, "I think Montolors would serve well. His loyalty is as firm as mine."

"I favor Montolors myself. Let him be the one to assist you. Are there any others whose loyalty to Ankaria and to me you consider beyond reproach?"

Jalander recited six names, hesitated for a moment, and added three more. "Of these I can be certain," he said. "Of the rest of the apprentices, I have no more grounds to trust them than I do to doubt them."

"Then your first task is clear. A time of decision is at hand, Jalander. We must know our friends and our enemies." At Bellenzor's last word, Jalander looked up, his expression troubled, and the wizard said firmly, "The word is not too strong. The Empire is in mortal danger, and there is no neutral ground. Those who are not completely loyal are enemies."

Jalander nodded. His uneasiness was apparent, and when he spoke at last, his words seemed forced out. "Forgive me if I am presumptuous, Master... but I am troubled by what you say."

"Speak freely, Jalander."

"I am pained to say it, Master, but your brother Gariel... I have heard him speak scornfully of Ankaria, and mock those who believed. When I tried to learn his true feelings, he was evasive."

"I am aware of Gariel's feelings. I appointed him my assistant in spite of them, Jalander. I knew that I must have a trustworthy man at my side and none seemed more trustworthy than my own brother. I was certain that in time, he would come to believe as I do."

"Only a few nights ago, he did not."

"Tonight, Gariel first comprehended the full power of Ankaria. He doubts no more."

"I am glad to hear it, Master."

"Does anything else trouble you? Is there anything more you would ask?"

"Nothing, Master."

"Good. Bring Montolors to me after the evening meal tomorrow, and I will give you my instructions. There is much to be done, and the time is short."

When Jalander had departed, Bellenzor returned to the fireside. He settled into a chair, sighed deeply, and let his head fall back like a man utterly spent. As he sat unmoving, his form and outline wavered for a moment, like a blown candle flame. After a time he slumped forward and covered his face with his hands, breathing deeply and wearily. He dropped his hands and stared into the fire, and faintly whispered, "Gariel, forgive me. It must be this way." Then he sank back and went into a deep sleep.

• • •

Winter came and passed, and in early spring the main forces of the Empire left the city to confront the Alliance of the Nine Lords once again. The early reports were disheartening. The standards of the enemy now flew over lands no conqueror's foot had ever trod before, and their camps stood where once the Empire's outposts had risen. Some of the richest territories had been seized, or laid waste. Ruins and abandoned farmsteads were all that remained of once-prosperous regions.

But in early summer, word of a victory came to the White City. Easy progress had made the forces of the Alliance overconfident and disdainful of their enemy. The armies of the Empire, on the other hand, were goaded by shame and humiliation; they fell on the invaders in a wild fury impossible to withstand. Throughout the summer, the outlanders fell back before the fury of the Empire; at last they dug in, determined to hold, and in a bloody three-day battle, they held. After that clash, neither side was strong enough to mount a new attack in force. Skirmishing in the autumn was cautious, and when the first snows fell, the situation was little different from what it had been in the spring. The armies of the Empire had regained some conquered territory, but the outlanders had strengthened their hold on other areas. Their victories had cost the Empire dearly. When all reports had been heard and evaluated, it was clear to the Thirty-three that the fall of the Empire had been postponed, but not averted. At best, they had bought a year or two, and they had bought them dearly.

In their deliberations on the most recent campaign, the Thirty-three revealed the deep division among them. Behind the leadership of an honored veteran, a few stood firm for a fight to the death. If the city were to fall to the Nine Lords, they declared, it must be a ruin of blood and flame. No prisoner must be taken, no trophy must be defiled by the invaders' hands, no building must remain standing to shelter them. If the Empire was fated to fall, its last act would be to snatch the joy of victory from the enemy.

A smaller minority rejected this view with abhorrence. They urged immediate negotiation with the outlanders in order to seek an honorable peace. Better to talk than to fight, they said; better to live, even in defeat, than to die and lose everything. Future generations would bless those who made this decision;

THE TIME OF THE ANNIHILATOR

make any other, and there might be no future generations.

The spokesman for the peace seekers, the venerable Alnore, cast one final look of appeal at his assembled peers and resumed his seat. Bellenzor rose to speak for the largest faction. His views were well known, and his powers of persuasion were respected. On this occasion, his speech was brief.

"We have debated long on the future conduct of the war. The time for debate is now over. We must talk no more of surrender, and we must drive all thought of self-destruction from our minds. Victory is within our grasp. We must seize it!" he said, looking at Alnore with a challenge in his eyes, then turning his gaze on Vesvigan, spokesman for those who would destroy the White City and its people rather than have them fall into the enemy's hands.

"The defeat of the Empire is inevitable," said Alnore wearily. "Your prescription for victory would end in the destruction of both sides. It might well consume all the life in the world. You would unleash a magic beyond all control. Only our way can save the Empire."

"The power I summon will be our servant, not our master, Alnore. But what of you, Vesvigan?" said Bellenzor more gently, turning to his other adversary.

"I'm no mage, but I have some knowledge of magic. It seems to me that Alnore speaks sensibly," said the grizzled warrior.

"If you believe so, how can you withhold your support from me? If I am right, we would have victory. If Alnore is right, we would not die without destroying the enemy as well as ourselves."

"True, but... but we must not risk destroying everything, Bellenzor. If we die bravely, and bring the Empire down around us, we will be remembered. Our courage and our sacrifice will live on to inspire those who escape and survive. One day our revenge will come."

"Why 'one day'? Why not now? You speak bravely, Vesvigan, but I think you are as fearful as Alnore."

"Do not say such things of me," Vesvigan growled, and his supporters murmured angrily.

Raising his hands in a pacific gesture, Bellenzor said, "Your courage in battle is well known, Vesvigan, and no one questions it. I say that you fear the power of magic."

"If I do, I'm not alone. Once the destructive force of magic is loosed on the world, it can never be contained. What will be the good of our sacrifice if no one lives to recall us?"

Smiling patiently, Bellenzor said, "And do you think our enemies are so sensitive to honor that they will keep the memory of your sacrifice alive? They are politic men, Vesvigan. They want no future generations rising to avenge the fallen. They will besmirch your name and your honor with lies, call you cowards, say you crawled and begged for mercy as they smashed your city to rubble."

"No!" Vesvigan cried.

"Yes. Your sacrifice will be forgotten, and your enemies' children will live to laugh at you."

Vesvigan's little group of adherents clustered around him. Bellenzor's words had struck them to the heart; if he spoke truly, all their courage would be mocked, and their enemies would enjoy the ultimate triumph they had hoped to withhold. The last defenders of the White City would be forgotten or, worse still, remembered in dishonor.

Seeing the effect of Bellenzor's speech, Alnore rose and in a clear voice cried, "Let us hear no more of this council of destruction! Bellenzor recommends a desperate act of suicide worse even than the policy of Vesvigan. Let us agree instead to seek an honorable peace. If the Nine Lords demand territory, or treasure, we have them to spare—only let us shrink from bringing the world to ruin before the blast of the Annihilator. Let this ancient abomination remain forever exiled from the world of men!"

Bellenzor turned a cold gaze on him, and Alnore shrank away. Bellenzor's outline flickered for an instant, his eyes remaining fixed on Alnore all the while. The old man drew himself up and raised an accusing finger to point at him, but not a word came. Instead, Alnore clutched at his chest and cried out in pain. He doubled over with a dying moan, fell to the floor of the chamber, and lay still.

Alnore's supporters rushed to his side. They turned him over, and saw that he was beyond their help. One by one, they raised their eyes to Bellenzor, who stood opposite them, arms folded, face impassive.

"He is dead," said Bellenzor.

• • •

THE TIME OF THE ANNIHILATOR 65

When the Thirty-three met again, Alnore had been replaced by Jalander. No talk was heard of negotiating with the outlanders. Vesvigan abandoned his position soon after. The Thirty-three were unanimous in their acceptance of Bellenzor's plan, and at Jalander's urging, they placed the conduct of the war entirely in Bellenzor's hands.

From that time on, Bellenzor seldom was seen outside his chambers. He had few visitors. Only Jalander and Montolors came and went regularly, and they were seen more than once to emerge trembling and pale. They acted as Bellenzor's deputies, and carried his orders to the Thirty-three and elsewhere about the city, but they spoke to no one of the things they saw and heard in his chambers. Those few who heard the sounds that penetrated the heavy oaken doors, and glimpsed the shadows of the forms that visited the chamber from somewhere within, wished to know no more.

When spring came, the field commanders were given their orders. They were surprised—and in view of their diminished forces, many were relieved—to learn that they were to avoid major engagements. They were to hold fast, but not to attack. The enemy appeared to have adopted similar tactics, and the war settled into a stalemate.

There was some dissatisfaction among the Thirty-three. Bellenzor had promised the destruction of the outlanders, and there had been scarcely threescore enemy casualties in the year's time. Along with the dissatisfaction there was a sense of relief at the possibility that it might not be necessary to invoke the Annihilator after all. Each of these views was held quietly and privately, and expressed only with great caution. Something about Bellenzor and his silent, observant minions made those who disagreed with them reluctant to speak. The memory of Alnore's death was vivid in their minds.

Late one night at the end of winter, Bellenzor summoned Jalander to his chamber. When the doors were sealed, he drew the younger man to a cleared space at the center of the room.

"Ankaria comes tonight," he said. When Jalander looked at him fearfully, he went on, gripping the younger man's sleeve tightly, "You must stay. I require another, and I am able to trust no one else."

Jalander swallowed loudly and nodded. "Will it come here, to this chamber? Will it ... appear to us?"

"I have found the spell to pierce the last barrier and permit Ankaria to reenter our world. Whether it will do so, I cannot say. What form it might take, how it will look upon us... I know none of this. But it will come, in all its power, and that power may be ours."

"May be ours? *May* be...? Do you doubt?" Jalander's eyes were wide, and his voice small with fear as he said, "You promised that Ankaria would befriend us—would serve us!"

"And I still believe it will. But I do not prescribe for a being like Ankaria. It will do as it wishes."

"Then let it stay beyond the barrier," Jalander said, pulling free of his master. He raised his hands defensively and backed away. "You spoke as if you knew... as if you could control... but the thing that Alnore feared, and tried to warn us about ... it might come about! You must go no further."

"We have passed the point where we can choose to stop," Bellenzor said with cold contempt. "Ankaria comes. We can hesitate. We can delay its coming—perhaps—but it will come. It has penetrated to our world before, but only fitfully. Now it comes to remain among us. Will you have it come in anger? Would you meet Ankaria as its betrayer?"

Jalander was beside himself with fear. His face was pale and his hands shook. "Before? Has Ankaria been here before? When?"

"To plant a lingering death in Valimagdon's breast. To crush the heart of Alnore. To remove those who stood in the way of its return."

Jalander staggered backward, as if stricken, and clutched at a chair to steady himself. "I'm afraid, Bellenzor, terribly afraid," he said in a low, tremulous voice. "If we stop now, perhaps ... perhaps Ankaria will not come. Even you can't be certain. There's a chance we'll escape. But if we go on, and Ankaria comes, we'll be helpless before its power!"

"We will go on. Take up the book on the table behind you, and read the passage marked in red," said Bellenzor. When Jalander still hesitated, he snapped, "Do it!"

Jalander started from the chair and all but collapsed over the table. A black-bound book lay open on a low reading stand, and he looked down upon it dumbly.

"Take it up and read!" Bellenzor commanded.

Jalander's voice was weak at first, but the power of the incantation seemed to give him strength. His voice soon steadied and deepened to a low drone that echoed through the chamber.

As Jalander read, Bellenzor stooped to complete a figure marked on the stone floor. When the figure was sealed, he took up a scroll that lay in the center and raised it overhead. Slowly and distinctly he uttered three phrases, timing them to serve as responses to Jalander's recitation. At the third phrase, the tip of the scroll burst into flame.

Jalander was silent now, his role in the ritual accomplished. He watched as Bellenzor outlined a form in the air, mimicking the pattern drawn on the floor. The light of the burning scroll hung in the emptiness, burning with lurid brilliance, until a complex many-sided figure glowed in the air between them.

The light spread slowly inward until a single plane of crimson hung before Bellenzor. The wizard reached forward and thrust the scroll into the plane. As he did so, the scroll was consumed, and he spoke the final phrase to summon forth Ankaria.

The light quivered and flared up and began to enfold Bellenzor, who stood unafraid to accept its embrace. Jalander watched it close around his master. Bellenzor was clearly visible through the curtain of fire, standing motionless, arms upraised, like one in ecstasy. His outline dimmed and wavered; then, in an instant, the light was gone and Jalander stood blinking in darkness made doubly black by the sudden absence of brilliant light.

When his sight began to clear, Jalander saw Bellenzor outlined in the glow of the sinking fire in the grate. "Bellenzor ... are you all right? Did the fire harm you?" he asked in a faint voice. When no response came, he asked again, "Bellenzor, is all well?"

The figure before him moved, throwing out its arms and tossing back its head, stretching like a man rising from a long sleep. Jalander heard deep, slow laughter.

"Bellenzor, Master, speak to me!" he cried.

In a voice that sounded like the wizard's echoing through cold empty spaces, the figure before him said, "Bellenzor is gone. I am Ankaria."

Jalander had time to utter a single soft moan of terror before the master stretched forth its hand and extinguished him as one crushes a fly beneath a fingertip. Looking down on the lifeless body, the thing in Bellenzor's form gave a soft sigh of repletion, like a man who has dined well after long fasting.

PART TWO

7

Flight

Gariel awoke to darkness. He drew a breath, and then another. The air stank of death.

He was naked, and chilled. Cold, yielding things pressed against him on all sides, and lay across his legs and his chest. With a great effort, he worked himself free, thrusting off the weight that held him down.

For a time he lay still, drained of strength, breathing deeply of the tainted air. He was alive, in his body, and that body was whole. He remembered the sight of a desiccated form, the sensation of sundering, rising apart from his flesh and then falling into darkness. His mind raced, a whirl of fragmented memories. He understood nothing of what had happened to him.

Shivering, he pulled himself to hands and knees. As he started forward, his hand came down on a face. He drew it back quickly, but there was no outcry, no motion, no reaction of any kind. Reaching out cautiously, he touched the face again. The flesh was cold to his touch. He groped wildly, and his hands fell on arms, legs, breasts, faces, all of them waxen and cold. Smothering an involuntary groan of horror and revulsion, he dragged himself forward until he came up against earth. He stood, feeling his way up the barrier, and as he reached its full extent, his fingertips curled over the top. He pulled himself up, out of the charnel pit, and lay for a time shuddering and gasping on the dank ground.

Far away, a fire burned. Two men sat by it, conversing. The low murmur of their voices was just audible in the surrounding silence. From time to time, one of them drank from a jug and passed it to the other. Once they laughed, softly and privately, and the ordinary sound seemed horrifying in these surroundings. Gariel lay shivering, looking on in a paralysis of confusion and terror, until he felt a rat run over his outstretched hand. He was suddenly aware of the fluid scurrying of their humped bodies all around him, and the squeak and chittering of their commerce.

He realized where he must be. He was still weak, and his mind was like a shattered mirror, but he knew that he must bestir himself and get away.

His eyes had by now grown accustomed to the faint light, and he saw a pile of clothing near the edge of the pit. He worked his way to it. Crouching in its shadow, he lifted off garments and a heavy cloak, and felt for boots to fit him. There was a risk to touching these things, he knew, but he had no choice. Once dressed, he kept the pile of garments between him and the fire and, stooping low, he made his way into the darkness on the far side of the pit, away from this tainted ground.

The burial of the dead was a ritual of solemn significance in the White City. Masters, councilors, and others of prominence had special burial places within the city walls; the rest were placed in the appropriate spot on the surrounding plain. All were buried upright, their faces turned to the west.

The exceptions to this practice were criminals, beggars, and those who died of a contagious sickness. For them, a special place was reserved beneath the city. The broken remains of executed criminals were dragged there and buried flat on their stomachs, with a tablet bearing words of execration laid on their backs. Beggars and victims of disease were stripped and laid in a deep pit, facing upward; lime, and then dirt, were shoveled over them, and a tree, symbol of the Nurturer, was marked in the soil that covered their remains. Their garments were burnt, and the ashes buried with the corpses of their former possessors.

It was to this place of burial, in the ancient vaults beneath the city, that Gariel had been conveyed. He still did not grasp what had happened to him. Memories all the more terrible for their vagueness crowded and jostled in his mind. He knew he had seen his own shriveled corpse, and felt separation and oblivion; yet he was not dead. A dead man would not feel the rough garments against his flesh, nor the chill on face and hands. He would not gag at the rank carrion air, nor blink at the light, nor suffer the consuming thirst that made his mouth and throat feel dry as a fistful of sand. Gariel lived. He had escaped the touch of the Annihilator. But how, and why, he could not begin to imagine.

He had long known of the labyrinthine ways that lay beneath the White City, but he had no first-hand experience of them. The work of these places was done by others. Now, with his mind shaken and his memories disordered, he had to reach back to a time of quiet study that seemed like a mythical lost age of innocence to try to recall the turnings and windings marked on the ancient tablets from the early ages.

He stumbled away from the fireglow, feeling his way along. The rough wall under his fingertips turned smooth, and the yielding ground firm. Soon he was in a dry tunnel. The air was cold and dank, but free of the smell of the dead. The floor sloped gently upward.

He came at last to a set of ancient steps, concave in their centers from the slow wear of generations that had ascended and descended on long-forgotten business. The steps were faintly lit from above, by light coming through a series of barred openings high in the walls. He climbed cautiously, quietly, but with a growing sense of deliverance, exhilarated by his ascent from the subterranean darkness.

He finally emerged in a ruined storehouse near the eastern wall. The day was on the wane, and he thought it best to leave the city at once. At this hour, the gate guard would be least watchful.

He drank deeply from a fountain near the gate. The quenching of his thirst only made him more aware of his hunger. He searched in the clothing he had taken and found a few coins, which he spent on food for his journey. The guards at the gate took one look at him—a poorly clad figure, a mud-spattered, hollow-eyed beggar by the look of him—and let him pass, glad to see him gone.

He followed the road east for a time, then turned north. It meant hard traveling at this time of year, but he had little choice. The enemy had overrun the southern territories, and battles were still being fought in the east and west. Most important, the only home he knew and the only friends he had lay to the north.

Travel was slow, and harder than he had anticipated. He avoided all the settlements near the city, fearing discovery, and he saw no other human for twenty days. At that point, starving and half-frozen and desperate, he begged a meal and a sleeping-place at a farmstead in a tiny hamlet. He stayed for nine days, working in exchange for food. When he insisted on leaving, the farmer gave him a castoff cloak and a pair of sturdy boots, old but with good wear left in them. The farmwife packed a generous stock of food for his journey.

When he reached the pass, dry, powdery snow was falling, blowing in spectral curls along the stony uplands. A flood of memories came back to him, and he sank down, weeping, while the snow eddied and swirled about him. Once before he had come this way, when he was young and blessed with love, and waiting to begin his life. Now he was alone and broken, seeking a quiet place to await the end.

Moarra and their children were dead. Valimagdon was dead, and Bellenzor, his last living tie to the human race, was worse than dead. He himself was dead in spirit, dead as a mage, as a husband, as a man. For a moment he felt a great desire to lie down here until the snow covered him, burying all his pain and loss beneath its white mantle, bringing him peace at last.

But he could not do that. He climbed to his feet and made his way through the pass. A few days' travel would bring him to the settlement, and there he would stay to the end of his days. He had failed Valimagdon, and the Empire, and all mankind, if the old wizard's fears were right. In the settlement, at his forge, he would at least be useful and dependable, among friends.

Deepening cold and the dwindling of his scanty food store goaded him on. In five days he came to the river. He gazed across and found the reason why he had seen no smoke rising from the chimneys when he looked down from the last hilltop. The settlement was in ruins.

He walked across the frozen river slowly, numbed by the final tragedy, and made his way through the remains of the settlement. The work of destruction had been methodical and unhurried. Every house had been burned until only charred fragments of wall and heavy corner posts remained. Stables, barns, woodsheds, and outbuildings had all been burned or smashed apart to serve as fuel for greater fires. His own house and small cottage were a tumble of blackened wood, no portion standing higher than his shoulder. The forge, being of stone, had fared better. The walls stood, but the doors had been wrenched off and the burnt roof had collapsed.

Gariel climbed the rise, and found that the outlying farmsteads had also been put to the torch. Snow had fallen since the raid, and the smooth white ground showed no trace of the brutal events that had taken place. The setting of black and white against the dark background of the evergreens even had a kind of stark beauty. Only the reek of burnt wood attested to the devastation.

Gariel shouted repeatedly, proclaiming his return and his wish to help old friends and neighbors, but no reply came. Whether they had all been taken off somewhere into the forest and butchered, or fled in terror, or been led off into captivity, he could not tell. The settlement was destroyed, the inhabitants gone. That much was clear. The rest was mystery.

He wanted to visit the graves of his wife and children, but after setting out twice and turning back, confused, he realized that he could not remember the way. He was very weak, and his head swam. His food was gone, and there was none here.

Returning to the forge, he crawled into a sheltered niche where a portion of the fallen roof lay against a wall. He felt that he had come to the end. He would have preferred to die by Moarra's graveside, but the forge would do as well. Nothing mattered now. He wrapped his cloak tightly around him, laid his head on his arms, and fell into a deep, exhausted sleep.

He slept long, and awoke with a raging hunger. In growing desperation, he searched through the ruins, but found nothing. He remembered his garden, and groped in the snow behind the cottage until it occurred to his befuddled mind that the garden

had not been planted last season. He stumbled to Strolsse's
garden then, and scraping away the snow, he managed to unearth
a few shriveled roots overlooked in the harvesting. He bolted
them down and returned, wet and shivering, to the forge.

He lost track of time after that, as fever gripped him and
his strength failed. Waking and sleeping seemed to merge, day
and night to blend into a single featureless grayness. Then one
morning he awoke clearheaded but very weak, with scarcely
the strength to pull himself from his sleeping alcove and struggle to his feet. The sickness in his body had passed, and some
of the sickness in his mind was gone, as well.

He had to have food, and the only source he knew was
Strolsse's garden. It was scarcely two hundred paces distant,
but he had to pause for rest three times on his way.

When he came in sight of the garden, he froze at the glimpse
of things moving in it. Working cautiously closer, he saw that
woodfowl had ventured into the ruins and were scratching where
he had uncovered the dirt in his earlier effort.

Here was food, if Gariel could catch it. He could not afford
to lose this chance. Woodfowl were timid creatures, easily
frightened off. He did not trust himself to throw a stone ac-
curately, and there was no other weapon at hand. He began to
move slowly toward the birds, stopping after every step, until
he was within reach of them.

Lunging forward, he seized one woodfowl, and with a wild
grasp, caught a second by the foot as the rest took to flight
with short, sharp cries of alarm. He wrung the birds' necks at
once, and brought them to the forge. His ravenous hunger made
him want to tear the birds apart and eat them on the spot, but
his reason was beginning to reassert itself. He knew that his
stomach would reject the raw flesh, and he would be worse
off. A little patience, and he would have a sustaining meal.

He kindled a small fire. Plucking and drawing the birds, he
skewered them and set them over the fire to cook. He forced
himself to wait, and to eat slowly, and to leave one of the
woodfowl for a later meal.

With the strength of this food, he would be able to hunt
and set traps. There were edible roots to be found in the woods,
and perhaps a few handfuls of dried and shrunken berries might
still be gathered. A man could live if he had the will to go on.

Warm food in his belly raised Gariel's spirits. He found a

pot and filled it with snow, then placed it over the fire. By the charred doorpost of his cottage he gathered dried, close-furled timmery leaves from a low bush and added them to the hot water. The sharp tang of the infusion filled him with a sense of well-being and a new confidence. He wanted to live, and he was going to work to assure his survival. He would live.

He dug in the ruins of the cottage and uncovered three traps and a pair of hunting spears. The traps needed repairing, and the spearpoints were rusted, but all could be used. Settling in a spot sheltered from the wind, where the sun could warm him, he began to work on the traps.

He tried to focus his mind completely on the work of his hands, but an idea kept intruding. It was preposterous, but he could not force it from his mind. He wanted to live in order to face the Annihilator once again, and drive it back to its place of exile. Despite the awesome seriousness of the situation, he could not suppress a smile, for there came into his mind the image of a flea threatening to demolish a mountain. Gariel knew that he had no better chance of success than the flea, but he found that that did not matter. He had lost everything he cherished, and still he lived. For his life to be meaningful, he had to find a new purpose. He had found one, and however fantastic it might be, it was the only thing that could sustain him. He had no idea how he would go about it, but he did not concern himself with methods. All that would come in time. Right now, he must survive and build his strength.

He worked on the traps until nearly sundown, then returned to the forge and built up the fire for the night. After finishing the second woodfowl, he placed the collected bones in the pot of melted snow, and set it to simmer. The broth would give him strength to hunt in the morning.

He stretched out near the fire and went quickly to sleep. His sleep was deep and peaceful, free of dreams, until he awoke with a start in the night. He had heard his name.

He raised himself on one elbow and looked around. The moon was near full, and light streamed into the roofless forge. He saw nothing. He had dreamt after all, then; but he remembered no dream, only the sound of a voice calling his name, faraway but clear.

Perhaps someone had returned to the settlement. He rose and drew his cloak close against the night chill. No one was outside, and there were no footprints but his own in the snow.

He heard his name called again. With a sudden shiver of wonder, he recognized the voice.

"Valimagdon! This is Gariel, old master—I hear you!" he cried.

"Gariel... forgive..." said the dry, distant voice.

"Forgive you, Valimagdon? You've done me no offense."

"Forgive me, Gariel," the voice repeated.

"I do forgive you, if you ask it. Show yourself, Valimagdon. No need to conceal yourself from me."

The air before the forge began to shimmer and became bright, and the brightness deepened and took form. Gariel saw his old master standing before him like a column of cold light. He was filled with feeling, but no trace of fear.

"You trusted me and did my bidding, Gariel, and I failed you. I sent you against one too strong for all my power," said the wraith softly, sadly.

"I'm still alive. It didn't destroy me."

"My magic was sufficient to deceive the enemy and to save your life, but too weak to vanquish it."

"What is the enemy, Valimagdon? Is it really the Annihilator of the ancient cult?"

"It is the Fourth Child and the Annihilator, the Avenger of Chaos, the dark twin of the Lifegiver that seeks to gather all life to itself. It is all these, and other names, but it is more, more. I did not know, Gariel, I did not suspect. Now I have passed among those who know, and I am ashamed. In my pride, I sent you to destruction."

"But it didn't destroy me, Valimagdon! It hurt me, and shook my mind and my will. I've taken long to recover even this much, but I'll recover and I'll face it again."

"It has overcome. All will fall before it. The desolation you see all around you is its work," said the mournful voice.

"Surely this was the work of soldiers, Valimagdon."

"The thing you faced is the force behind the war, this war and all wars and every act of cruelty. It thrives on destruction and death. It caused the Nine Lords to grow envious of the Empire and rise against it, and it incited the emperors, and after them the Thirty-three, to vow to exterminate the enemy. It urges men on to ever more brutal deeds. It shrivels all com-

THE TIME OF THE ANNIHILATOR 79

passion, drives out all mercy. It is the Annihilator," said the spirit of the old mage.

"Is there no way to stop it?"

"It has devoured empires mightier than ours, and laid waste all the earth. The First People, with all their power and wisdom, fell victim to it. We cannot escape."

"We can call upon our guardians. Surely the three of them together can withstand the Annihilator and save us."

Valimagdon's voice echoed like the closing of a final door. "The guardians are a dream and a delusion. The Sower of Worlds is far away. Only the Annihilator is here, and it must overcome."

"No, Valimagdon!" Gariel cried, overcome by anger and frustration. "We are here, and even if we stand alone, we must find a way to resist it, and drive it off forever."

A note of hope was in Valimagdon's voice as he asked, "Would you confront the Annihilator again, even if you stood alone?"

"I would."

"Then perhaps there is a chance, Gariel. You will need knowledge that I lacked the courage to seek. The way is hard."

"Tell me where the knowledge is, and I'll seek it."

"Hear me first," said the shade.

"No. If I hear of danger I might weaken. Show me the way, Valimagdon, and I'll seek out what I need."

The figure of light grew brighter. The spirit of the old mage smiled and said, "Then I will be your guide. Come, Gariel."

8

Voices Out of a Dead World

With no sensation of change or movement, Gariel found himself in a flat place ringed by high walls that soared upward and disappeared into darkness. Whether the walls met overhead or were joined to a roof he could not tell. He saw no stars when he looked up, but he felt no sensation of enclosure. The air was cool and dry and a light breeze was blowing. All was silent.

The floor of the immense arena in which he stood was smooth, with slabs of differing sizes rising from it at irregular intervals. Some were barely above floor level, but others stood chest-high or higher, though none appeared to rise above his head. The slabs were of black stone, unadorned, with smooth surfaces and rough-hewn edges. He could not guess their purpose.

The surrounding walls were pierced by oval openings. They were dark, and Gariel assumed that they were entrances to rooms or galleries, but no stairs or ramps led to them; they opened onto nothingness, and the highest of them was higher than the top of the Masters' Tower in the White City.

He looked around and found that he was alone. He had no knowledge of where he was, or how he came to be here, or where he was to go. Of Valimagdon there was no trace. He could see clearly, for the place was illuminated by a bluish light that pervaded the lower portions and cast a faint shadowless glow high up the walls. The light seemed almost alive; it was in constant flux, flaring here, dimming there, but it maintained a level of brightness throughout the great space.

Gariel felt warmth against the flesh of his breastbone, and reaching inside his shabby tunic he drew out an amulet. It was a single smooth stone, pale green in color, slightly larger than a man's thumb, wrapped in a wire of some base metal and hung on a leather thong. It warmed his hand as he grasped it, and the warmth filled him as he felt Valimagdon's presence unlocking the magic that still slumbered deep within him.

He walked with immediate certitude to a knee-high slab some distance away. Mounting it, he seated himself cross-legged and spoke a phrase. The slab rose, light as a leaf in the wind, and carried him up and into one of the dark openings in the wall.

He traveled for a long time at what felt like great speed. Sometimes he moved through tunnels so narrow that he could have touched both walls at once merely by extending his arms; at times the floor of the tunnel dropped away with sickening abruptness and he felt himself crossing an abyss that stretched away on all sides into infinite emptiness, only to be suddenly enclosed in a confining passage once again. The slab came to rest at last in a domed chamber. It touched down gently, and Gariel stepped from it.

He stood at the center of an amphitheater. Tiers of benches rose all around him, curving upward until they joined the dome that hung overhead, an immense featureless hemisphere of pale light. He could see that the benches were occupied, and he raised his hands in salutation, but no sound or movement acknowledged his greeting. He stepped forward, across a smooth floor, and as he approached, he noticed with a pang of horror that the benches were filled with mummified human forms, grinning mirthlessly down, empty eye sockets turned upon him. Opulent robes hung rotting on their shrunken frames, and jeweled diadems and coronets tilted crazily over their shriveled brows.

For a moment he faltered, but the warm throb of the amulet assured him that he was not alone. He walked on, and even when the forms began to stir, and the rustle of their movement was joined by the dry sibilance of their voices, his tread was firm until he halted before a stepped dais on which sat three throned skeletons. He bowed to the golden-robed figure on the central throne, then he stood with folded arms to await its response.

The skeletal thing pointed at him with a staff held in its bony hands. "Who are you?" it whispered.

"I am he who will vanquish the being that destroyed you. It walks in the world still, and now it would destroy another empire, and all things living on earth. You must help me," Gariel said, in words that came to him unbidden, as if they had lain waiting within him for this moment.

"What is all this to us? We are no longer creatures of earth," the central figure whispered.

In low rustling voices, those on either side added their messages. "Let all empires fall," said the one on the left, and the other said, "Let all things die, and be as we are."

"You have forgotten much," Gariel said. "I came to you seeking knowledge, but I wonder now if all your knowledge is lost."

"We forget nothing! We are wise!" said the figure on the central throne in an angry hiss.

Gariel laughed softly and shook his head. "You have been gone from the earth too long. You forget that all empires must fall and all things must die, and come to this."

The skeletal form to the left of the high throne rose and pointed at Gariel. "This we know, and have said. If it is so, why have you come to mock us? What have we forgotten?"

"You have forgotten the fitness of things. Empires rise and fall, and creatures live and die, all in their proper season. It is not fit for one creature to subject all things to its whim, to topple kingdoms and empires and snuff out the lives of their people merely for the pleasure of exercising its power."

"If all must fall, what does it matter by whose hand they fall?" said the central figure, and the others echoed, "What does it matter?"

"Then I am right. You have forgotten."

"No! We remember all! We are wise!" The cries went up in a sibilant rush all around him, like a sudden gust of winter wind through a grove of evergreens.

Gariel turned as he spoke, so he might address his words

to all. His voice carried clearly to every dry and withered listener. "Do you remember the pleasure and pride you had in your empire, and the pain of having it all torn from you? I think not. Do you remember the feeling of flesh on your bones, and breath in your body, and the sun on your face? Do you remember love, and friendship, and joy? I think not." The assemblage sat silent and motionless, intent on his words. Softening his voice, he went on, "Do you remember the sunset over the water, and the sound of the waves, and the purity of winter? The green of spring, and the ripening of summer, and the golden richness of autumn—do you remember anything of these? Do you remember what it is to laugh aloud for sheer wordless happiness? I think you have forgotten all these things, for if you remembered even the least of them you would rise up and hurl yourselves against the monstrous thing that would purge the earth of all life, all feeling, all beauty, and leave it a sterile memorial to its own hunger." He paused, and waited in the silence of their eyeless scrutiny, then he flung up his arms and cried, "Do you remember?"

The stillness was profound. Gariel could hear his own heartbeat and the rhythm of his breathing, and no other sound. Then an awful cry, a wail of utter desolation, shattered the silence as a ragged misshapen husk bound in chains, a heavy iron collar around its gaunt neck, struggled to its knees at the bottom step and turned to him. In its shriveled face Gariel saw a despair that shook him to his soul. He averted his eyes from the sight, and the creature sank to the ground with a low moan and did not stir or cry out again.

After a time, the figure on the central throne stood. Cradling the scepter in its arms, it asked simply, "What do you seek from us?"

"Your knowledge, to help me overcome the thing that calls itself the Annihilator."

In a whisper hushed with fear, a single word arose from the tiers all around: "Ankaria."

"Yes, Ankaria. It moves among men now, inciting them to their destruction. I know nothing of its true nature or its origins, only that its power is immensely greater than mine. But I know that for a time, you withstood it. Your knowledge passed from the world long ago, and now I come to seek it."

"Ankaria came to us as a deliverer. We gave it our worship

and it laid waste our homeland and our world. But before the last of us fell, we learned something of our destroyer."

"I would know it," said Gariel.

"Come forward, then."

Gariel climbed the steps to the foot of the central throne. The sceptered figure gave a command, and the thing huddled at the base of the dais lifted its head. Another command, and it began to work its slow way upward in a grotesque writhing motion, whimpering with pain as it came.

"This wretched creature knows Ankaria well. He will reveal all, from the beginning. Can you bear the sight of him, and his touch?"

"I can," said Gariel.

The chained figure struggled to his feet and stood awkwardly before Gariel. One of its limbs was free to the elbow; the hand was a shriveled, twisted claw. At a sharp word from the master on the throne, it raised the ruined hand and reached out to Gariel.

Gariel did not shrink from the touch of the cold dry fingers on his temples, nor the empty gaze of the eyeless sockets. He submitted. He unlocked his mind and loosed his will. Closing his eyes, he felt himself drawn away, rushing at ever greater speed into the past. Empires and cities and campsites winked by as he sped to the time of the First People and far beyond, to a time unimagined in his own age. He was in a world where the moon loomed larger overhead and the air was thick and steamy, and the only living things were so small that he could not see them with his eyes.

He plunged into a blood-warm sea, deep into its darkness, and became one with the life that swarmed about him. There he dwelt, no longer the mere human Gariel. He became an empathic sensibility, observing and waiting. And at some point in the long undifferentiated darkness came the flash of revelation: *I am I. I am a self alone and apart. All else is the other*.

Thus it began, in simple awareness. It was a small, weak creature then, one wriggling insignificant mote in a sea teeming with life. But this mote was different from all the rest. At first it sought for others like itself, but it found none. It was alone. The great gift of awareness set it apart from all other living things.

Awareness gave it some advantages, but awareness alone

could not confer safety. Danger was everywhere in those murky waters. Only speed, strength, and cunning brought safety, and even then, chance hovered above the mightiest to strike them down in their moment of victory.

It learned to divide the other into two kinds: those that hunted and those that fled. Through the early ages, it numbered itself among those that fled. Its quarry were few, and those that hunted it were many and ubiquitous.

It was cautious by instinct, but also curious. In time it knew the ways of hunter and hunted better than the creatures themselves. With that knowledge began its long ascent.

Under the sunless, timeless sea it flowed and darted with the swarm of its fellow creatures, amid them but no longer one of them. It could turn to snatch one up in the midst of headlong flight, and it knew to keep the swarm always between itself and the pursuer. It grew, and learned. Each escape added to its little stock of knowledge. Each quarry taken brought new strength. It went on growing until the swarm were no longer its fellows, but its food.

It left the swarm and spent more and more of its time alone, a solitary predator that darted from nowhere, struck, and was gone before its victims could scatter. As it grew, it changed. New senses developed and old ones became more acute. Its size and shape and physical structure altered. But these changes occurred so slowly, over such vast stretches of time, that it was unaware of them, knowing only that it must hunt, and feed, and avoid its enemies, and live on. It was already unimaginably old.

For long it was the unchallenged lord of all that swam in those dark seas. All things were its prey, and fled at its approach; the other had become one, the victim, the thing to be pursued and devoured. Through unchanging ages it moved under the waters, hunting and feeding and growing ever stronger.

A day came when a great storm took it by surprise and washed it into shallow water. It darted about, filled with unaccustomed fear, and hurled itself, thrashing, into the thin coldness that hung above its world. Eventually it found its way back to the open sea, and not until long after did it approach the land again. It stayed longer in the shallows this time, curiosity overcoming its fear. It returned again and again after that, and at last became a dweller in the fringes of the sea.

The ages passed, and change went on, and finally there came a day when it drew itself up onto the shore, out of the all-embracing sea. Pain drove it seaward again, but something forced it back to the land. It emerged.

It suffered greatly for a time, but it endured. It longed to return to its warm, food-filled dominion. From time to time it revisited the old dark world to hunt and feed as before, but the seas were becoming an alien place. Its visits became shorter and less frequent, and eventually they ceased.

It was a creature of the land now, and it no longer needed its first home. It knew, without understanding, that the age of the seas was ending and its life would be lived henceforth under the pale sky. Other creatures, too, had emerged from the waters, and now the land was filled with life. All things that moved on that turbulent, steaming world were its prey. It lived on as it had lived before, hunting and feeding and slowly changing.

The first change of its life of which it was fully and immediately aware came on a day of pain and slaughter. It had hunted, and was feeding contentedly when it had a sudden sensation of acute danger. The warning came too late. Even as it turned, two huge-headed, razor-toothed carnivores thundered into the little sunlit clearing, cutting off the fastest escape route, while two others crashed through the forest to emerge at its back.

It knew these creatures and their ways. Speed and agility had always enabled it to escape a single one, and it had never known them to hunt other than alone. Now it was faced with four of them, in a narrow space with little room to maneuver. The scent of fresh blood and warm flesh was heavy in the humid air, and their hunger and ferocity were aroused. The wisest course was flight.

It dropped low and moved smoothly to the edge of the clearing, where boulders were thickly strewn and hiding would be easiest. Their attention would be on food; it would make its escape as they homed in on the carcass.

But one of the great beasts caught the flicker of its motion and charged. The others instinctively followed. It could not reach the boulders, and it could not flee. It attacked.

Scuttling under the trunklike legs of the nearest, it ripped open the creature's underbelly and struck directly at the next with the same tactic. The wounded creatures turned on one

THE TIME OF THE ANNIHILATOR

another, and the third hurled itself into the wild broil. It slashed at the last of its assailants, gutting it as easily as it had the others, but as it broke free, one of the struggling trio, reeling blindly in its death throes, trampled on its rear leg, splintering the bones and all but tearing the limb from the socket.

It dragged itself off. The ramping and roaring of the dying carnivores faded in the distance, and still it clawed its way ahead, seeking a dark, safe shelter. At last it came upon a shelf of fallen rock with a clear field of vision before it and no perceptible scent of life. It dragged itself within and sank into oblivion.

It awoke with a start of fear and pain, and slashed out wildly at the little sharp-toothed creatures that swarmed over the rent in its flesh. Those that escaped its stroke scuttled out of reach, squatted down, and waited for it to sleep.

For the first time in all the ages of its dominance, it realized that it, too, could die, just like the other, and that it would be dead very soon if it did not find a secure shelter and a supply of food for its recovery. A great anger came over it, and a hatred for all the stupid, mindless life that swarmed over the earth, and it raged at the thought that it, the master of all, might die while they lived on; die foolishly and pointlessly, by mischance, and hunt and feed no more. It turned all its wrath and pain and hunger on the creatures seated in a half-ring around the entrance to its den.

The nearest of the little flesh-eaters rose unsteadily to its feet, staggered, and slumped to the ground lifeless. One by one, the others did the same. When they all lay still, it felt its hunger sated, as if it had eaten its fill. The pain in its leg was slightly lessened.

It drew back into the cool darkness, awed by the impossible sight it had witnessed. It had killed without slaying, and fed without eating, and it had taken into itself the strength of the other without consuming the other's flesh. Such things had never been, could not be; and yet they were.

Through all the innumerable ages of its existence, it had used the unique power of awareness for no other purpose than to hunt. Now, crippled and forced into immobility, it turned that awareness upon itself.

It remained in the rock den for a long time, mending its body and testing its new power. The putrefying carcasses that lay before the den drew others to them. It let them feed to gorging, then took their life and strength with a single stroke of will. The fallen creatures drew new hunters, and these, in their turn, became its prey.

When at last it came forth to claw its way over the tangle of crushed and whitened bones that palisaded its den, it walked upright. Now it feared no living thing.

It crossed and recrossed all the world's ways. It refined and perfected the new power it had found within itself, and learned that it was not necessary to seek out victims: predators and natural events provided them in abundance. It learned to snatch the flicker of life from a fallen creature just as the hunter's jaws shut, or the water or earth closed over it, and it found that these lives taken in the moment of ultimate terror had a savor missing from those lives it had taken in the ordinary way.

No creature could withstand it, but it soon realized that the world was a turbulent place, and that flood and earthquake and avalanche could be as deadly as any predator. It saw no way to protect against them. It could only be vigilant.

But one day, as it passed through a rocky defile, it felt the ground tremble under its feet. A roar filled the air all around it, and it looked up to see the wall above it crumbling and falling. It could not flee; there was no shelter; it flung up its forepaws to ward off the avalanche, desperately willing it away. Before its astonished eyes, the boulders and dirt divided, and flowed to either side. When all was still again, it stood at the center of an empty cone ringed with rubble. Not a single pebble had touched it.

It was safe, and it was stunned by this manifestation of a new and unsuspected power. But it staggered in weakness, and fell senseless to the ground, emptied of all strength. It lay in a coma, utterly helpless, protected by the rocks towering all around it, and awoke racked with hunger, tormented by delirium.

Long it lay too weak to move; then a pair of lizards peered over the crest of the debris ringing it and scuttled down to investigate the still form below. It snapped up their lives as soon as they came into view. In a little while, it was strong enough to rise. It sensed other small creatures nearby, and drew them closer and took their lives, building up strength to escape.

THE TIME OF THE ANNIHILATOR

It wanted safety and solitude in which to study its newfound power.

It wandered far from this uncertain place of shifting stone and came at last to the shores of an inland sea, in the midst of which rose a rounded hump of land. It stepped forward, and paused at the first touch of the blood-warm water. Then the ancient memories revived; it filled its lungs and plunged in, making its swift way to the islet.

Life abounded on the islet and in the lake, and for some time it did nothing but feed and rest, building strength for the test it had in mind. When its strength was what it had been at the time of the avalanche, it went to the crest of the islet, where a boulder stood poised at the head of a long slope. Squatting down a safe distance off, it willed the boulder to move.

It felt the power surging within itself, rising and flowing outward, draining strength and vitality; but the rock did not move. Exhausted, it dragged itself away. Again it fed and rested, and relived in its mind the moment when it drove off the avalanche. When it felt ready, it returned to the rock and took up its efforts. Again it was unsuccessful. It fed and rested and returned, again and again, determined to master the power within it. For a long time, nothing happened. Then, one day, the rock quivered slightly.

The islet became its home. There it studied its powers, delving ever deeper into the forces within itself and in the world around it, seeking to control them.

At first it was profligate with its power. It leveled the crest of the islet and built itself a rounded shelter, fusing the stones to one another by its will, smoothing the surface beneath its feet, shaping apertures through which it might observe the tiny lights that shone overhead in the night. The work was slow, and emptied it of strength, but it took pleasure in the sheer exercise of its ability. As time passed, it acquired ever greater control, and learned to husband its energies. It could focus narrowly, concentrate on a single objective, and leave its power but little diminished.

The third great change in its life came not suddenly, but as the culmination of long thought and searching. It had lived incalculable ages; it possessed the power to sustain and protect itself to immortality, and the ability to shape the world to its will. All knowledge, all wisdom, lay within its eventual grasp. From an insignificant atom of random sentience at the dawn of life, it had become an all-powerful being poised on the threshold of the infinite. It could not divine its origins, but it could remember eons of life, ever-changing and ever-growing; and contemplating its long development, convinced that its rise could not be purposeless, it sought the goal of its existence.

In time, that purpose became clear. It was its own fulfillment. *I am life, and all that lives is mine.* This was its law and its purpose, the reason that it and the other existed, the explanation of all things.

When it left the islet and went forth into the world again, it found many things changed. Only then did it realize how long it had spent in isolation and how greatly its own physical form had altered. It was smaller now; bulk and brute strength were no longer necessary for its safety. It walked easily on long hind legs. Its forepaws had developed into agile members, and it found a certain satisfaction in performing tasks with its fingers that it could have accomplished instantly with an act of will.

Most of the familiar creatures were gone from the face of the earth; those that remained were so greatly changed as to be new species. The towering, smooth-skinned, many-toothed carnivores had given way to smaller warm-blooded beings with shaggy coverings. Life beat in these new creatures at a faster pace, and their minds were quicker and more alert. The shape and texture of the land was different, and new things grew on the earth. Even the air was drier, and cooler against its skin.

For long, it went shielded only by its own powers. It could walk untouched through blinding sheets of rain and scouring hail, remain cool and shaded under equatorial sun or warm in the teeth of the north wind. Its physical body was safe from discomfort and danger. Out of curiosity, it tested its ability to protect itself by physical strength and dexterity alone. After many trials, it learned to remove intact the shaggy outer covering of certain creatures, and to treat the skin with substances that helped preserve it and make it supple. It shaped the skins to its own form and put them over itself. Henceforth it wore such garments, and to cover its head, it wore the cleaned, preserved head of its victim.

It perfected other skills. It learned to make shelter from

heaped stones, or from branches hacked off with the aid of a sharp-edged stone and laid in rows. It took fire from where it smoldered in the forest and kept the flame alive, feeding and preserving it. Though it did not feed on flesh, it learned to hunt down and trap the fleet creatures of this age instead of drawing them to it. All these things it might have done easily with a mere blink of its will, but it sensed a greater goal ahead, and felt the wisdom of husbanding its power against a time when it might need reserves.

It became aware of a new kind of creature, which it studied with growing interest: beings formed much like itself, only more crudely. But what impressed it was not mere physical structure, but the creatures' apparent ability to reason. Their rationality was of the most rudimentary kind. Nevertheless, they could work together in ways that other creatures could not. They could use tools, and they seemed to plan for the future.

It observed them closely, and saw them struggling to achieve the very things it had taught itself to do. For the first time in countless ages, it felt kinship to another living thing.

It traveled about the earth seeking out these creatures, watching their development, intruding unseen where it felt its interference necessary. Something about them fascinated it, made it feel that its destiny and purpose were somehow bound up with theirs. Goaded on by obscure urgings, it sometimes placed obstacles in their path, and sometimes conferred its bounty on them. Some it preserved from destruction; others it destroyed as unfit. The creatures developed rapidly, and soon reached the point in their development at which it saw that it might reveal itself to them.

It came to each group in a different guise. To all it brought fire, and new tools, and weapons, but it manifested its power in a different way to each tribe. To one, it came in the terrifying darkness of a midday eclipse, bearing fire in its cupped hands. They worshiped it ever afterward as Lightbringer. It appeared to another in the midst of a hurricane, walking upright into a blast that leveled trees, stilling the wind at its command, and they worshiped it as Master of Weathers. A third tribe attacked it on sight, and the way it punished them was remembered forever in the name they gave it: Twister of Bones.

In time, it was known everywhere in the world where the

early races of men gathered. It was god and demon; spirit of light and bringer of darkness; healer and scourge, consoler and slayer, builder and destroyer. To some, it was a creature like themselves in appearance but possessed of gifts beyond imagining; to others, it was a fearsome thing half-human and half-animal; to a few, it was a shapeless, formless power that paralyzed their bodies and gripped their wills with terror. It was worshiped, propitiated, besought; and in the end, wherever it passed it left destruction, for it still drew its power from the lives of others, and when it hungered, it fed. As it grew ever more ancient, it fed at longer intervals, but its hunger was greater. Individual lives no longer satisfied it. It required tribes, nations, and eventually entire races.

It watched men stumble and fall and rise again and again, dragging themselves a little higher each time, and it was amused by the pretensions to reason of these creatures that had become its primary sustenance. But a time came when these weak and clumsy creatures learned to deceive. They tricked it into wasting its power, and when it was exhausted they turned against it magic of their own, and overcame. They were not strong enough to destroy it; they cursed it in the name of every god they knew and imprisoned it in a dark close cell deep under a mountain on a world far away, there to dwindle and die.

It did not die. For long it lay dormant, slowly regenerating. The race that had vanquished it passed away and was forgotten, but still it did not come forth. It studied itself, and explored its powers and its weaknesses. In its prison, it learned the slow strength of patience from the surrounding rock that was its entire universe. It craved revenge, but it waited.

When it returned, it had learned to be subtle. It saw that for all their efforts at reason and their pride in its exercise, men were creatures of emotion. It explored the workings of will and imagination, and found ways to use human emotions to serve its own ends. Life was all it required, and that could be reaped without effort. Humans could easily be led to consume themselves in great banquets of mutual destruction for its benefit. It had only to arouse the proper passions.

In a great and flourishing kingdom, it stirred up ambition among the nobles, pride among the sorcerers, and envy among the commoners. It breathed hatred and suspicion into all, and then it waited for the holocaust.

The destruction exceeded its greediest hopes; so much so that when the last blow had been struck, all the world lay waste and still, and it was long before men gathered together and laid stone upon stone, and once again began to build a civilization. In its long wait, it forgot the lesson of patience, and this time it fell victim to a spell that sealed it off from its prey for another hungry age.

But now it knew the ways of men, and their machinations. It was ready to feed, and it would wait no longer.

9

The Sign and the Weapon

Gariel woke as from a trance. The thing in chains had dropped its withered hand and stood before him in a posture of abject despair. Gariel's mind was still filled with the presence of the Annihilator, but at the sight of a creature so wretched, he felt a surge of pity that purged his consciousness and restored him fully to himself.

As if it had read his thoughts, the figure on the central throne said coldly, "Have no pity on this traitor. Once he was Darra Jhan, a wise and good man, but envy led him to become the destroyer of his people. He sought out the enemy and offered himself as a vessel for Ankaria's power."

"And is he punished still?"

"His punishment is scarce begun."

"Then I cannot help but pity him," said Gariel, thinking of what might be in store for his brother.

"Did you learn what you hoped to learn?"

"I know now what Ankaria is, and why it consumes life, but I learned nothing to give me hope. Ankaria is old beyond imagining and immensely powerful."

"Yet once it was overcome, and nearly destroyed."

"The race that did it vanished from the earth before yours began. Their secrets are lost."

"We were close to their knowledge when the end came. We learned enough to wall out Ankaria from our world, but we could do no more. With more time, we would have found the secret, and overcome the enemy."

"Tell me what you learned. I must have some weapon to use against Ankaria."

The withered figure before him hesitated, and then said, "The price of knowledge is great."

Gariel felt the amulet throb in warning, but he would not be dissuaded. "Give me the knowledge and I will pay the price," he said.

All the rest of that long-dead audience had been still and attentive, but at these words of Gariel's a low soughing sigh rustled through the tiers of watchers, and their dry bodies bent toward him. The amulet beat like a heart, and he laid his hand over it to still it. The dried, grinning remnant of a face before him seemed to grin more broadly in anticipation.

"Understand, we did not find all we sought. We can place a weapon in your hands, and give you a sign, but we can do no more. You must find the last secret for yourself. I tell you this so you will not think we deceive you," said the figure on the throne.

"What is the price?" Gariel asked.

"You spoke to us of the world, and the things it holds, and you made us remember. We have been here long, and forgotten all you named, and we have been at rest. Your words disturbed us. They made us hunger, and until the hunger is sated, we will not rest again. We would enjoy the things of the living, and only you can provide them."

"How?"

"One drop of your blood for each of us. Only one drop, to taste and smell and savor in memory through the ages to come."

Gariel looked at the ranks of skeletal forms, and shuddered with revulsion at the thought of their touch. But he said with a firm voice, "I will pay your price. But first, show me the sign and place the weapon in my hand."

From the dry throats and shriveled lips there went up a thin purring exhalation. The mummified watchers strained forward, but their ruler stilled them with a flourish of his scepter.

"It will be so," he proclaimed in a loud voice, for all to hear. "First the sign and the weapon, and then our price."

He goaded the chained prisoner slumped at his feet, and Darra Jhan struggled erect and raised his dried claw to touch Gariel once again. Hunger glowed like a beacon on his gaunt face. Gariel felt the amulet burn against his chest and took heed. Stepping back, he pointed an accusing finger at the bearer of the scepter.

"You mean to betray me," he said angrily.

"No!"

"Yes. You intend to take my life and give nothing in return."

"No, it is not so. The thought came to me, a momentary temptation, nothing more. I would not give in to it."

"Attempt to trick me, and you will all be sorry," Gariel said, and as he spoke, he began to glow fierce red, then white, and at last erupt in a column of flame that made the dry and withered forms shrink back, shrieking and gibbering in terror of immolation. The flame sank and vanished abruptly, and he stood as before. "You will take your price, and not a drop more, but only after you have fulfilled your promise and returned me to the world of the living. Betray me, and every drop of my blood will become an inferno to consume you for the rest of eternity."

"We will do as you say," the chastened figure on the throne assured him.

Darra Jhan slouched forward at his command, and its sunken face showed only despair and fear. The shriveled hand touched Gariel's temple, and the amulet gave no warning; only a distant voice deep inside, fading as it said, *I have given all I can, Gariel, and I must rest. It is in your hands.*

There was darkness for a time, and a sense of headlong motion, and then he stood alone on a rocky slope. The air was cold, and a chill wind swayed the dark trees below. Snow lay luminous under a moon nearing the full, and the path ahead curved up the slope like a ribbon of light. He glanced over his shoulder and saw that no trail led downward, so he began the ascent.

The crust gave under his feet, but the snow was not deep and the slope was gentle, though it grew steeper as he climbed. When he reached the crest, he was gasping for breath, both from the effort of the climb and the thinness of the air. He sank to one knee on the bare, wind-scoured rock of the summit and knelt unmoving until his breathing was regular, and then he rose and looked on his surroundings.

He stood on the central peak of a range of hills that glittered like crystal under the cloudless sky. This was the highest point; he felt as if he stood at the summit of the world. All was at his feet, still and bright and timeless, and the austere beauty of the scene touched him to the heart.

But he had not come in search of beauty, he had come seeking a sign and a weapon to use against the Annihilator, and he saw neither in this bleak majestic setting. He no longer feared betrayal by that long-forgotten race; he feared it from his own ignorance: The things he sought might lie before him, plain as the mountains and broad as the skies, and yet go unnoticed.

As he stood wondering, he heard a sound like distant thunder. He raised his eyes, and beheld a light in the sky. It was coming toward him, brightening rapidly as it came. The rumble grew louder and seemed to set the air to trembling before it. Still it came, ever brighter, ever more deafening, like a missile of fire aimed at his heart, and he was afraid.

Dizzied by the noise that filled the air and drove all thought from his mind but a frantic desire for escape, he covered his ears and took a step back, then another. He lost his footing and fell backward, rolling and tumbling down the steep slope until he came to a halt in a drift. As he lay breathless and confused, the light burst with a terrible roar, shaking the ground beneath him. A profound silence followed.

Gariel struggled to his feet. He stood dazed for a time, then he made his way slowly to the summit, where the light from the heavens had struck. A shallow bowl was scooped out of the ground, and dust curled upward from the bottom.

Gariel stepped down into the depression and began to dig with his hands. In a very short time his fingertips scraped a hard surface. Clearing away the dirt, he uncovered a gray stone. It was warm to the touch, but not hot enough to burn; indeed, its warmth was comforting in the chill night.

He took up the stone. It was of a size to fit comfortably in his two hands, and heavy for its size. As he raised it and inspected it in the bright moonlight, he saw that it was unlike any stone he had ever seen before. It seemed more like a rough ball of metal, and he recalled legends of metal fallen from the sky, and stones from the heavens, legends he had always treated with scorn. Now he saw that they might be true, and he marveled at such wonders.

He tapped with his knuckle on the stone, and took up a small chip of rock and tapped with that, and satisfied himself that this was truly a bit of metal that he held in his hands. It had the ring of iron, and the look and texture of the metal he had worked at his own forge.

Holding this heaven-sent object in his hands, he had a flash of insight. The true dimensions of the struggle seemed to unroll before him like a great scroll, and he saw that the war against the Annihilator was not one battle but a conflict reaching over ages of time and covering the face of the earth. He was a single small figure in a design too vast for comprehension, but here and now his role was crucial. If he failed, the burden on the men and women of future generations would be crushing; if he succeeded, their way would be easier, though never truly easy.

Cradling the metal to his chest, he started back down the trail for the shelter of the forest below. Though the future of this long war flashed through his mind, his own present role in it was not yet clear to him. This ball of heavenly metal was significant, but was it sign as well as weapon? Could it be both? Was something still to be seen, or experienced, before he could begin to understand how to proceed? Beneath his cloak, the metal felt warm and alive, but it remained an enigma.

He reached the timber line and continued down. These stunted upland trees afforded little shelter, and there was no dry fallen wood to burn. Nearly halfway down the mountain, he came to a shallow niche beneath an overhanging rock. The ground within was dry and free from snow, springy with a deep layer of dried needles. He cleared a spot before the opening, gathered wood, and kindled a fire. The dry wood ignited easily and burnt with a furious quick heat that soon dried his cloak and boots and warmed him to the marrow.

Wrapping himself snugly in his cloak, he settled deep into the shelter, his face toward the warmth of the sinking fire, and slept. His sleep was deep and dreamless, but he woke after a time with an uneasy feeling. The fire was cold. The moon had set, but day was not yet breaking. Gariel shuddered and pulled his cloak more closely around him. He listened, but heard no sound from the forest.

Then shadows began to close around him like leaves falling, fluttering down to bury him under something insubstantial yet suffocating. A dry whispering filled the little hollow, growing louder until he could distinguish a multitude of voices crying, "The price! We will have the price! Pay us the price!"

Gariel sat upright, with a low groan of fear and loathing. The shadows swooped and swung about him like bats, but he felt no touch.

"We kept the bargain, and you must pay the price. Pay us the price!" the whispers repeated.

"You promised a sign and a weapon," Gariel said.

"You have seen the sign. You hold the weapon. You must pay the price. Do not betray us." The thin rustling of the voices filled the little space.

"Have you told me all that you learned?"

"You know all, all. Pay the price!"

Gariel swallowed and shuddered. He drew back the sleeves to expose his wrists, and threw back his head, baring his neck. "Take your price," he said.

For an instant, the voices were still. The shadows hovered about him, barely moving. Then, with a shrill exultant cry, they enfolded him in darkness.

He awoke with a start, crying out, and winced at the pain of morning light in his eyes. He lay half out of the shelter, near the ashes of last night's fire. For a time he felt too weak to rise, but thirst finally drove him to climb to his knees and take up a handful of clean snow. He blew on the embers until they glowed, and then he built up the fire and sat by it until the deep chill was driven from his body.

His wrists were swollen and discolored, and his neck was tender to the touch. The price had been horrible to pay, but he had what he sought, the sign and the weapon, and the world was no longer helpless before the will of Ankaria.

He still did not fully understand the sign, nor did he know how the metal was to be used as a weapon. Any ordinary weapon would be useless against such a thing as Ankaria, he was certain. This iron could not have been sent from the heavens merely to be forged into a blade or a spearpoint like any other.

He sat for a time enjoying the warmth of the fire on his face and chest, and the sun on his back. The wind had not risen, and the warmth and silence put his mind at peace as it eased his body. About midday he rose, extinguished the fire, and took the downhill trail to the plain below, where he headed toward the shore.

At dusk he saw the faint wink of fire in the distance, where low rounded huts stood in the shelter of the bluff overlooking the sea. It was a village of fisherfolk. Long narrow boats were hung on parallel racks between the huts, and from the number of the boats and the paucity of empty racks, Gariel judged that the village was full. A sea breeze brought him the aroma of cooking, and he hurried on with the last of his strength.

The villagers gave him food and shelter with the unquestioning generosity of those accustomed to uncertain fortunes, and when he had eaten his fill they gave him a warm sleeping-shelf and furs to cover himself. He was left to his own company until the next night, when they were all gathered around the fire after eating. The leader of the village, a wiry gray-haired man named Cossaran, with sun-narrowed eyes and skin browned and wrinkled by the weathers, asked Gariel if his strength had returned.

"It has, thanks to you."

"You looked weak and weary when you came. Lucky you were to find us," Cossaran said.

A woman at Gariel's side said, "We see few strangers here. Did you come from the sea?"

"From the mountains. I was in search of a certain metal."

A dark-haired man who resembled a younger, stockier version of Cossaran said, "Then you've had a hard journey for nothing. There are no precious metals in those mountains."

"I sought no precious metal, only a piece of iron."

"Iron is easily found elsewhere. No need to come here for it."

"I was sent here."

"Did you find it?"

Gariel reached into his tunic and drew out the ball of iron. He held it out to the dark-haired man who took it, inspected it, and passed it to Cossaran. It made its way from hand to hand until it was returned to Gariel. He sensed a new attitude on the part of the villagers, partly fearful, partly curious.

"You've come a long way to find a bit of iron. What will you do with it?" Cossaran asked.

"Tell me this: Have you a forge in the village, where I can work this metal?"

Cossaran exchanged a silent glance with the dark man, who nodded and said to Gariel, "I am Tassran, the smith. What do you want with my forge?"

"If you permit me, I will make something for the village and something for myself."

Again the two men exchanged a look, and this time Cossaran said, "In the morning, my son will take you to the forge."

When the others left at sunrise for the day's fishing, Gariel went with Tassran to a hut slightly larger than the others, where he found a small, crude, but serviceable forge. As Tassran displayed his tools and examples of his work, and Gariel showed his own knowledge and his approval, the tension that Gariel had sensed between them the previous evening began to ease. Tassran turned the forge over to Gariel, but asked his permission to remain and observe, which Gariel willingly granted. In a short time, Tassran was assisting him, and by midday, the two were working in cheerful concert.

They worked at the forge for three days. On the third night, after all had eaten, Gariel took out a roll of soft skin, laid it on the floor of the hut in the firelight, and opened it to reveal three gleaming spearheads. They were different in design from anything the fisherfolk had ever seen, and showed the craft of a master in their fine workmanship. Cossaran gave a low cry of approval and reached for one.

"Be careful. The barbs are very sharp," Gariel warned.

Cossaran tested one of the barbs gingerly against the ball of his thumb and nodded. "They're good. No fish will work free of these," he said.

"I helped to make them. I'll be able to make more for us," Tassran said proudly. "He showed me how to do it."

"We're grateful. Will you show me what you made for yourself?" Cossaran asked.

"I took most of the remainder and hammered it into a torc. I'm going to make something else out of it someday, but I'm not yet sure what it will be. I made this for myself," said Gariel, drawing out an amulet on a leather thong and removing it from around his neck.

It was a thin disc of polished iron. A simple design around its border enclosed a ring of symbols. At the center was the green stone. Cossaran took the amulet in his hand and studied it closely. After a time he looked into Gariel's eyes in the same searching way, as if he were looking for something that lay there unknown to Gariel. He dismissed the others with a word. They all left the hut quickly, as if they knew what was about to happen, and feared to be present.

When they were alone, Cossaran asked, "Is the stone yours?"

"It is."

"And the markings on the amulet—where did you learn them? Have you seen them before?"

Gariel hesitated, because the truth was strange; but in this strange setting, it seemed almost reasonable. "I've never seen those markings before. The design of the amulet was in my mind when I awoke this morning. I don't know where it came from—I had no dreams that I could recall and no visions; I heard no voices. I awoke this morning, and the amulet was there in my mind, every detail, as if I'd always known it."

"Then you are the one," Cossaran said, "and I must take you to the woman of silence."

10

Panorn of the Silence

Mist lay over the village in the morning, so dense that one might walk five paces from a hut and be unable to see even its outline in the milky air. Cossaran fretted impatiently, growling at everyone, until the mist began to clear and he and Gariel were able to depart. They took sufficient food for four days' travel and set out to the east, keeping to the top of the bluff that ran along the shore at the limit of the water's reach.

It was a bleak setting for a journey into the unknown. The changing winds moaned in the dry grass of the bluff. The sea was a sullen grayish-green, with an ashy gray sky lowered over it like a shroud. Inland, the mountains rose a deeper gray to ice-covered crags. In this barren wind-flayed landscape there was no sign of life, and little relief for the eye. To Gariel, it possessed a cold beauty all its own, far different from the forest's ever-changing progress from season to season, like the beauty of a diamond opposed to the beauty of a human face. He observed in appreciative silence.

His companion appeared less moved. Cossaran was silent for other reasons. He had said nothing more about their journey after his cryptic announcement the previous night. Gariel did not press him, assuming that the mystery would be made clear before long. They walked in silence until the last hut passed from view, and then Cossaran spoke abruptly, as if resuming an interrupted conversation.

"I don't know anything about her, that's the truth. I wouldn't know she was here, but for the storm. We avoid that part of the coast—it has treacherous currents, and rocks like hatchets on your boat—but I was carried up by a storm that came out of nowhere. I thought I was lost when the boat broke up," he said all in a rush, then paused as if uncertain whether to go on.

"Did she rescue you?" Gariel asked.

"Yes. Yes, she rescued me," Cossaran said hesitantly. "I don't understand how, and I'm still not certain just what happened. When I try to remember, my thoughts get mixed up. I was finished, no hope of getting to shore, and then all of a sudden everything went quiet. The storm was still blowing bad as ever, but I could only see it and feel it—all the noise faded away and in no time at all it was gone, and I was...." He stopped, shaking his head in confusion, and said, "You'll laugh at what I tell you. No one would believe it."

"You didn't laugh at what I told you. I won't laugh at you."

"The rest of them would laugh. I told them nothing of this. Only Tassran, and I didn't tell him more than I had to."

"Tell me, Cossaran."

The old fisherman nodded, heaved a deep sigh of resignation, and went on. "It was like a tunnel over the water, all silent and calm, and the storm raging all around without a sound to be heard. A woman stood at the end of the tunnel, on the shore, right at the water's edge, holding out a hand to me, and I began to swim toward her. I felt no winds, no waves, just smooth water all around me. She was dressed in white, so pure a white that it seemed to shine, and her hair was black as a crow's wing. A beautiful woman, but...more than a woman...different," said Cossaran uncomfortably.

"In what way?"

"There was a silence all around her. Around me, too, when I crawled up on the shore and stood before her. I was gasping for breath, but I wasn't making a sound. Shells were crunching under my feet; I felt them snap, but I heard nothing. The waves broke, and the wind blew, all in silence. Even when she spoke, she didn't really speak. I heard her words inside my head... like my own thoughts, only they weren't my own thoughts, they were from outside me, and they were in a woman's voice." Cossaran glanced at Gariel and then looked down, shaking his head. "I tell you, I was afraid. I thought I'd died and gone to the keeping of the Woman of the Waves, who takes all those who die at sea. She didn't look the way I've heard her described, all green, with green hair and webbed hands, but I couldn't think of any other explanation for what was happening."

"What did the woman say?" Gariel asked.

"Ah, it was strange. First thing she did was tell me that I was still alive. Then she studied me and sort of shook her head, as if I had disappointed her. 'You are not the one,' she said, 'but he will come to you, and you will bring him to me.' Before I could ask what she meant—and maybe I couldn't have asked, maybe I would have been as dumb as the wind and the sea and all else in that place—she described you. You'd come to us when a great light burst over the Crystal Hills, she said, and so you did."

"Why did you wait to bring me here?"

"She told me that you'd stay with us for a time and give us gifts of your own devising, and then you'd show me a green stone ringed with markings that you didn't understand. I was frightened when she said that. I keep clear of magic, and this sounded like magic stronger than any I'd ever heard of. But she knew what I was thinking! She smiled, and touched my hand with both of hers—and they were warm and dry, not like the hands of the Woman of the Waves would have been—and I knew that very instant that it was all for the good, and I'd do as she said. After that I don't remember anything but waking up in a hollow under the bluff. The storm was over, and two days' food lay in a pack beside me."

Gariel had nothing more to say, but much to wonder at. The two men spoke very little the rest of that day and the next, confining their remarks to the weather, the path, and the time. Early on the second day, a strong offshore wind rose. Cossaran and Gariel left the bluff and followed along its foot, out of the wind. Later that day, Cossaran stopped to point out a shallow depression under the bluff as the place where he had awakened after his encounter with the woman of silence.

"She must be close ahead. This is near the place where I came ashore," he said.

The shoreline changed soon after that point. The strand narrowed, and they ascended once again to the ridge. A short distance farther, they could look down directly into the water. When the bluff ended in a high curl of sand against a sheer rock face dropping straight into the sea, Cossaran halted and looked dubiously at the steep and rocky way inland.

"I thought we'd find her before this. I don't know my way here. None of us does. It's not a good place," he said.

"But this is where she is," said Gariel.

"She has to be here. All she said was that I should bring you to her, and where else would I bring you? She's up in there somewhere."

"Then I'll find her. You can go back."

"Would you go on alone?"

Gariel laughed. "I've gone far worse places. I have food and a good warm cloak. I can find my way back easily enough, if I have to."

"She said I was to bring you to her," Cossaran said, clearly torn between his debt to the silent woman and his desire to flee this place.

"You've done as she commanded, Cossaran. Go back to the village," Gariel said.

"If you think it's right, I'll go. You must tell her that it was your wish that you go to her alone."

"I'll tell her."

"I would have gone on with you, if you'd asked me," Cossaran said, backing off a few steps, then halting to add, "You must tell her that."

"I will tell her of all your help to me. Go, Cossaran, and take my thanks."

Gariel watched with relief as the fisherman's figure dwindled and was lost to sight in the distance. His nerves were tingling with impatience. He could sense someone awaiting him, calling to him, drawing him unerringly to a destination at which only he and she could meet. Cossaran had obviously been insensible of the summons, but Gariel felt it all around him. He breathed it in the dank air, and felt it brush his face and stir his hair and beard and pluck at his garments. He turned and made his way up the rocky slope as confidently as if he had been following a high road.

She was waiting for him at the lip of a hollow among the rocks, a scooped-out bowl with a rounded hut of rough stone at its center: a woman all in white, with the blackest hair he had ever seen tumbling in long waves below her shoulders. Her complexion was fair, with spots of color on the high cheekbones. She stood with her hands at her sides, smiling to welcome him. As he walked toward her, sound grew fainter and fainter, and then ceased.

I am Panorn of the Silence. I knew you would choose to come to me alone, said a sweet voice that came to him from within himself, like remembered music.

"How did you know?" he asked, and though he felt the breath leave him, and his mouth speak the words, there was no sound. Nevertheless, she replied.

I once worked magic in the service of the Nine Lords' Alliance. I left them for the same reason you left the White City. Alone, I had no hope, but now I begin to hope.

"The same reason?" Gariel asked uncertainly.

A force stronger than themselves is drawing them to the use of forbidden magic to destroy the Empire. Any who try to warn them of the danger are called enemies, and condemned. They worship a new god, a being that they say will come to purify the earth for its loyal followers, and they please it by sacrificing its enemies' lives.

"This god sounds very like the new guardian of the Empire. Its followers call it Ankaria, the Annihilator."

She held out her hand to him. *They are the same, I think. We must share what we know of this creature. Perhaps together we can defeat it, or at least deny it total victory. Come inside.*

He took her hand and followed her to the crude stone shelter. He sensed the magic surrounding them, and knew that what he saw was not all that existed in this place, but he trusted Panorn. Her grip was firm, and her hand warm.

Gariel ducked to pass through the low, narrow entrance. He blinked in surprise when he saw where he was. The interior was an immense hall of smooth white stone, ceiled in soft light. Smiling at his astonishment, Panorn led him to a doorway. It opened on a spacious chamber lined with shelves on which lay tablets, scrolls, books, and a number of unfamiliar objects, several of which seemed to return his scrutiny.

This place was created long ago by one driven into exile. She gave much magic to building it, and it holds wisdom long forgotten in the changing world.

"How did you learn of it?"

Panorn looked at him, and her eyes, of a green as bright as the stone of his amulet, clouded at a painful memory. She lowered her gaze, and did not look at him as her words formed in his mind. *I sought her among the dead, and found her. She told me of this place, and of you, and of what we will do together.*

Gariel was beyond surprise. He accepted the fact that his life was no longer in his own hands. Whether he could still refuse to serve, and could shake off the influence of these unknown forces, he did not know. He had no wish to do so. He believed Valimagdon, and the mage of the dead race, and this woman. His sole wish was for greater knowledge of his mission—their mission, it now appeared—and the means to accomplish it. He surveyed the room, and turned to Panorn.

"Somewhere among all this, there is knowledge of our enemy, is there not?" he asked.

I am told that there is, but I fear that I might not recognize it if I found it.

Gariel gave a short mirthless laugh. "We haven't been told much, either of us. I've been given a sign and a weapon—given them at a high price—but I can't decipher the sign and I don't know how to use the weapon. I only hope I can learn all I need to know in time for it to be useful."

The sign was the fire from heaven.

"I thought so, but what does it mean?"

I was told no more than that. The fire was the sign, and it was to place the weapon before you.

"It left a ball of metal in the ground. I made some things from it, at a forge in the fishing village, but they're not the last I'll make, I'm sure. I'll make them into something new ...some weapon... but what the weapon will be, and who's to wield it, I don't know."

It is one more thing for us to learn.

He gave a soundless sigh and shook his head ruefully. "We have too many things to learn, I fear. Too much to learn, and too little time. The Annihilator is impatient to begin its work."

THE TIME OF THE ANNIHILATOR

She came to him, smiling, and took his hands in hers. *One thing I know, Gariel. Those who wield the weapons will be our descendants.*

Her hands were warm, and her smiling face moved him with its beauty. Gariel had wanted to be close to no woman since Moarra's death. Her loss had burned something out of his life. He had given himself to his work, first at the forge, and after in the White City. But the closeness of Panorn shook his resolve. It was not just her beauty that moved him—he had seen beautiful women in the White City—it was the aura of perfection that surrounded her, as silence enfolded her. She was like no one else on earth. Yet even as he felt himself drawn to her, he realized that she suggested the impossible.

"How can you speak of descendants? There's no time, Panorn. I've felt the terrible hunger of the Annihilator. It might be upon us at any moment. If we had children, and the Annihilator struck before we knew how to fight back, they'd be consumed," he said earnestly.

You were chosen for me, and I for you. Why do you question what must be?

"I've seen what must be. I've felt it, and it nearly destroyed me. I had children once, Panorn, and they were taken from me. I don't want that to happen again, not to me, not to them."

After all you have seen, you still have no trust. Do you think that the power that rescued you from the Annihilator, that conducted you safely through the kingdom of the dead and brought a sign from the heavens into your hands, will abandon you?

"If some power is guiding us, why can't it make things clear? Why all these mysteries? I'm willing to do what I must— why can't I simply be told outright what it is?" said Gariel impatiently.

You have been chosen, Gariel, as have I. Trust the power that chose you.

"I can't believe that I'm so very special."

You have proof that you are. Ankaria has chosen your brother, your closest flesh and blood, to be its servant, and has helped bring about the death of those close to you. It fears you, Gariel.

"But why?" he cried. "Who am I, to be singled out like this?"

Enough that you are. You need know no more.

"But I want to know. Why me, and why you?"

Her green eyes flared. *Does the thought of taking me in your arms distress you?*

"No, Panorn, no," he said quickly, abruptly aware that her feelings, as well as his, were involved. "It's not that at all. Any man would be happy to have your love. But haven't you been told why this must be?"

I can only guess. You and I have had similar lives, Gariel, but our lives have been very different from the lives of the other men and women around us, and from those who practice our art. Like you, I once abandoned my magic for someone I loved. For a time, I was very happy, but I learned that happiness is a passing thing. Those I loved, even the child of my body, were taken from me and slain. I was almost destroyed by one I trusted and loved. I cannot tell myself that similarity between us is mere chance. There is a plan, and we must accept it and follow it.

When she had finished speaking, Gariel said slowly, reluctantly, "I know that I've seen and done and experienced things that few people before me—perhaps none—have known. And I want to see the Annihilator defeated, Panorn, believe that I do. But I'm an ordinary man, the son of ordinary parents. I'm not a great mage. I confronted the power of Ankaria once and nearly was killed. All the power that was given to me barely sufficed to keep me alive, and it took me long to recover. Even when a sign is sent to me, I don't understand it. It seems like terrible presumption to imagine that I could have been singled out for such a mission."

You have had glimpses of what must be. Accept your role in the work.

In his agitation, he had released her hands. Now he took them in his once again and raised them to his lips.

"I accept everything, Panorn."

Then come, she said, drawing him from the room of stored knowledge, *come and see our home.*

In the long days of study, as they pored over the ancient archives in search of the knowledge that would sustain them in the face of the Annihilator, Gariel found that Panorn had a formidable grasp of magic. He had the greater natural gift, but she possessed a tenacity that matched Bellenzor's and added to it a sympathy and understanding for those vanished mages that led her intuitively through the labyrinth of words and symbols in which they labored.

At night, in his arms, Panorn was as soft and loving as a girl, and she clung to him with single-minded passion when they made love. Silence enfolded them at all times, but her words sang in his blood and her cries of rapture echoed along his nerves. Her presence drove away all his loneliness and sense of loss, and he began to think, as he had once, long ago, that life was a good thing and the world was a good place. The shadow of the Annihilator seemed less menacing in this bright sanctuary, and the hope of the world seemed greater. The knowledge they sought was elusive, and they labored on, day after day, with much frustration, but nevertheless, Gariel felt his confidence growing.

In all the time that he spent in this silent place, Gariel saw no one but Panorn. Yet he felt the constant presence of other lives around them, benign and protective, like loving friends hovering just out of reach and out of sight. He spoke of this feeling to Panorn, and she confessed that she, too, had experienced it.

I felt their presence when I came here, Gariel, but now I feel it even more strongly—as if more were joining us every day, she said.

"But who are they? What are they?"

I think that they are others who resisted the enemy in past ages. They died long ago, but they have not ceased to exist. They carry on the struggle in a different way.

"So the struggle never ends, not even with death."

Is there such a thing as death, Gariel?

"There was for my wife and children, and the people of my village. And for your child, as well."

Perhaps not. This conflict is much greater than we know, or can imagine, and we play only a small part in it. It may be that all who live are in the struggle forever, on one side or the other.

"I find that small comfort. There must be rest sometime. No one can fight forever."

Would you rest while Ankaria thrives? Panorn asked. He looked up sharply and she laid her hand on his, saying, *Then believe that others may feel the same.*

He took her hand and held it for a time without speaking. At last he said, "I think I'm beginning to understand. But why are they coming here now?"

She placed his hand on her belly, and smiling, said, *It may be that they come to welcome a new partner in the struggle, and to protect us all.*

And it was true that when the time came for Panorn to give birth, Gariel felt the unseen presences quicken with a contagious excitement. They hovered about him, setting the air gently aglow, almost tangible, a protective canopy over mother and father, and when Gariel took up his infant daughter he felt the dwelling-place filled with a sense of fellowship and love and joy that penetrated to the roots of his being. In that luminous company, a truth became clear to him: He had never truly been alone, except in his own unperceiving mind, and he need never feel alone again. Unseen and unheard, this fellowship of light would be forever with him, with Panorn, and with their child.

11

The Fourth Child in Glory

Resident within the mind of Bellenzor and clothed in his flesh, the Annihilator moved in the White City, among the Thirty-three and the apprentices, in the person of that hapless master. The usurpation was complete; no outward sign betrayed the elemental being present within the mortal frame.

Bellenzor had never been loved, but he had won respect as a man apart from his peers, aloof in his manner and austere in his life. Those who knew him marked his dedication to the Empire and his great sacrifices on its behalf, and overlooked his coldness. But now his bearing became arrogant, his commands sharper, his anger quicker, and though none in the White City suspected the cause, they saw the change and began to fear him.

He seemed to sleep and eat as an ordinary man no more. His assistants were worked to exhaustion, and broken in his service. Only one, an obscure apprentice named Morodel, endured; he seemed to flourish where others had declined. The two became inseparable, and when Bellenzor took to walking in the city, observing and questioning the people, Morodel was always at his right hand, a pace behind his master, ready for any command.

Bellenzor's dedication to Ankaria was well known, and now it assumed a more active form. On his rounds of the city, the mage spoke sometimes of the guardians Ilveraine, Teleon, and Ebanor. He did not attack them, or their followers, or mock their beliefs; indeed, he praised the steadfast faith of those who had believed so firmly and so long with no evidence that their guardians heard or cared. He seldom spoke without reference to the burgeoning power of Ankaria, which, he revealed, had lent its might to the armies of the Empire and brought them victories where the old guardians had been unable to stave off defeat.

The Thirty-three seldom ventured among the people, and these appearances of Bellenzor—who, as all were aware, had little time to spare from his duties—drew crowds to hear and follow him. More and more, the crowds consisted of Followers of the Fourth Child. As those who did not accept the new guardian withdrew, the crowds surrounding Bellenzor became, in effect, the legions of the Annihilator and Bellenzor, in turn, became more outspoken in his advocacy of Ankaria. He was heard to speak slightingly of the elder guardians, and say that the Protector had ceased to protect them, the Illuminator had left them in darkness, and the Nurturer had cast them aside. Only Ankaria heard their desperate prayers, he told the listening crowds; only Ankaria would reward their sacrifices.

Some among the Thirty-three disapproved of his talk, but they were silent out of prudence, remembering the fate of Alnore. Others agreed with Bellenzor's words but were uneasy with his tactics, holding that it was not good for one of their number to go so often among the common people and speak so openly to them. This group, too, remained silent. Many of the Thirty-three, worn out by the war's demands, were glad to leave things in the hands of a vigorous leader who, whatever his shortcomings, promised hope of victory.

As Bellenzor's influence in the White City grew, the cult of the Fourth Child grew also in influence and in numbers. The symbols of the old gods were no longer seen so frequently on buildings, or signs, or in the public places. The tree with its burden of fruit, the sun, and the armed figure were withdrawn from common view and relegated to private worship. Nothing replaced them. The Annihilator had no symbol but emptiness.

The worship of Ilveraine, Teleon, and Ebanor became secretive. The few remaining public meeting places of their cults, now abandoned, were first defaced and then destroyed by zealots among the Followers of the Fourth Child, who trampled the ruins underfoot and condemned them as the fanes of false gods.

These changes took place in a very short time. The men who had marched to battle in the early spring with invocations to the Protector sounding in their ears and Ebanor's signs of the tower and the wall traced on their weapons or tattooed on their shoulders and forearms heard no reference to the god upon their return. The tree of Ilveraine that had been carved or painted above half the doorways in the city had vanished, and nothing now stood in its place. The soldiers trudged wearily home from battle in the gray days of early winter to a city stripped of its old shrines and newly dedicated to the worship of the Annihilator, and they found Ankaria a harsh god. Before they returned again from the battlefields, Ankaria's reign had grown harsher.

Bellenzor was in constant activity during this time, and all in the White City wondered at his endurance. Only Morodel knew of the days and nights when Bellenzor collapsed suddenly and entered a sleep so deep as to border on death. Motionless and rigid, scarcely breathing, pale as a corpse, he lay sometimes for three full days and nights before springing instantly awake and returning to his rounds.

Morodel had his suspicions, but he kept them to himself. As an apprentice, he had learned to be a careful listener and a close observer, and to keep silent. Above all, he had learned the value of discreet obedience. He had watched his master in those early days, and the Bellenzor he now served was a different man—if indeed he was a man at all.

For something seemed to have taken possession of the wizard. An occasional observer would not see the changes that were plain to one whose every waking moment was passed at Bellenzor's side—the tentative and fitful motions, as of something learning to make its way in an alien body; the casual expenditure of titanic power for no sake but its own exercise; the deathlike sleep as sudden as the extinguishing of a candle, and the instantaneous full wakefulness after. These were traits and powers beyond the human.

Morodel said nothing of his suspicions. He feared Bellenzor, or whatever lived in Bellenzor's body, and he trusted no one. He could only watch, and serve, and wait, and these things he did. Despite surmises that sometimes terrified him, Morodel enjoyed his proximity to power. The being that he served had raised him high, and he was willing to serve it loyally rather than sink back into obscurity; but he could not help wondering.

On those occasions when Bellenzor lay as one entranced, Morodel kept up the illusion of unceasing activity in the tower and barred all visitors, even the Thirty-three, from entry. His master was deep in the toils of a magic to safeguard the Empire, he told them, and none could approach him in safety. The callers left, and few returned. Morodel kept watch, and waited for his master's return.

Morodel's explanation to intruders, which he considered a serviceable lie, was in an ironic sense true; for when the ravaged form of Bellenzor lay untenanted, Ankaria ranged among the forces of the Nine Lords' Alliance. Whether the Annihilator's visitations helped or hurt the outlanders' cause might have been hotly debated, had anyone known the truth.

Though their speech and their appearance were similar, the people of the Alliance were different from the people of the Empire in their customs and manners. Their organization was diametrically opposed. Instead of a unified body with a single tradition and a single home, the outlanders were a loose and ever-changing aggregation of tribes, families, and fighting companies, each under its own local leader, each with its own beliefs. Their loyalty to the Nine Lords who were their titular leaders—all of them long dead—was mercurial, their unity fragile. They were steadfast only in their hatred of the Empire, though even the wisest among them would have been hard put to state the exact cause of the long enmity. It had always been so, and would be so until one side destroyed the other. No one asked to know more.

To the fierce outland wanderers, Ankaria came as a whispered promise of victory. In a short time, the worshipers of wood and stone and cloud, of dead ancestors and monstrous phantasms, had all begun to speak of a new power, something from beyond that would give them the strength to sweep the world clean of its enemies, which were their enemies. It promised war, and awesome destruction, and total victory to those who served it, and the outlanders quickly came to embrace its ways.

It was a god without a name. To some, it was a wind to blow down the strongholds of their enemies; to others, it was flood or fire; to all, it was an annihilating force greater than they had ever imagined. Those who served it faithfully would live and triumph; all others would be swept away.

Now and then, Ankaria turned one of the bands against its neighbors and feasted on the ensuing destruction. The feeding was pleasant, but Ankaria did not act out of hunger alone. After long exile, utterly isolated and walled out from all life, it again had creatures to bend to its will. They obeyed blindly, convinced of their own power and independence and magnificence; they mouthed proud words and prophesied greatness, and stirred others as foolish as themselves to follow them. And in a little while they were gone, forgotten, fodder for the Annihilator. Ankaria found this amusing.

When its visitations among the forces of the Nine Lords were done, Ankaria returned to the body of Bellenzor to resume its work in the White City. It was pleasing to move and act in a corporeal frame once more, though Ankaria found the housing of flesh in some ways constricting. Human clay was not strong enough to contain its informing essence; the feeble body of this creature that had brought Ankaria forth from exile was already breaking down. It would have to be kept alive for a time, but when the Empire and the Alliance were gone and the world lay open before it, Ankaria would take a new form. Man or woman, or perhaps beast; a forest or the sea; a plague or a storm; all were possible, and Ankaria passed some idle moments weighing one against another.

But these were mere speculations. There was much still to be done in the White City.

Through the hard winter, families huddled by their firesides and ventured forth infrequently. The worship of Ilveraine, Teleon, and Ebanor was conducted in privacy, behind closed shutters, among small groups of worshipers well known to one another. Though no threats were voiced, and no open enmity was shown toward them, the followers of the old gods sensed that it was prudent to conceal their beliefs from those who followed Ankaria.

In spring, when the fighting companies left the city, the symbols of Ebanor, the wall and the tower, were seen on few shields. The tree of Ilveraine stood in effigy in no fields or gardens that spring and summer, as it had for generations past, and no scholar wore the sun of Teleon as a medallion around his neck. As the White City came to bustling life after the winter, the followers of Ankaria seemed to be everywhere, and they spoke more bluntly than before. Now it was not only the zealots among them who dared to call the old gods frauds and their worshipers dupes. In a short time they ceased to speak of dupes and spoke instead of traitors. At this point occurred the first open clash between the two factions.

A group of Followers of the Fourth Child were holding forth in one of the smaller squares of the White City, accusing Ebanor of deserting the Empire in its time of greatest need. In the midst of the harangue, a grizzled old soldier named Forlan, a veteran of the forest campaigns and the three battles of Cleft Hill, stood up and angrily denounced them and their god. There was a scuffle that quickly became a melee. When it was over, one of Ankaria's followers lay dead on the stones, and two others were beaten so severely that they died before nightfall. The rest fled headlong to safety.

Forlan's outburst seemed to fan something long smoldering within the people. For several days, the White City was the scene of pitched battles between the adherents of Ankaria and the worshipers of the old gods, with Ankaria's followers getting the worst in every clash.

Forlan found himself overnight the leader of a large and angry faction. He had no plans and no aims, only a simple faith in Ebanor and a wish to see the Protector honored, as in the old days. To end the turmoil, he proposed a peaceful procession to the citadel of the Thirty-three, bearing the symbols of the city's traditional gods. At the citadel he would proclaim an end to the fighting on condition that those who believed in Ankaria ceased their attacks on Ilveraine, Teleon, and Ebanor.

His suggestion was received with enthusiasm. Two days later, a procession of over a thousand set forth from the western quarter to the center of the White City. All went peacefully, even joyously, until the towers of the citadel rose in view ahead, and as they turned a corner, Forlan and the others at the head of the procession saw Bellenzor. He stood alone, robed in black, his arms extended to either side, barring the way.

What happened next was never clear; no single version of the events was agreed on.

The procession halted at Forlan's command. As those in the rear, unaware, continued to march on, the marchers began to crowd together. Suddenly, from the very head of the procession, came screams of horror and wild shouts; a shudder went through the crowd, as if it were a single organism, and then it disintegrated into a thousand separate fragments intent on flight. Scores were trampled to death and hundreds injured in the panic. Most fearful of all was the fate of Forlan and the man and woman who had walked on either side of him. They lay untrampled, as dry and withered as corpses baked by the desert sun. It was whispered in the White City that the touch of the Annihilator had fallen upon them.

After that day, the followers of Ankaria spoke openly and without interruption, and their words were strong. The old discredited gods, they said, had revealed their true natures at last by rousing their followers to rebellion. They had turned decent people, one of them a warrior of great courage and proven loyalty, against their leaders. They had incited murderous plotting against Bellenzor, without whose efforts the Empire would lie helpless before its enemies. After such manifest deceit and treachery, the evil Ilveraine, Teleon, and Ebanor deserved nothing at the hands of the Empire but hatred. Let their shrines be thrown down, their symbols destroyed, their names effaced from memory, cried the Followers of the Fourth Child, and in their place let Ankaria be sole guardian of the city, the Empire, and its people.

No one dared voice an objection. The sight of the three desiccated corpses displayed before the citadel, and the grisly accounts of their death that circulated among the people, stilled all opposition.

Many of the citizens found it as easy to worship Ankaria as any other god. Some of the more thoughtful, though they found the rant of its cultists distasteful, were impressed by the obvious fact that Ankaria protected its followers. Bellenzor lived and thrived, while those who marched under the protection of the old gods had been blasted and scattered like sheep before a bolt from the heavens. If Ankaria could do the same thing to the forces of the Nine Lords as it had done to Forlan's mob, it deserved worship.

There were some who spoke no word against Ankaria, but removed the symbols of the old gods to some hidden place and worshiped them in secret. These few kept to themselves, and did their duty, and were tolerated for a time.

When the armies returned from the field in early winter and learned of what had happened, there was some grumbling. Forlan's old comrades, in particular, were angered by things that were said against his name. Bellenzor offered to meet with them all, and they accepted his offer. No one learned what was said at their meeting, but from that time on, the armies were loyal to Ankaria.

In the following spring a proclamation came forth ordering the destruction of all remaining signs and symbols of the false gods. A few people shamefacedly produced carvings, hangings, amulets, and other items. These items were burned in public, the penitents forgiven. After this, there was no more forgiveness. A second proclamation was issued shortly after the first, this one declaring the possession of any artifact signifying the false gods Ilveraine, Teleon, and Ebanor to be an act of treason. Again there was a public burning, but this time it was not objects alone that were put to the torch.

The immolation took place in the open space before the citadel in the presence of a great crowd. They watched the flames rise, and they heard the screams of the two men and three women chained to the pyre, and when it was over they returned to their homes without speaking, for it seemed that the wisest course in these times was to be silent.

12

Out of Sanctuary

Panorn named the child Ciantha. It was a name unfamiliar to Gariel, and he was puzzled by the choice. He had never heard it in the White City, nor among the people of the forest settlement, and he was certain that it was not a name from the east, whence Panorn had come. He made no inquiry; but she, sensing his puzzlement, explained that it was a name from an earlier age, a time now lost to memory save for a few clay cylinders impressed with markings none but Panorn could decipher, and she only with great difficulty.

The people of that time did not think like us, and their scribes wrote in a way hard to understand, she explained, *but I know that Ciantha was an enchantress of much skill. Her powers turned back Ankaria for a time, until she was betrayed.*

"Have you been able to learn what magic she used against the Annihilator?" Gariel asked.

I could not. The rest of her story has been lost.

"So much has been lost," said Gariel wearily. "I sometimes wonder if what we seek still exists."

It exists, and we will find it, Panorn replied.

"I've come to feel more confident about our search in recent days, but when I think of the scope, the unimaginable amounts of time...." Gariel fell silent, and shook his head sadly.

121

We are not alone.

"No, but the spirits I spoke with were from an age so distant it's scarcely known, and they told me of knowledge that was ancient when their race was young. It's hard to believe that knowledge can survive so long, and still be found, and understood."

They faced the same challenge and they overcame. They learned enough to hold Ankaria back until our race grew strong enough to resist it. If they had survived a little longer, they might have overcome it completely and driven it from our world forever.

"But they didn't overcome. Time ran out. They failed, and their race was destroyed."

We must not fail. We must search until we find the knowledge they lacked.

In frustration, Gariel cried, "They couldn't even tell me what to look for, Panorn! The sign they sent was cryptic. The weapon they gave me is a mystery to us still. It may all be deceit!"

Her reply cut into his mind, hot with indignation. *You know the truth, and yet you speak of deceit! When we come upon the knowledge, we will recognize it.*

"It might turn out for us as it did for them. We'll come close, and then Ankaria will strike and we'll have no more time to look. We'll have to fight it unprepared."

Then we will resist it as best we can.

"And be crushed, as the others were."

Before we fall, we will add all we know to the ancient lore, and leave it for a later generation to find and use.

Gariel sighed and said wistfully, "I wish I could believe as firmly as you do. Sometimes I do, but then I start to doubt."

Trust the power that sent the sign, and put the shape of the amulet in your mind, and brought us together. It is greater than those ancient mages, greater than Ankaria.

"Can anything be greater than Ankaria?"

If no greater power exists, why has Ankaria been thwarted? Why does it not rule? Why do we survive to resist it? Something protects us, Gariel.

"But what is it? The Sower of Worlds is not concerned with our problems. The spirits that dwell with us are only people like ourselves, in a different life. Ilveraine, Teleon, and Ebanor offer no hope against the Annihilator, nor do the gods of the east. All of them together could not withstand Ankaria."

Yet Ankaria has not overcome. It has known defeat, and learned to fear.

"The thought of a power beyond Ankaria frightens me as much as it heartens. If we're part of a struggle between such adversaries, we're like insects on a battlefield."

Panorn came and stood behind him. Leaning over, she put her arms around his shoulders and laid her cheek against his. *I understand your doubts. But we have not been called to this task only to be abandoned in our greatest need. You must know that,* she said.

He took her hands in his, and savored the sweetness of her voice in his mind. "I do know it, Panorn," he said, "but I feel the importance of what we're doing so much more acutely now. I have others to care about. When I had no one, I didn't care what happened to me, or to the world. I never dwelt on it as I do now. It didn't matter." Rising, he took Panorn in his arms, holding her close. "That's all changed. Now I care very much. I've lost a family, and I fear I've lost my own brother, and I don't want to lose you and Ciantha." He was silent for a time, then he sighed and said, "I thought this new life would make me stronger. It appears to be causing me more doubts than before."

Keep to the search, and have no doubt. Ciantha will be well cared for.

"Not if we fail."

She smiled and kissed him gently. *You will see.*

Gariel returned to his work and remained at it almost without respite. Panorn was ever at his side, urging and encouraging him in the moments she was not working herself. In their silent sanctuary, time had no demarcation; their labors ended only when they were too weary, their eyes too tired to read on.

They gained some important information—a hint of weakness in Ankaria found on some ancient tablet, a spell to shield against the Annihilator's withering blast copied on a crumbling scroll—but the great answer eluded them: How could this life-consuming entity be fought and overcome, and the world secured forever from its undying hunger? They marked their discoveries, and worked on.

Their way was like a journey through some dark and ancient labyrinth where the single path to the light had been trebly concealed by design, time, and chance. The tablets and cylinders of clay were fragments, chipped and eroded; scrolls and books were dry to the point of crumbling at a touch, and their markings were faded and dubious. These bits and scraps of age-old lore, transcribed in cryptic lines of obscure languages, written in some cases long after the events they described, mixed observation with surmise, knowledge with superstition, ripe wisdom with childlike fancy. Yet Gariel and Panorn had no other source to turn to. What they sought was here, or it did not exist.

One day Panorn looked up from a shard of clay tablet with an exultant light in her eyes. She seemed to derive strength from the very desperation of their task, and Gariel had drawn encouragement from her presence. Now, as her words came to him, he glimpsed success within their grasp.

It's a verse—an incantation—it's not complete, but it speaks of Ankaria, I'm certain!

"Read it!"

'*... for the Hungerer, Eater of Souls, will ... will suck the life from the world and spew up living stone to ... to serve it. All hope will die ... the sea will be still ... dust will be thick on the holy place. But if one comes forward to give the Sign of Denial ... fires ... a great fire ... will strike from the heavens and the might ... of the Consuming Beast will be shattered, and from that day, all. ...*' *There's no more, Gariel, but think what it must mean!*

He was at her side in an instant, tracing out the sculpted symbols with cautious fingertips. He sensed the excitement growing in Panorn even as it rose within him.

"It speaks of a sign—and fire from the heavens."

And those names, the Hungerer and the Consuming Beast— they must refer to Ankaria.

"But the Sign of Denial ... I don't understand that."

The amulet! Look on the amulet!

Gariel plucked out the amulet that lay against his chest, and together they examined the symbols that ringed the green stone, twisting and curling in upon themselves, interlacing like the tendrils of a vine. They were as different from the angular markings on the clay tablet as a reed from a stone.

"There can't be any link between these two languages. I don't even know if the inscription on the amulet is in human script, Panorn. It came to me in a dream."

Perhaps it is the language of the dead race you spoke with.

"That's possible. But so many things are possible, and there's so little time," Gariel said in frustration.

We know now that someone found the way. The words speak of shattering Ankaria's might, even in its moment of triumph. We can do it, Gariel, if we can learn the Sign of Denial!

Gariel took some comfort from her words. They spent no time celebrating her discovery, but bent at once to resume their search, now more narrowly focused. Perhaps, in time, they could piece the answer together from these fragments. But time was running away like water between their open fingers, and the day came when the time for searching was over.

Gariel awoke one morning late in winter from uneasy sleep. He lay staring upward, frowning, trying vainly to recapture the fleeting fragments of a troubled dream, and then he turned with a sigh and saw Panorn looking at him intently.

You have heard the summons, too.

"I had a dream. It frightened me, but I can't recall...."

Ankaria is astir, and we must leave this place.

Gariel did not respond for a time, but at last he said, "Yes. Ankaria plans some great destruction to feed its strength... and we must prevent it. That was in my dream. But how can we leave this place?"

We must.

"Our work is incomplete. We may be able to defend ourselves against Ankaria, but we still don't know how to defeat it. And what of Ciantha? We can't leave her here unprotected, and we can't take her with us if we're going to confront the Annihilator," said Gariel flatly. "I don't care what kind of summons we receive, we're not endangering Ciantha."

She will be protected. The spirits are here to care for her.

"How will she live, Panorn? Spirits may be able to guard her from evil, but a spirit can't be parent to a child."

She smiled at his concern, and reached up to stroke his cheek gently. He assured Panorn that his objection was in earnest, and she told him that all would be well.

Some days later, as Gariel was making a final survey of the old volumes, Panorn came to him leading a young couple. To

Gariel, they looked to be scarcely more than children, but they bore marks of suffering. The woman carried an infant bundled in rags, and a child just able to walk clung to the man's hand. He smiled in uneasy greeting, ducking his head respectfully, and Gariel welcomed them. The woman did not acknowledge his greeting.

Panorn drew Gariel aside and said, *They will care for Ciantha as their own child.*

"Do they understand what might happen?"

They look at this place and see a cottage, the home they have dreamed of finding since their own was destroyed. They are unaware of the spirits dwelling here, but the spirits will protect them. If we fail to return, Ciantha will grow up as an ordinary child and marry among ordinary people. But our blood is in her, and from her descendants will come others to fight Ankaria.

"Then our mission becomes clear. We'll delay Ankaria, but we won't defeat it. The struggle will go on," Gariel said.

Perhaps we will overcome. I only say what I was told. You yourself spoke of forging a weapon for some future adversary of Ankaria—does that mean that you have no hope of victory?

Gariel spread his arms wide and shook his head hopelessly. "I'm not sure what anything means, Panorn, even my own words. For years, I stood at my forge and used a hammer and tongs and an anvil. I never wondered what the hammer thought, or whether the tongs understood my purpose, or how the anvil felt. Now I feel as though I've become one of those tools. Something is using me—that power greater than Ankaria, I think—and I can only obey. But if it will save Ciantha, and help deliver the world from the Annihilator, I'll follow to the death."

We will follow together, she said, embracing him.

The young man's name was Roak. His wife, even younger than he, was named Mabshe. They had come from a forest village far to the south that had been attacked and destroyed in a night raid.

They were still fearful, and the enveloping silence of the place froze them with awe. Mabshe clutched the infant to her breast, and the toddler clung desperately to Roak's leg, while husband and wife stood close to comfort one another. To avoid frightening them more, Panorn suggested that Gariel speak with them outside, beyond the sphere of her magic.

Since he and Panorn had met, Gariel had not been from her side; the only sound he had heard in all that time was her voice speaking within his own mind. Now he heard the sounds of the world once again. The wind blustered about the rim of the depression in which he stood; pebbles grated and clattered underfoot as he walked; sea birds called overhead. At the first sound of his own voice, Gariel started. Then he laughed, and the sound of his laughter was a tonic to him, and to the fearful family near at hand. Roak gave a nervous, tentative smile, and the child at his side joined in Gariel's laughter. The mother and the infant in arms did not react, but stood silent, unmoving, absorbed by some inner concern.

"I have some knowledge of healing, Roak," said Gariel. "Let me look at your injuries."

Roak held out his left arm, which was wrapped in a filthy makeshift bandage. Another dirty bandage was around his brow, covering one eye.

"What happened?" Gariel asked as he gently undid the wrappings.

"Men tried to take our food. I had to fight them off. I think I killed one, but they cut me badly."

Roak's wounds were deep but clean. They had already begun to close. Gariel washed them and applied salves to speed their healing. As he worked, he tried to draw out the couple's story. Roak was willing to speak, but Mabshe was silent, holding tightly to the infant in her arms, rocking it with stiff, jerky movements. The child made no sound, and Gariel began to suspect that she clung to a corpse.

"We just heard shouting and then screams, all bursting into our sleep in the middle of the night so at first you'd think you were having bad dreams. But seeing the flame and smelling the smoke, you knew it was no dream," said Roak.

"How did you escape?"

"We just grabbed up our clothes and the little ones, and ran. It was our luck to run into no raiders. Didn't none others escape, only we two and the little ones. We hid in the forest three days and nights, and then we went back to look for kin, and try to find some food and water. Everyone was dead, all of them piled in a heap in the center of the village, and everything around broken and burned. That's what scared us most. They didn't even loot, they just destroyed."

"Have you any idea who they were, Roak, or why they destroyed your village?"

Roak shook his head slowly. "They was raiders, that's all I know. That's what raiders do to us villagers."

The simple account stirred painful memories in Gariel. It was indeed what raiders do, as he had learned when he had been living a simple life, like Roak's, fancying himself remote from the struggles of empires, ignorant of the powers that incited men to brute deeds. The sheer wanton destructiveness, the killing for killing's own sake, bespoke the influence of Ankaria, who drew life and strength from the deaths of men and women. The Annihilator was indeed astir in the world.

Gariel finished ministering to Roak and turned to Mabshe. The young wife looked at him dully and drew back from his touch, pressing the tiny bundle against her. Gariel caught the reek of death in the air, and felt a gentle touch on his shoulder.

"She won't put the child down, Master. Little one died three days back, but Mab won't give her up," said Roak softly.

Gariel's heart went out to her. He remembered kneeling in the forest, looking down on the bloated, blackened remains of his own children, and he knew that only one medicine could cure Mabshe, and that it lay in his power to dispense it. He raised his open hands, palms forward, and smiled at the young mother to reassure her.

"I won't touch your child, Mabshe," he said. "Only let me wipe your brow and give you water to drink."

She shrank a little, but did not back away. Gariel touched his fingers to her forehead and spoke the phrase that brought oblivion. Mabshe's eyes shut, and her head lolled from side to side like that of a troubled sleeper. Her fingers loosened, and Gariel took the bundle from her grasp and gave it to Roak.

"Take her over beyond those rocks. I'll help you dig a grave," he said.

"What of my wife, Master?"

"She'll remember none of this. She'll know she lost a daughter, but she'll think it was some time past."

As Roak went off, Gariel lifted Mabshe in his arms and carried her inside to where Panorn waited. Leaving the women, he went to assist Roak.

When Mabshe awoke, she found herself in a snug cottage. She had been washed of the dust of long wandering, and was newly dressed in a plain white robe of soft material. The scratches and bruises on her arms and legs were healing under soothing salves, and her bruised and lacerated feet were wrapped in clean dressings. She had vague memories of a time of struggle and suffering, and of a loss that brought her sorrow, but they were all far in the past, and now she felt safe and warm and secure from all pain, as if she had come to a home that had long stood waiting for her.

Roak sat in a chair by the fire, nodding, and their son slept on his lap. Mabshe stirred, and the slight sound brought him awake with a start. Smiling, he rose and came to her side, with the child in his arms.

"Roak, we're home, aren't we?" she asked.

"We are, love. This is our home now," he said, seating himself at her side.

"We've had a bad time, but it's over now. It is over, isn't it, Roak?"

"It is. We're safe here, Mab. Master Gariel promised me that, and he's a healer and a great mage."

"I remember him, Roak. And there was a woman, too. She moved in silence, and never spoke, but her words sounded inside me. She ... she ..." Mabshe struggled to recall, then blurted, "She gave her child into my care, Roak!"

"She did, love. We're to care for the little one as our own until they return."

Mabshe sat up. She looked wide-eyed about the room, and her gaze fell on the cradle near the hearth.

"Is she sleeping, Roak?" she asked softly.

He went to look, and told her, "She's just lying here quiet, looking up at me. She's a pretty little thing, Mab."

"She must be hungry. Bring her to me," Mabshe said, extending her arms eagerly.

Gariel stood on the ridge overlooking the sea, listening to the booming of wind and waves. Panorn, at his side, touched his hand and smiled up at him.

"You like the sounds of the world, Gariel. Have you missed them much?" she said.

"When I was with you, I seldom thought of them. But I like hearing your voice this way, and not inside me. You've a lovely voice."

"It's best we be two ordinary people for a time, I think, and use our power only when it's needed. I fear we'll have to use it soon enough, and often, too, if we're to stop Ankaria."

"Where is our way, Panorn?"

"We'll follow the strand. We can stop at the village, and get directions from the fisherfolk. They know the way to the White City."

"Is that safe? They'll be sure to recognize me, and Cossaran may remember you, too."

She smiled and shook her head. "He was too frightened to look into my face. Besides, I'm an ordinary woman now. The villagers will not study me closely."

"You can never be an ordinary woman, Panorn. The villagers have never seen so beautiful a woman. They will study you closely, believe me."

Laughing, she said, "Then I will be plain. Have no fear, Gariel."

"They might remember me. I spent a few days among them, and met them all."

"You forget that time has passed, Gariel. Your hair is grayer now, and your skin is pale. And you are dressed as a mage, and not a vagabond."

Gariel wore a cloak of gray, trimmed with a pale gray fur. His shirt and loose trousers were of a deeper gray, and his high boots a shade darker. He laughed softly and said, "It's true, I look almost wellborn. As do you," he added, for Panorn wore a longer cloak, similarly trimmed, and the iron torc, deeply graven with symbols, hung at her neck.

They walked at an even pace along the strand, and came at last to the site of the fishing village. Nothing remained but a tumble of blackened stones, charred fragments of boats and bodies, and a few scraps and tatters of bloodstained fur and rag.

"Raiders," said Gariel.

"Not raiders," Panorn responded. "Ankaria."

13

A Silent Vengeance

Amid the desolation and the carnage, a startling change came over Gariel. As Panorn spoke the enemy's name, Gariel saw—not with his eyes but with some hitherto unsuspected sense within him, newly manifest—a mist forming over the ground. On some places the mist was dense and sulphurous, while in others it was no more than faint tatters of pale yellow. It was everywhere around them.

Gariel gasped and reached for Panorn's hand. He knew that he was seeing the lingering spoor of evil. It lay over the land, folding in upon itself in turbid undulations, thick and slow and loathsome, and his heart sickened at the sight.

"Gariel, what's wrong? You're trembling!" Panorn cried, looking fearfully up into his pale face.

"Can you see it? It's like a poisonous fog rising all around us," he said in a whisper.

"I see only the ruins of the village."

"I can see the evil that destroyed it."

The mist began almost at once to dissipate, and in a short time it was gone. Gariel felt warmth against his breastbone, and drew out the amulet. The green stone was pulsing with light.

"Valimagdon has awakened this power in me. But to what purpose?" he said, perplexed. "I don't need to see evil as a presence before me in order to know that it exists."

"Perhaps it's to serve as a warning. Ankaria may be nearer than we know, and stronger."

"Perhaps," said Gariel listlessly. He seated himself on a pile of stones and slumped forward, burying his face in his hands. The experience had shaken him.

Panorn laid her hand on his shoulder. "Let's leave this place. Even if I can't see the evil as you do, I can feel it all around us."

He looked up helplessly. "Where shall we go? Without the fisherfolk to guide us, we'll be wandering like lost children."

"Our magic will guide us."

"We can't use magic. Ankaria would be aware of us at once. There's no sense in bringing it down on us any sooner than we must."

"We'll follow the coastline as far as we can. It will be longer, but it will take us to the Empire eventually."

They walked on, day after day, and saw no one. They passed a second devastated village near the shore, and one day they saw thick smoke rising from deep in the wood. The aura of evil was sensible to Gariel on both occasions.

At a place where the level strand ended in cliffs that plunged almost vertically into the sea, they turned inland until they came upon a trail through the forest. They proceeded warily, and the time came when they knew that they were being watched and followed. In a small hillside clearing they came face to face with a trio of armed men. The foremost commanded them to halt.

Gariel saw the shadow of evil hovering faintly about the three; but it was not evil they had done that marked them, it was evil they had suffered. He whispered to Panorn to withhold her magic, and raised his open hands in greeting.

"You're a brave pair, to walk these ways alone and unarmed," said the leader of the little band.

"We go to the White City," Gariel replied.

"Are you followers of the Annihilator, then?"

"We are not."

"Then you'll be no safer in the White City than you are here," said the leader, stepping forward to examine them more closely. "By the look of you, my good master and mistress, you come from no fishing village."

"We have been living in the mountains."

"Thought you'd be safe there, did you?"

"We were safe, for a time."

"Well, no one's safe now. Not in the mountains, not in the White City, not anywhere. We've all learned that, and it was a hard lesson," said the man, and his two companions showed their agreement by the bitter expressions on their faces.

"We have passed scenes of terrible destruction along the way," said Panorn.

"Our homes, maybe. But we'll be repaid."

"How can anyone repay you for the dead?" Gariel asked.

"We're following the raiders who destroyed our homes and slew our families. They're well armed, and they outnumber us, but we know this countryside. There's a place in the trail ahead where a score of men could butcher a hundred. When they reach that place, they'll feel the hand of Banseele. They'll learn what destruction is."

"You must not do that. Whatever you do, you must not kill them," Gariel said.

"Don't preach to me. I'll have my revenge."

"What you think will be revenge will only strengthen our enemy. You must not kill."

Banseele drew his sword and brandished it before Gariel's face in a rage. "Be quiet, old fool! You tell me to spare these butchers—you'd talk differently if you'd lost a family of your own!"

"He has lost his family to raiders. So have I," said Panorn.

Banseele looked at them dumbly for a moment, then sheathed his blade. With lowered eyes, he said softly, "I'm sorry for my words. But you're nobler spirits than I am if you can foreswear your revenge. I mean to see blood shed, and so do all who follow me."

"Every death, every drop of blood shed, makes the enemy stronger. The enemy is Ankaria, and it feeds on lives," said Gariel.

"Then it's well fed. The raiders kill out here, and Ankaria's followers sacrifice the lives of unbelievers in the White City. And the war goes on."

"All the more reason to kill no more. I'll stop these raiders, if you bring me to them, and they'll suffer for their deeds. But they will not die."

"I'd as lief have them live and suffer," said one of Banseele's companions thoughtfully, and the other nodded in agreement.

"I agree with my men. If you can make them live and suffer, we're glad to help you. But forgive me, good master, if I point out that one man can't stop a hundred warriors," Banseele observed.

"Three men won't slay a hundred, even from ambush," Gariel replied.

"I have enough men to carry out my plans," Banseele said.

Gariel closed his eyes for a moment, as if in meditation, then he nodded and said, "Perhaps you do. I count twenty-six besides yourselves."

"How do you know that?" Banseele cried.

"I know that four more stand among the trees on our left, with arrows aimed at us. There are three on our right hand, and six behind you. The rest are spread out behind us. Three are in the tree that overhangs the path."

"You have sharp eyes, but you're still only one man."

Panorn said, "There are two of us."

"One man and one woman, to stop a hundred? Don't mock me, or you'll regret it."

"One man and one woman with the power of magic can overcome an army," Panorn said.

The three men exchanged apprehensive glances, and before they could respond, Gariel said, "I was a mage in the White City, one of the Thirty-three, until I clashed with Ankaria. Its power nearly destroyed me, and I fled. Now I've been summoned back to confront the Annihilator once again."

"And I, Panorn, once wrought magic for the Nine Lords, until I learned that the true enemy was not the Empire of the White City, but the monstrous being you call Ankaria, which urges men to slaughter one another only to feed its own hunger."

The men before them wondered at these assertions so calmly delivered, and Banseele, with faltering voice, said, "But Ankaria . . . Ankaria's a god, more powerful than all the other gods of the Empire. No one can withstand its power. No one dares!"

"Ankaria is no god, only a hunger that feeds on life," said Gariel. "Once it hunted, like a beast, and killed as a beast kills. Now it's learned how to feed on the killing done by others."

"It caused the raids that cost the lives of your families, and ours," Panorn said. "It will never let the killing stop, because its life and power flow from the deaths of others."

Banseele looked from one to the other in growing confusion. "If you speak the truth... if this is so, what hope is there? I thought to fight men... but a thing so powerful...."

"Ankaria is not unconquerable. An older race of men drove Ankaria from this world and barred its return. It was defeated once, and can be defeated again," said Gariel.

"But if it was defeated, walled out... how is it so powerful today?"

"Men sought it out, and worked magic to bring it back among us."

"Why? *Why?*" Banseele cried wildly.

Panorn came forward and laid her hands on his arms in a soft gesture of reassurance, saying, "Ankaria feeds on life, and this gives it great power. Some men feed on power, and would willingly exchange all else for the promise of it. Ankaria's great strength lies in human weakness."

"Then there is no hope at all."

"There is hope, Banseele," said Gariel, coming to the warrior's side. "We know that men on both sides have sought to loose Ankaria in the world, but we don't know how far they've succeeded. If we can reduce the killing—or better still, prevent it entirely—Ankaria's source of strength will be cut off. It will be forced to move more slowly, and we'll have time to rally the knowledge we need to drive it off forever. Do you understand now why I urged no more killing?"

Banseele nodded, but did not speak.

"Then take us with you," Gariel went on, "and when you find the raiders, let us deal with them. I promise you, they'll shed no more blood when we're done."

Though there was no more sign of danger now than there had been throughout this long expedition, the Red Harriers observed all customary precautions. Scouts were sent ahead, where the forest track narrowed and turned abruptly to enter a steep-sided pass that formed an easy ambuscade. While the main body rested under the trees by the roadside, guards stood watch at close intervals.

Heggren, commander of the troop, was a careful man. Now,

with a successful expedition all but complete, he wanted nothing to go wrong. He had done his work well, but he looked forward to the end. Heggren was a warrior, and this expedition had involved not war but slaughter; no prisoners, no plunder, only total destruction.

He did not doubt that it was necessary slaughter, nor had he shrunk from it. These remote settlements harbored fugitives, shrinkers, malcontents, and traitors, and served as bases for spies and assassins. The people had no loyalties; they expected the Empire's troops to protect them while they themselves betrayed the Empire for profit; they were a worthless, stinking, half-savage lot, still shivering in superstitious fear of unseen things that lived only in their ignorant minds. He smiled coldly at the memory of dying curses calling upon the moss giants, or the black boar, or the Woman of the Waves to be avengers. The simpletons had learned at Heggren's hands that there were things more to be feared than ghosts and shadows.

The return of the scouts recalled Heggren's thoughts to the moment. The way was clear, without a sign of an enemy. He gave orders for the troops to make ready and summoned his subalterns to set the marching order. The temporary encampment was filled with sudden brisk activity; everyone knew that the high road to home—to rest and rewards—lay only ten days beyond the other end of the pass.

Before the first subaltern reached him, he heard a cry go up, and a trooper ran to him to report, "There's a man and a woman in the mouth of the pass, Commander. Just the two, and unarmed."

With an angry curse, and a silent vow that the scouts would pay for their carelessness with a flogging, Heggren turned and strode to the pass. The men were dumbfounded as he pushed them aside, and he himself was surprised by the appearance of the pair.

The man was big, with a breadth of shoulder that suggested strength, but he was pale as a scholar, and well past his youth. He was dressed in garments far richer than were customary among the people of this remote land. The woman was beautiful. She, too, was attired as someone of high rank. No need to kill her, thought Heggren, until we've made good use of her.

She stood tautly, with her hands pressed against her thighs, the fingers spread wide. The man stood at her side with folded arms. Neither of them spoke or acknowledged his presence. They returned Heggren's challenging glare coolly, without a trace of fear. The woman raised her hands and traced a figure in the air, and Heggren gave the command for his men to seize them.

The command did not come forth. He shouted again, and felt the cords of his neck grow taut and his jaw stiffen, but still there came no command. With a pang of terror, he realized that he heard no sound at all; a pall of absolute silence had descended upon him. Turning, he saw his men staring in astonishment and growing fear. Their mouths moved, and their faces reddened with the strain of shouting; their swords and shields struck against one another; their booted feet cracked twigs and shifted stones underfoot, yet all was silent.

Heggren felt a needle of ice go through him, and gave a silent cry of fear. Out of instinct, he drew his sword; he shrieked unheard to find in his hand a serpent that coiled up his arm and bared fangs in his face. Tearing at the apparition, he saw that the entire wood had come alive with misshapen hulking things that reached out for him and his men. Roots burst from the ground to entangle him, while branches lashed raging at his eyes. As he struggled, a mound of dark green rose up and towered over him, black mouth gaping and moist, dirt-clotted arms outflung, and he tore free from the clinging roots to hurl himself aside, rolling in the dirt, away from the moss giant's grasp.

All around him, his men were helpless with terror. They ran blindly into the forest, or retreated down the path, colliding with one another, stumbling, scrambling along the ground in headlong flight. Vengeance had burst upon them, and there was no hope but to run until their legs could carry them no further. Worst of all was the silence, deeper than the silence of the grave, the tangible silence that seeped into the soul and the blood and permeated the body, smothered the will and darkened the mind. It drove away all power of thought and reason, and left only the desire to flee.

When the last trooper was gone, Gariel breathed deeply and passed his hand across his forehead. Hearing the soft rub of flesh against flesh, he glanced at Panorn, who returned his look with a smile of relief.

"I've lifted the silence," she said.

"I reached every man's mind. They'll run until they drop, and they'll never kill again," said Gariel.

"Do you feel weak?"

"No," he said thoughtfully. "I once did something like this, and it drained all my strength. But now I feel as though I've used no power at all."

"I feel the same. Something has made us strong."

Panorn's fingers went to the iron torc that she wore around her neck. At the same instant, Gariel's hand closed on the amulet. They looked at one another, instantly recognizing the truth.

"We've found our weapon," he said.

One by one, Banseele and his band emerged from the wood to look in awe on Panorn and Gariel. Weapons and equipment were scattered in wild disarray on the ground. Fragments of clothing sagged from bushes and branches where they had been torn off in flight; cloaks and tunics lay where they had been stripped off and flung aside. They might have been standing on a battlefield, except that there were no wounded and no slain.

"Take what you need," Banseele ordered his men. "There's food in those packs, and healing stuffs that we can use. The cloaks will be welcome in cold weather."

"Take everything but the weapons," said Gariel. "Leave them here to rust. You'll have no more need of weapons."

The men looked to Banseele. He nodded to Gariel and told them, "Do as he says. Leave the weapons." As the men went about their work, Banseele asked, "What do we do now?"

"Do you know the way to the outposts?" Gariel asked.

"We can find them. That's dangerous traveling, though. It's where the fighting takes place."

"That's where we have to go, if we're to stop it. And we'd better move quickly."

Banseele left them to supervise his men and organize the march. When they were alone, Panorn said, "You think Ankaria is aware of us."

"It's possible. If Ankaria isn't aware of us now, it will be soon. We must do all we can to limit its power before it realizes what we're doing and seeks us out. Every battle avoided, every army scattered, is strength lost to Ankaria and time gained for us."

THE TIME OF THE ANNIHILATOR

* * *

In the White City, Ankaria looked out through the eyes of Bellenzor at the thin white column of smoke rising from the marketplace, where another enemy of the Fourth Child was meeting a slow death. Each day at evening the flames rose around a screaming, terrified victim, and each time Bellenzor looked down from his tower while the entity within his body consumed the frenzied life with greater satisfaction.

It was long since Ankaria had fed so richly. The eagerness it had felt in those first moments back on the ancient hunting ground of earth was moderated now, and it wished to linger a while, savoring every morsel of devoured life, before commencing the great feast it had dreamed of through those lean and starving eons of exile.

It had decided that this time it would destroy with fire, for death by fire lent a special piquancy to those expiring lives. But there would be no haste, and each step would have its pleasure to offer. Soon, with the return of the spring, would come the renewal of battle on the outskirts of the Empire. That, with the raids by both sides on remote villages and settlements, gave Ankaria the raw strength required for its work; these single deaths in the White City were more for pleasure than utility. Sporadic battles and slaughters would suffice for a few more winters; then would come the final clash of two armies, each desperate to survive and mad for vengeance, in a war of extermination. With both armies gone and its strength at a peak, Ankaria would throw aside this constricting human frame and fall upon the world as a wave of fire, consuming all in its path.

It would proceed slowly and deliberately, allowing a few to survive in its wake and breed new life for its next visitation; this much it had learned when once, long ago, it had given in too quickly to its hunger and left itself vulnerable. There would be no more vulnerability, only an eternity of triumphant life, feasting and growing ever stronger.

Deep in its dream of holocaust, Ankaria sensed a faint and distant disturbance. It was as if a single filament of some worldwide web had snapped, and the all but imperceptible tremor of its parting had at last reached the center.

Annoyed at the interruption of its reverie, Ankaria turned its attention to the warning: Magic had been used against its followers in a remote land. It probed no further. The matter was inconsequential. Some petty dabbler in magic was protecting his gold, or perhaps a sorceress was driving off a band of raiders. There was no danger here. No merely human power could threaten Ankaria, whatever magic it might attempt. Indeed, its followers were the better for an occasional reminder of what magic could do to men, even in the hands of a fellow human. It was a salutary lesson.

Ankaria dismissed the interruption and looked to the pillar of smoke. The moment of extinction was at hand, and Ankaria hungered.

14

Turning the Tide

Banseele sent six men to scout out likely sites of conflict and then proceeded with Gariel and Panorn and the main body of his men to a rendezvous inside the borders of the Empire. They saw nothing on the way but a barren countryside; the land and skies were empty and silent, as if all living things had fled. Water crawled sluggishly through clogged courses, and the wells were dry. They were soon grateful for the supplies taken from their enemies.

Gariel found the desolation ominous, a foreshadowing of the world under a triumphant Ankaria. He kept his feelings to himself, but Panorn could sense his uneasiness. She drew him aside, so they could speak without being overheard.

"Is something amiss, Gariel?" she asked.

"No. Why do you ask?"

"You don't look like a man coming from a victory."

"It was an easy victory, Panorn. The time for celebration hasn't come. We have a long struggle ahead."

"We know that, and so do Banseele and his men. Something else troubles you, Gariel."

"It's this. All this," he said, encompassing their surroundings by a sweeping gesture. "The desolation. I knew this region.

There was life here—people, livestock, animals, crops. And now everything is dead."

"A long war does such things."

"As you once reminded me, the war didn't do this. Ankaria did. And if all this life has gone to feed Ankaria, we'll face a powerful enemy."

"We will be powerful, too."

"I know that. I don't fear for us, Panorn, I fear for the world. Since we started out, I've felt my power increasing, and my confidence growing along with it. I knew we were going to scatter those raiders. I knew it before we set eyes on them. I could feel our power, great enough to make armies flee in terror."

She smiled and said, "Then you know the world is safe. You need worry over it no more."

"But I worry all the more," he said earnestly. "If we confront Ankaria, think what such a clash of powers might do to the world and all that lives in it! We might bring about a destruction greater than the one we're trying to avert."

After a pause, Panorn shook her head and said, "That cannot be."

"I wish I could think so, but I'm afraid, Panorn. Ankaria recognizes no limits. It will do anything to prevail. Even if we do no more than protect ourselves, terrible forces will be loosed. And if we fight back—if we seem likely to overcome —Ankaria would as willingly destroy the world as be driven from it."

Panorn walked in silence for a time. At last she said, "I think not. I think Ankaria would spare the world in hopes of returning in the future, when we are dead and the world has forgotten our times, and the struggle." Suddenly brightening, she looked up at him and went on, "This is why you had the premonition of forging some new weapon out of the iron from the heavens. If Ankaria should come back in some distant age, there must be a weapon waiting for those who stand against it."

Gariel did not reply for a time. "I don't know, Panorn," he said with a sigh. "We face a thing that isn't human. It lives on death and destruction. I can't believe that it would hesitate to destroy the earth rather than lose it. Yet... in the moment I was in Ankaria's presence, I felt its hunger. Perhaps it would spare the world if it believed that it might return and conquer ... for it has learned to wait."

"I think it would wait again. Even such a thing as Ankaria must be capable of hope."

"And which is worse? A few generations might live in peace ... people will forget ... and then Ankaria will return, stronger and more determined."

She took his hand. "And our descendants will be ready."

The first scout to return told of a sizeable force of warriors, more than two thousand of them, making for an outpost of the Empire manned by twelve hundred seasoned veterans. If a seige took place, the carnage would be terrible. The second scout had observed a small force of the Empire's troops digging in to await a raiding party. Here, too, there would be slaughter. Gariel and Panorn questioned both men closely, then sent them off to eat and rest, with instructions to be ready to set out the next morning.

They went first to the smaller engagement, where they found attackers and defenders preparing for a clash at dawn. In the middle of the night, Panorn covered both camps with silence and Gariel flowed from mind to mind, infixing panic. Men threw down weapons that had suddenly become objects of horror, and shrank from comrades who now were monstrous figures; they screamed, but their screams did not come forth. Unable to reason, stripped of their courage, alone in the grip of fear that turned their wills to water, they had no thought but to fling aside encumbering arms and flee.

When the field lay empty under a moon that glinted off abandoned weaponry, Gariel sent the second scout back to Banseele with instructions to meet them at the outpost in three days' time. Then, without pausing to rest, he and Panorn set off with the first scout.

Three days was ample time to reach the outpost, but a storm that flooded the lowlands drove them out of their way and the scout, who had not traveled by this route before, lost his bearings in the night. They came to the outpost just as the war cry arose and the forces came together in the shock of battle.

Forgetting their weariness, heedless of the danger, Panorn and Gariel raced to the field. Their work was quickly done, but this battlefield was not emptied. It was strewn with the dead and the dying. When Panorn lifted the silence, the groans of wounded men came from every quarter. The worst slaughter had been prevented, but scores had fallen in that first clash.

There were more injured than dead on the field, and Gariel drew on all his healing skill to save them. Some were beyond help; but many, only slightly wounded, were compounding their hurt in frenzied efforts to flee. Only when he had brought sleep on them all could Gariel proceed to care for them.

When Banseele arrived, he found the outpost transformed into a makeshift hospital where blood enemies reclined side by side in the sun, chatting like brothers, oblivious to generations of hatred. He had no time to marvel at the sight, for he had news from his scouts.

"No word from the north, Master," he said. "I fear the men who went that way were taken. But there's an army gathering in the south."

"How big?"

"As big as this one. Maybe bigger."

"And where are they headed?"

"Going northwest, when my scout saw them. But there are no outposts this size in their path, only the Fortress of Sarbex, and that's too big for them to attack."

"Did your scout learn of any other forces?"

"None. It may be that this lot plans to break up into raiding parties. They could do a lot of damage."

Gariel nodded. "We'll have to reach them before they can start."

"You look weary, Master. Will you rest before you go?"

"I'll rest if I can. Some of these men need care."

"We have healers among us, and all the supplies we need. Leave the work to us, and rest for a time, you and the mistress," Banseele urged.

Gariel weighed the offer for a moment, then agreed, for he was weary to his bones, and his eyes burned from long sleepless watches. "Look you care for them well, all of them," he said. "Every life we save is lost to Ankaria."

He and Panorn found a quiet chamber in one of the towers and slept deeply until well into the night. Rising refreshed, they sought out Banseele and his scout, and listened to a full report of the conditions in the south as they ate.

THE TIME OF THE ANNIHILATOR 145

"We must leave tonight," said Panorn.

The scout looked at her imploringly. "Mistress, it's a long and weary way, and dangerous, too."

"There's no need for you to come. Is there, Gariel?" she asked, turning to the mage. "The man's done his work, and done it well. He need only give us the directions."

"But will you be safe, just the two of you?" Banseele asked, clearly concerned.

"We'll be safe," Gariel assured him. "And you'll be safe here for a few days more. After that, you'd better return to the first camp. We'll rejoin you when our work is done."

They left at the midpoint of the night, wrapped in traveling cloaks and bearing seven days' food and water. The way was as long and weary as the scout had foretold, but they were accustomed to travel. The comfort of one another's company and the urgency of their mission hurried them on, and on the morning of the sixth day they reached the landmark they had been seeking. Soon after, they found traces of an encampment.

Looking down, Gariel saw lying over it, like thin mist on an autumn morning, the spoor of evil. It was not the dark trace of deeds, but the paler trace of evil willed but not yet accomplished. As Gariel knelt in the dust, he found tangible signs that were more disturbing: This had been the camp of a small force, not the thousands reported by the scout.

Panorn realized the import of this as soon as he remarked it to her. "Then they've divided," she said. "There may be twenty or thirty bands harrying the countryside."

"And we must find every one. We'll never do it before lives are lost."

"We'll stop them eventually. And many lives will be saved, Gariel."

"True. For all my warnings about easy victories, I allowed myself to grow too confident," Gariel said as he rose.

Two days later they came upon a scene that chilled their hearts. Gariel had had warning when he saw the air above a little wood thicken and grow murky with the effluvium of foul deeds. The reality was grim beyond his expectations. The air was loud with flies, and stank of putrefaction. The bodies of sixty-four men, most of them soldiers of the Empire, lay unburied under the sun, swollen and blackening.

Some of the men lay where they had fallen in battle, bloodied weapons still tight in their hands. An equal number, all of the Empire, were heaped in low mounds, butchered at the victors' leisure.

Nothing could be done here. They left in haste, and that night, as Panorn slept, Gariel climbed to the top of a rise where he could see the countryside all around. Faintly at first, then ever more distinctly, he perceived the breath of evil, willed and done, staining the air of a hillside, a grove, a valley, an abandoned village. He marked the whereabouts of nine bands, and then descended to awaken Panorn.

Before dawn they had scattered the first patrol and were closing on the second. Twenty-four days later, as the sun sank, the last of the nine bands of harriers was in terrified flight. Alone in the camp where fires still burned and food, though trampled in the dust, was yet warm to the touch, Panorn and Gariel sprawled by the main fire to rest.

"That's the last of them in this part of the country," Gariel said, rubbing the small of his back.

"But there are others," Panorn said.

"If the scout was right, there are. We've accounted for about twelve hundred. There could be nearly that many more at large."

"Where?"

"To the northwest. He said that they were headed that way. We can only hope that they haven't done too much killing."

"We must rest, Gariel. I can't go on without rest."

He took her hand. "Nor can I. We'll stay here for a day—nothing will come near this place—and then head northwest. Is that agreeable to you?"

"I hate to lose even one day, Gariel, but I'm too tired to go on."

"It's odd, though... I'm as exhausted as I've ever been in my life, and I ache from head to foot, but it's all physical weakness. Despite all the magic we've used, I feel my power stronger than ever."

Panorn nodded and said, "I've been too busy, and felt too tired, to think about it... but yes, I feel the same way."

"As if our power were growing even faster than we can use it."

"Just so."

They were silent for a time, then Gariel said thoughtfully, "I'd heard of iron falling from the skies, though I never believed it until I held such iron in my hands. It must have happened before, perhaps many times. Yet a piece came to me, landed almost at my feet, and I knew exactly what to do. I still don't understand how I knew, but I knew."

"Must you always understand?"

"I must try."

Gariel rose and gathered cloaks, tunics, and blankets from where they had been flung by their bearers with no thought but of unhampered flight. He piled them up to make a comfortable bed by the sinking fire, and he and Panorn stretched out. She was asleep almost at once, but Gariel, despite his physical fatigue, was mentally stimulated and could not sleep.

A thought had come to him, and he could not put it aside and rest. He still found the consequences of a clash with Ankaria dreadful to contemplate. Panorn might be right; it was conceivable that Ankaria, seeing this attempt fail, might leave the world and its occupants unscathed in hope of capturing them in some distant age; but Gariel feared that the Annihilator would remain true to its name and its nature, and destroy what it could not possess. The meeting of such power as Gariel felt within himself and that which he had glimpsed in Ankaria would shake the world to its foundations even if destruction were not its primary aim, as the trampling of giant beasts in mortal combat crushes smaller lives all around it.

Gariel no longer feared defeat by Ankaria; he dreaded the devastation of battle, and pondered over a way that it might be avoided. Though there had been bloodshed, and would surely be more before he and Panorn could touch the last band of warriors, there had been less than in the past. To some extent, then, Ankaria's power must be diminished. In such circumstances, even such a creature as the Annihilator might be reasoned with.

If he saw Ankaria face to face, an equal, unafraid, he might offer terms that would be scorned if they came from an ordinary adversary. The prospect of that cold presence was unnerving, but it seemed the only chance of sparing the world great suffering. Gariel drifted into deep sleep with the thought of peace in his mind.

The next day they headed northwest, and Gariel's mind was turned to the immediate problem of locating and neutralizing the remaining marauders. One by one, they found the harrier bands. Three times they were too late. A village was utterly obliterated, and two small Empire patrols were overcome with great slaughter before the last troop of raiders fled unmanned and terror-stricken before their wizardry.

"It's done," Gariel said as he looked about the abandoned encampment. "There'll be no more fighting in this sector."

"There's fighting elsewhere. And they'll fight here again in the spring," Panorn reminded him.

"Perhaps not," said Gariel. "I think there's a way of stopping it all now."

"Tell me."

"It's your idea, actually. I've been thinking about it since you mentioned it," he said, helping her to a seat in the shade of an oak and settling beside her. "You said once that Ankaria might spare the world from destruction if it had reason to hope for victory in the future."

"Yes, I remember. But you did not agree."

"I've thought about it since. We can't promise Ankaria the world, of course, but if it sees that it faces opponents as strong as itself—perhaps stronger—it might choose to withdraw. That would give us time to find the spell to block it out forever."

"You never sounded this confident before."

"I don't want to sound over-confident, Panorn. Ankaria is a terrible opponent, and it may have powers we don't suspect—powers we can't even imagine. I'm well aware of that."

"And yet you would face it."

"I think I must. It must be aware of what's happening on the frontiers, and if I confront it while I'm at the peak of my power and its own power is waning—if I remind it of what befell it once before—"

"You speak as if you would confront it alone," Panorn broke in.

"Yes. I know a way into the city and the citadel of the Thirty-three. I can get to Bellenzor's chambers without using magic. I'll appear there without any warning. And if I fail," he said, breaking from her intent gaze, "you'll be left to carry on our work."

She shook her head firmly. "Neither of us can do the work

alone. Our magics complement one another. We both wear the iron from the heavens. We must not be separated, Gariel."

"I've faced Ankaria once. It's awful, Panorn. It's too dangerous."

Matter-of-factly, she said, "If it is dangerous, all the more reason to go together."

15

A Second Reunion

After six days' travel, Panorn and Gariel saw the first distant glint of the walls and towers of the White City. Two nights later, in the dark of the moon, they slipped through a concealed opening in the outer wall and worked their way down to the maze of passages underlying the city. Gariel led the way, moving much of the time in utter blackness, with only an occasional far gleam of lantern light as they skirted the fetid charnel pits and the dungeons, crossed the deep cisterns, and rose at last to torchlit corridors awhisper with the faint echoes of distant footsteps. A narrow, twisting staircase took them up for three hundred and forty steep steps. They moved hand in hand along a narrow passage to another, narrower set of steps, and here they halted.

Placing his lips close to Panorn's ear, Gariel whispered, "Bellenzor's chambers are just on the other side. Ankaria may be there, and it may attack us on sight. Be ready."

She responded with a quick pressure on his hand. He touched the fastening of the door and, as it opened, stepped quickly into the dimly-lit chamber, Panorn following close behind.

All was still. They scanned the chamber warily, but saw no occupant or guardian. Yet a candle burned beside a low chair, and bracketed torches cast a wavering light. Books, scrolls, and tablets lay on a long table ready for perusal. Despite the warmth of the summer night, a low fire burned in the deep fireplace. Gariel moved stealthily about the chamber, puzzled and uneasy. He saw a drawn curtain, and gestured to Panorn. She nodded silently to signify her readiness.

Gariel drew the curtain back and gasped at the sight of Bellenzor. His brother lay still as stone, but life still beat faintly in his ravaged body. The face was pallid and deeply scored, the lips dry and cracked. One gaunt hand clawed at his breast and the other lay twisted and misshapen at his side. Bellenzor looked like a man dying under long torture.

A pale aura of distant long-ago evil lay about him, slowly fading as Gariel watched. He put his hand on Bellenzor's and looked with pained eyes at Panorn. A faint rasp of breath from the supine figure brought Gariel to his knees, face close to his brother's.

"Speak, brother. It's Gariel. I've come back. I'll help you any way I can," Gariel whispered urgently.

"Kill me. Destroy this body," came the barely audible response.

"Bellenzor, hear me. It's Gariel. I don't want to hurt you, I want to help."

"Kill me," Bellenzor repeated, his lips scarcely moving. Gariel looked up at Panorn, who gestured helplessly, and the dry whisper came again, "Ankaria has possessed me... works through me... horrible...." another pause, and then Bellenzor's body shook spasmodically and he cried, "Horrible!"

Gariel remembered the shadow he had seen come over the form of his brother when they last stood face to face in this chamber, and the change it had wrought. The man who lay on the couch was his brother, in agony of mind and body; the thing that had possessed it once possessed it no more.

"Kill me... before Ankaria returns," Bellenzor pleaded. "Kill me... burn this chamber. Destroy all."

Gariel could not. He touched his fingertips to his brother's brow and spoke the words that gave oblivion. Bellenzor gave a great sigh and his body relaxed. His eyelids slowly opened, and he turned his dark eyes on Gariel; they were pained, yet innocent, as a child's who suffers and knows not why. After a moment, Bellenzor closed his eyes and seemed to sleep again.

Rising, Gariel said, "I don't know what to do, Panorn. I never thought this might happen. If I can save him from Ankaria, I must."

"What can we do?"

"I don't know! I can't kill my own brother, even though he begs me. I want to save him, not kill him. If we take him away from here, Ankaria will follow, and then there can be no peaceful meeting. But if we just leave him here...." He shook his head.

"You've given him oblivion. He won't remember his suffering."

"But when Ankaria returns, it will begin again. And I know no magic to protect him."

They moved away from the sleeping figure. Suddenly Bellenzor came fully awake; he rose, and his dark eyes blazed with rage. "Who are you who dare enter my chamber?" he demanded in a deep strong voice that seemed to speak through him from beyond.

"We would speak to Ankaria," said Gariel, stepping forward.

"You presume too much." The figure rose and leveled its hand at Gariel. A silent, invisible blast of life-shriveling power poured forth, and broke on Gariel's unmoving body as a current breaks and flows around a rock.

Ankaria lowered its hand, and Gariel calmly said, "You're wise to husband your power."

"Who are you?" Ankaria demanded again. It was confused, for it had returned to a body from which all memory of its possession had vanished. It felt like one who reenters a familiar house in broad daylight and finds it shuttered and dark, emptied of accustomed things. It knew that this man and woman were responsible, and it swelled with rage to realize that they not only dared such a deed, but could accomplish it.

"We are your enemies," said Panorn, and Gariel added, "But we have not come to destroy you."

"I am indestructible."

"You are not unconquerable."

Ankaria looked out through Bellenzor's dark eyes at these two mortals who confronted it so coolly. An aura of power surrounded them. One of them seemed familiar, but when Ankaria probed the memory of its host it found a curtain of oblivion enshrouding all that had taken place since it occupied this body. The magic of these mortals was potent.

"If you would speak with Ankaria, then speak," it said.

"We have little to say. We know that you have been in this world since the beginning of life, and that you have been driven from it by the magic of men. You were recalled from exile by that foolish man whose body you have usurped and are destroying," said Gariel.

"What is this to you?"

"You do much evil in this world. You bring war and the shedding of blood to feed your insatiable hunger, and you drain life from all you touch."

"This world is mine. I do in it as I please."

"You must leave. Swear to leave, and we'll swear not to attack or pursue," Gariel said flatly.

"I will never leave my world!"

"You are an intruder here," said Panorn.

"I am the rightful lord of this world!" cried Ankaria. "Ilveraine, and Teleon, and Ebanor—these are the intruders, false gods who seek to lure my subjects into weakness and death. Men follow me instinctively, and always return to me in the end."

"Men are turning away from you, Ankaria. Few have died in battle since the spring, and now the armies are scattered, and the raiding bands have thrown their weapons aside. Your age is over. Leave the world now, before all your power is lost," Gariel said.

Ankaria weighed the words of this pair, and realized that there might be truth in them, for the battlefields had grown quiet in recent days—awareness of this very change had drawn Ankaria away, and left its untenanted body to be found by these strangers. They had appeared without warning; their purpose and the extent of their power were unknown, but they were strong, and might be some danger. Surprised and disoriented, Ankaria required time to think on the situation.

"And what do you offer me—a peaceful departure, and nothing more? That is little to give in exchange for a world," it said.

"You have heard our terms," Panorn replied.

"Not terms but an ultimatum. You must give me time to reflect."

"It takes no time to give an answer," she pressed.

The man held back, silent, and Ankaria sensed the weakness in him—a concern for the creature in whose flesh it dwelt—and quickly moved to use this to advantage. It addressed its words to him, speaking now without arrogance, and in a conciliatory tone. "I have been kept from this world long, and my exile was painful. I cannot lightly part from my world again." The man and woman exchanged a glance, and Ankaria went on, "Let the seasons go their rounds once more. When the sun stands where it did this day, I will leave the world."

"Many people can die in that time," said Panorn coldly.

"I will swear to restrain the armies and the raiders. Not one drop of blood will I cause to be shed in battle from this time to that."

"There are other ways of taking life. You must foreswear them all."

"I will do so. And you must swear to leave me in peace to enjoy the world until then."

Gariel said, "We will swear." He could not keep back the words. Quibbling would be foolish; it was time to bind Ankaria with an unbreakable oath, before it reflected and recanted. Here was victory, bloodless and free of destruction. The Annihilator would reside in Bellenzor still, but the horror of the past was over.

Panorn looked at Gariel sharply when he spoke. She wanted assurance, not a hasty oath that might bind them to their regret. But she had seen Gariel's concern for his brother, and she understood.

She felt that Ankaria had yielded too quickly. So easy a victory over such an adversary made her suspect treachery. Yet she knew that Ankaria's strength had not been renewed by the slaughter of battle; she and Gariel were the stronger now, and perhaps they always had been; Ankaria feared them. Perhaps she had never fully appreciated the extent of the power conferred on them.

"Let us swear now. You know the unbreakable oath," Gariel said, gesturing to a dark tablet that lay on a high shelf, covered with a generation's accumulation of dust. He took it down and placed it on the table, quickly tracing the requisite figures and markings. Ankaria placed a hand in the figure. Gariel put his hand beside it. Panorn, smothering her misgivings, laid her hand in place with theirs.

They repeated the ancient words that bound them to their promise as firmly as the mountains were rooted to the earth and the stars to their heavenly paths. When the last phrase was spoken, Ankaria turned to Gariel. The voice that came forth was so very like Bellenzor's that Gariel thought for an instant that his brother's old self had returned; but the words were Ankaria's.

"Perhaps it is well that this is done. I have been on this earth too long, always hungering and never sated. It may be that now I will find a peace I never found before."

Until this moment, Gariel had thought of Ankaria with loathing and dread, seeing it as the wellspring of all the world's suffering. Now the creature's words filled him with sudden deep pity. For millennia it had waded through blood and feasted on death; wherever it passed, all was desolate; and at last it seemed to be looking in on itself, and seeing its deeds in their true light.

"I hope it can be so," Gariel said.

Panorn took his hand and drew him away, saying, "We must go now." To Ankaria, she said, "We will meet here on the appointed day."

"Not here, I beg you. Let it be in some distant place—in the Valley of Standing Stones."

"Very well. We will meet there," said Panorn.

Ankaria bowed. "I will come at the setting of the sun."

Panorn and Gariel left the way they had come, and made a circumspect departure from the White City. They traveled to the northeast, walking steadily until dawn, speaking seldom. No one pursued, and no one appeared to bar their peaceful passage. At first light they paused to rest.

"The sun seems to shine more brightly," Gariel said, his face radiant with happiness. "The very air smells of peace. We've broken Ankaria's grip on the world, Panorn."

"Ankaria remains," she said.

"But the killing and the dying are over. Even Ankaria dare not break the oath we swore."

"I want to share your joy—truly I do—but it all came about

so quickly. It was too easy a victory, Gariel."

"Now you've become the doubter," he said, taking her in his arms. "In a year's time, Ankaria will leave the earth forever. It will be so, Panorn."

"What if it chooses to fight us?"

"If it did not resist us last night, when its strength was great, it will not resist when it's weaker. Ankaria is incredibly ancient, Panorn. We can't comprehend what it must be like to live so long. I believe Ankaria truly longs for rest."

"It spoke with your brother's voice. That does not mean that it spoke the truth."

"I think it did. We'll be watchful, of course, but I'm sure that this will be a year of peace, and when the appointed day comes, Ankaria will meet us in the valley."

Panorn sighed and nestled against him. Her breathing became regular, and she slept. He kept watch, too happy to sleep.

Ankaria had been stopped, and Bellenzor saved. The earth was free of the threat of annihilation. The long bondage was ended. Ankaria itself seemed relieved to have come to an end of slaughter; perhaps in the tranquility of exile, remote from the scene of its long ascendancy, it would come to repent its past. In time, it might even turn its powers—for it would always be a being of great power—to making atonement for those ages of evil.

As Gariel mused on these things, Panorn shuddered and cried out in her sleep, clutching at his robe. He drew his cloak around her and pulled her closer, stroking her cheek until she relaxed and slept peacefully.

When the intruders were gone, Morodel came from his hiding place and threw himself at his master's feet, imploring forgiveness. To his surprise, Bellenzor bade him rise, and showed no anger.

"They appeared suddenly, as if from nowhere, Master," Morodel explained earnestly. "I feared enchantment, and concealed myself."

"You were wise to do so. They would have swept you aside like a day's dust," said Bellenzor mildly. "Did you recognize them?"

"I had only a glimpse of them, Master. The room was but dimly lit."

Bellenzor said, "They are no strangers to this place. They knew the city and the inner ways of the citadel, for they came here without employing magic."

"There must be an enemy in the citadel!"

"There are many enemies around us, and I am aware of them all. Enemies can be as useful as friends, Morodel, when used properly. But these two were very different from the rest."

"Let me take our enemies and make them tell everything they know, Master!"

"They can tell me nothing useful. They know nothing of me, or of the real nature of this encounter." Turning his dark eyes on the servant, Bellenzor said, "Nor do you, though you have some suspicions."

Morodel, in sudden fright, raised his hands defensively and backed off a step. Bellenzor laughed drily and went on, "I am something more than you see, and something different. This body, this Bellenzor, is only an envelope of flesh in which to move about the city. I could have taken another form—yours, if it pleased me—been a child, or an old woman, or the citadel itself, or anything I chose to be. You know who I am, do you not?" The lulling voice suddenly cracked like a whip. "Speak my name!"

"Ankaria!" whispered Morodel.

"You are sworn to my service. Never forget that."

"I've served you faithfully, Master," Morodel said, falling prostrate before the unmoving figure.

"And you will continue to do so. I have a message for all commanders in the field: 'Hostilities have ended. Return at once to the White City and report to me.' Make copies, and I will place my seal on them. Summon the couriers and tell them to prepare for immediate departure."

Morodel's terror gave way to astonishment, and he stood frozen for a moment before scurrying off about his duties. To see the long war end so suddenly, and without a decisive victory, or negotiations, or the collapse of either side, was beyond all expectation. It could not be surrender; there was no mention of surrender, Ankaria could not surrender; but neither was there mention of victory. Hostilities had ended; the killing was over, but nothing had changed.

The intruders must have done this, Morodel concluded. No word of peace had ever been spoken before this night, but now, by the time the sun rose, the message would be on its way to all the Empire's forces.

He sent servants for the couriers, then returned to copy out the messages in his own hand. His mind was whirling. The man and woman had brought this about; but who, or what, were they? Ankaria admitted their power. If it had surrendered to them, and was now doing their bidding, they were powerful beings indeed, for they had turned Ankaria against itself. An end to the fighting; an end to killing; peace; these were abominations to the Annihilator, and yet it had ordered them to be.

Morodel finished the final copy and brought the messages to his master. He did not know what to expect, and could only hope that this had been some test of his loyalty, or a strategem too subtle for his understanding. But his master only glanced at the messages and then marked them with the seal of office.

"Give these to the couriers and tell them to leave at once," Ankaria said. Morodel bowed and turned to leave, but he stopped at the words: "You wonder at all this, do you not?"

"I do as I am bid, Master."

"You will always do my bidding—but this message troubles you."

"It is beyond my understanding," Morodel admitted.

"Listen, and you may understand. Tonight I swore an oath that cannot be broken. I will end all warfare and killing for one year, and at the end of that time I will depart from the earth. Do you understand that?"

"The words are clear... but you are Ankaria! You are lord of the earth!"

"Have no fear, Morodel. I will remember those who serve me. Quickly, now, to the couriers, and return to me."

The couriers were waiting. They took the messages, securely sealed, and left on their ways at once. Morodel returned to Ankaria with word of their departure.

"I will retire now. Keep careful watch. I do not wish to awaken in the presence of intruders again," said Ankaria.

When the curtains were drawn, the recumbent figure of Bellenzor shuddered once as a shadow passed over it, and then it lay like a dying man flung aside to await the end. Ankaria went forth, visiting the fighting bands of the Nine Lords' Alliance, bringing to each the message that the war was over at last.

THE TIME OF THE ANNIHILATOR

Some were stunned by the message that came from their seers and the keepers of their idols; some rejoiced, while others ground their teeth in frustration; but all obeyed. Everywhere swords were sheathed, spears were laid aside, bows were unstrung. The warriors struck their tents and returned to their homes, and the sounds of battle were stilled.

In the White City, the pyres burned no more. When spring returned, the symbols of the old gods, the tree, the sun, and the tower, were once again to be seen, and the worshipers of Ankaria passed them in silence, with averted eyes.

16

The Oath Fulfilled

As they made their way to the camp of Banseele, Panorn slowly came to share Gariel's belief. There was no sign of treachery, either by magic or the hand of man. They encountered no armies on their way, no raiding parties, not a single armed man. They came upon no new scenes of battle or devastation. The spoor of evil that had lain upon the land like pockets of stagnant mist was gone. All around them, the sounds of life were returning, growing stronger each day. As Gariel had said on that first morning, the sun seemed to shine more brightly on a world delivered from the power of Ankaria.

Even so, Panorn still felt a doubt about their victory. She gave it no voice, hoping that it would fade and eventually vanish as the year continued in peace, but it remained and she realized that she must reveal it to Gariel.

Banseele and his men welcomed them, and heard their news with unreserved joy. Their return became the occasion of a great feast. The fare was plain and the preparation simple, but the unfeigned happiness on every face atoned for the lack of elegance.

In the days that followed, Banseele's camp diminished as men left, in twos and threes, to return to their old homes, or to seek new ones in which to begin over. The day came when only Banseele and three companions remained with Gariel and Panorn, and as they sat by the fire on that morning, Banseele awkwardly and reluctantly announced that they, too, wished to depart.

"We want to go back north, to where we all came from," he said. "There's still time for a late planting, and we can have a house built before the first snow falls."

"Then you must leave soon," Gariel said.

"We'll go today, if you have no objection."

"We're happy that you're able to return to your old lives," said Panorn.

"We were thinking you might come with us; maybe settle near us," Banseele said hopefully. "We could help you to build a house."

Before Gariel could respond, Panorn said, "We would go with you if we could, but we still have work to do, and it will take us far from the north."

"We wish you success, then, Mistress, and we leave with our thanks."

The others joined their thanks to his and began to gather their few belongings. The leave-taking was brief but deeply felt on both sides. As Banseele gave one final wave of farewell and vanished into the distant trees, Gariel turned to Panorn and asked, "What work is this that lies ahead of us?"

"There are many sick and injured people who need our help."

"I'm not the only healer in the land, or the best. I would have preferred to travel with Banseele and the others, and go home."

"No. Not yet," said Panorn firmly.

"Our work is done. Don't you want to see Ciantha again, and start to live the life we thought was lost to us?"

"I want that more than anything, Gariel, but I'm afraid."

"Of Ankaria?"

"Yes."

"Ankaria swore the unbreakable oath. It can never recant."

Impatiently, she said, "Ankaria is older than the mountains and the seas, as old as life itself. Do you believe we can outwit such a being so easily?"

"I don't feel that we outwitted Ankaria. We faced it with a choice, and it chose wisely."

"Yes, wisely. Perhaps it chose more wisely than we know. We allowed it a year on earth—"

"A year in which it cannot replenish its power. When we meet again, it will be weaker."

"Much can happen in a year. It may grow stronger in other ways."

"So will we. In a year we'll have time to find the Sign of Denial."

"And will Ankaria be idle while we seek the final key to its downfall? No, Gariel, never can I believe that."

"It swore the oath. And I think, Panorn, that it came to realize what it has been, and done. I think it truly wants to be free of its past."

Panorn shook her head and angrily cried, "No, no! You think this way because you look at Ankaria and see your own brother. You look in his eyes, and hear his voice. You forget that the thing that looks out at you and speaks with you is not human. Because we saw this thing in human form, we think of it as human, but Ankaria never was human and never will be. It is something different from us." At sight of Gariel's changed expression she said earnestly, "Bellenzor was a stranger to me, yet I felt as you did. I saw a suffering man, and I pitied him. But Ankaria is not a man, does not suffer or feel as we do. I think it deceived us, and I fear what may come."

"But how? It swore the oath."

"Not even the strongest oath can foresee every possibility. If there is a single way for Ankaria to thwart us, we must be wary. This is why we cannot return to our home, Gariel."

Gariel nodded, slowly and thoughtfully. "Because Ankaria might follow."

"Yes. And however firmly you believe in our victory, if the slightest doubt remains we must protect Ciantha."

"You're right, Panorn," Gariel said softly, sadly.

She took his hand in hers. "I hope I'm wrong. I want to be wrong. But if there's any chance I'm right, she must be saved. If we should fail, Ciantha is the last hope for the future."

Gariel broke from her and sat by the fire, cradling his head in his hands like a man at the edge of exhaustion. After a time, he looked up sharply. "What about the books and tablets—all that ancient learning—what will we do without it?"

"We've studied every word and every symbol, and still we have not discovered the Sign of Denial. I think it would be foolish to look again where we've already searched so carefully."

"Where else is there to look?"

"Within ourselves. We may know without realizing that we know."

Gariel sighed and gestured in helpless surrender. "I believe that we've overcome, and that Ankaria will keep the oath. But you're right about my feelings. I want to believe, because I saw my brother's sufferings, and this would mean an end to them. I could be wrong. Ankaria might be plotting even now. We must do as you say. There is no other choice."

For the rest of the summer, and well into the fall, Panorn and Gariel traveled through the outskirts of the Empire, stopping to give assistance to all who had suffered in the long war. Gariel gave himself to this work with an enthusiasm that was close to desperation, using his strength, his knowledge, his skills, and his magic to help heal and rebuild. Panorn was less active; she spent much of her time alone, apart from everyone, deep in contemplation of their past studies, searching for the thread that would lead to the sign.

They passed the winter in a settlement at the border of the forest. Gariel worked at the forge during the day and sat until late in the night with Panorn, questioning and examining, helping her to probe their memories. Their understanding grew, but the one truth they sought still eluded them.

In spring they resumed their journey. By early summer, stories of a dark-haired prophetess and a mage in gray were circulating among the people of the Empire's outermost reaches. He was a man with the gift of healing. His eyes and his hair and his robes—everything about him, it was said—were the color of iron, and iron came to life under his hands at the forge, molding itself into shapes that were strong and useful and beautiful to see. The woman was like a shadow; and silence and peace followed her. Some who had seen them declared that they had been sent by the gods to rebuild the world.

As midsummer drew near, Panorn and Gariel turned their steps toward the Valley of Standing Stones. They had not found the Sign of Denial, the final assurance of victory over Ankaria;

but the time of their meeting was at hand.

They approached the rendezvous filled with hope. In all their travels they had heard of no fighting or killing; there had been no persecutions, no natural disasters, no epidemics. Peace reigned everywhere, and life flourished. To all appearances, the time of the Annihilator was ended.

Morodel stood before his master, awaiting instructions. He wore a dark traveling cloak and held a staff in his hand. In the scrip at his side, and in his pack, were food and water for six days.

"This is my last command to you," said the wizard. "You are to travel to the Valley of Standing Stones. There, in three days' time, you will meet the man and woman who came to this chamber a year ago. Tell them that Ankaria has fulfilled the oath and returned to its place of exile—"

"Master!"

"They will reward you," the wizard went on, heedless of the interruption. "Tell them that it is my wish that my power be passed on to you, and that you use it to assist them in renewing the world."

Morodel's eyes widened in amazement. "Then I . . . I am to be given your power, Master?"

"You have served me well. I promised you a reward."

Morodel fell to his knees and gave profound and heartfelt thanks. His master bade him rise, saying, "Speak to no one of these things. Afterward, you may do as you wish, but now you must leave the city and go directly to the Valley of Standing Stones, and reveal nothing of your purpose."

"I go at once, Master," Morodel said eagerly.

Morodel had not long been gone when the commanders began to arrive. They were experienced warriors all, hardened by the sights and sounds of battle, but they had heard rumors of things done and seen in Bellenzor's tower, and though they had all been here before, they nonetheless entered the mage's chamber like small boys venturing into a haunted wood.

Bellenzor greeted them with a dignified deference that reassured them. Wine and fruit and small crisp breads were brought by silent servants, and the commanders began to feel more at ease. They talked among themselves, and there was subdued laughter now and then. Some spoke with Bellenzor and found him, to their surprise, attentive and responsive to their words. The mood in the wizard's chambers became easy, and when Bellenzor at last addressed the commanders, they were eager to hear.

"Honored warriors, fellow servants of the Empire," Bellenzor began in that deep echoing voice, "for a full year, the war has slept. In all that time you have not drawn a weapon, nor have you shed a drop of blood in battle. The forces of the Nine Lords have kept the truce as faithfully as we. And in three days' time, on the Field of Nembar, they will lay down their arms in surrender and accept our terms for peace. The treaty is fair, for they were a brave enemy; but it is also severe, so they will never forget the price of defeat."

Pausing to permit the exchange of congratulatory phrases and affirmative nods among his little audience, Bellenzor went on, "The ceremony is in your hands, and the honor of that day belongs to you. I have assembled you here to add my thanks, and the thanks of the Thirty-three, to the gratitude already expressed by the people. And I wish to make one request. Now that the war is finally ended, I will return to my regular duties among the Thirty-three. But I would like to address the armies on their day of victory, to thank them for their courage and their sacrifice while I guided the Empire."

"They would be honored," said one man.

"You honor us all, Master," another added.

The score of commanders present were unanimous in their accession to Bellenzor's request. In this gathering, they had seen a different side of his character. The austere and forbidding leader who worked in isolation had shown himself to be a man with understanding of other men. The commanders knew responsibility; when they reflected on the burdens that had weighed on that gaunt frame, they marveled. They had fought, often to exhaustion, with the strength of their bodies and the quickness of their minds. Bellenzor had fought the war with powers beyond their imagining, and for him there had been no rest between battles. If any single man had earned the glory of victory and the right to stand triumphant over an enemy as the sword was laid at his feet, it was Bellenzor.

On the appointed day, the White City was a single great festival. The gates were flung wide early in the morning, and company after company of fighting men marched proudly out, past rows of cheering compatriots and friends. Shields and helmets, newly burnished, gleamed in the morning light. Banners snapped and fluttered in the breeze, and the rhythm of booted feet was a ground bass for the swelling cheers and shouts that filled the city.

Bellenzor looked down from his tower for a time, then turned to the four burly men who stood waiting, one at each corner of a large palanquin curtained in heavy red cloth that closed the interior off from view. He took up a dark tablet from the long table behind him and, without speaking, drew aside the red curtain and entered the palanquin. In the dark and airless interior he lay back, clutching the tablet to his breast. A faint shudder went through him, then he lay still as a corpse.

As the four bearers carried the body of Bellenzor to the red pavilion at the center of the Field of Nembar, the unfleshed Ankaria ventured far. It left the world behind and moved with the quickness of thought across time and space until it came to a dead gray world that circled a dying sun. Here it paused. Probing the lifeless stone with its inhuman senses, it found the narrow chamber at the cold center of the planet where it had lain powerless for ages in the distant past. Here it had learnt the price of defeat, and paid in anguish.

It turned from the place of pain and fled through the universe, groping for life on each world that flashed by. It seldom found any life at all, and what life it did find in these remote reaches was so bizarre as to be repellent; for Ankaria, different though it was from all other beings on earth, was yet a thing of earth. It had lived among humans, and in humans, for ages. By nature and habit it was closer to them than to anything else in the universe.

It journeyed ever onward, and still it found no life to sate its hunger. It went beyond the known, beyond the imagined and the imaginable, and on the borderline between being and nothingness it came to rest. It paused and scanned the mystery beyond, with its promise of oblivion and peace, and an end to the long craving. It need only plunge onward, and it would find rest.

It hung in the emptiness, deliberating. Then, with a wild inward cry, it turned its back on the void and began the long journey back to earth.

17

The Triumph of the Annihilator

The Valley of Standing Stones lay three days' travel from the White City. Travelers seldom visited this place of disquieting sights and sounds, where uncertain towers of jagged rock rose from the valley floor and its steep sides loomed like waves frozen in the moment of breaking.

It was a place of mystery. Those with imagination could study the heaped stones and see the shapes of men and monsters, of castles and strange beasts. The stones had been heard to crack and ring at the touch of sunlight, and moan under the caress of winds that set them to ponderous swaying. How they had come there, and why, and what reason could be behind their strange shapes and configurations, no one knew. Men blamed gods, or demons, or magic, and kept away.

Panorn and Gariel arrived here on the appointed day, when the sun was a forearm's length above the horizon. Slanting light and long shadows made the ragged columns of flat stone more stark and menacing. They entered from the shallow open end of the valley, and walked cautiously toward the center, keeping to the open ground.

"I've never been here before. It's very strange," Gariel said, his voice lowered.

"I came here once. I wonder why Ankaria chose it."

"Vanity, I think."

Panorn looked at him curiously. "What has vanity to do with such a spot?"

"It's far from the White City, and shunned by everyone. Even the mages among the Thirty-three seldom spoke of it. If Ankaria must accept defeat, it would do so in such a place as this, where no one would know."

"We will know," Panorn said.

"Yes, and we'll know soon."

The wind was still and all was silent. Gariel turned to the open end of the valley, and raising his hand before his eyes, peered at the sun through the narrow slits between his fingers. It was just above the horizon. The time was at hand.

"He is here!" Panorn cried.

Gariel turned and followed her pointing finger to the far rim of the valley, high above them. Between two uneven pillars of leaning stone stood a cloaked figure bearing a staff. After a pause, it raised the staff in salute and then began a slow descent of the steep, rock-strewn hillside. Gariel observed the figure closely, and saw an aura of greedy evil all around it. This creature, whoever it was, had done little evil but yearned to do much.

"No. This is not Ankaria," he said.

"It has betrayed us!" Panorn cried.

"Perhaps not. He could be Ankaria's messenger."

"Ankaria promised no messenger. It was to be here itself."

"I sense no evil power in this man, Panorn. He is only an ordinary man, nothing more. He can do us no harm."

They moved a few steps apart and watched as the man came closer. When he was within speaking distance, he halted, bowed profoundly, and pushed back his hood to reveal a homely, blunt-featured face devoid of expression. "I am Morodel, faithful servant of Ankaria," he announced.

"Where is your master?" Panorn demanded.

"Ankaria is gone."

"Gone? Ankaria was to be here on this day. It swore an oath."

"I am to tell you that Ankaria has fulfilled the oath and returned to its place of exile," said Morodel.

• • •

THE TIME OF THE ANNIHILATOR 169

In the red pavilion on the Field of Nembar, the body of Bellenzor came to life. Ankaria rose, and with the tablet pressed to its chest, it brushed aside the dark curtain of the palanquin and stood in the dimness of the pavilion. The sounds of men and weapons came through the thin walls, and it stood unmoving for a brief time, listening.

It took the tablet in both hands and raised it high. In a lowered voice, it said, "I swore that for one year, no one would die by my hand, or my will, or my command. I swore that on this day I would leave the world. I have kept the oath and am bound no more." Closing its fingers, it crushed the tablet between them and let the fragments clatter to the platform at its feet. "And now I hunger," it whispered.

It turned toward the pavilion wall that faced the White City. Extending its hands, it began to speak in a hushed voice. Its power and perceptions reached forth.

It saw the streets of the city filled with celebrating crowds. Sellers of sweets, flowers, and wine were everywhere surrounded by willing buyers. The apprentices had been granted the day off from study, and were to be seen here and there, faces lighted with unaccustomed gaiety. Even a few of the Thirty-three mixed with the crowds, accepting with dignity the praises and thanks of their people.

Ankaria felt the pulse of life flowing through the city like blood through the veins of a robust giant. The sensation was exhilarating, but Ankaria spared only an instant for the pleasure before turning to its purpose. It reached down, deep down, to the hidden fires of the earth and drew them to itself.

At the first slight tremor, people paused in their merrymaking. Song and laughter and conversation froze into sudden silence, and the wine cups stopped halfway to the lips. But when the tremor passed, the revelry burst out louder than before. Some even made a joke of their momentary fear.

Then the ground heaved like the cloak over a restless sleeper. The towers rocked, and showers of mortar and stone fell, scattering the crowds in panic, striking some down where they stood.

Over the rumble of the earth came the sound of anguished cries and screams of terror. Panic gripped the people of the White City and sent them rushing blindly from street to street, dashing indoors only to flee outside, thrusting one another violently aside, trampling the old and the fallen in their headlong flight only to fall and be trampled by others coming after.

The rending of the earth and the spurting forth of liquid flame added a new element to the terror of trampling crowds and falling rubble. Death was above and below and on all sides; it filled the very air, as sulphurous gases hissed from the spreading fissures, and the dark clouds of ash mixed with the smoke from burning buildings to blind the fugitives.

Towers toppled and walls crashed down, crushed and burying those in their path. The earth gaped to swallow scores at a time and snapped shut behind them like a hungry ogre's mouth. Fire and smoke and the frenzied clawing of their neighbors took the lives of hundreds.

Some reached the walls only to find the gates sealed by fallen rubble. As they turned to seek another way of escape more fugitives came, and still more, crushing those before them and then falling victim in their turn to smoke and fire and falling stone.

Ankaria passed through the city like unseen lightning, taking each life just at the final moment, gorging itself on terror and death. When the last vestige of life was gone and the city was silent but for the crackle of flame and the clatter of settling rubble, it looked around and down on the scene with deep satisfaction. All had been quickly accomplished, and a greater feast was soon to come.

It returned to the red pavilion and the waiting body of Bellenzor. There it abided until the first cries of alarm rose from the troops assembled outside. The cries spread and grew wilder, and still Ankaria waited. Only when the camp was on the verge of rioting did it burst from the pavilion, arms flung wide, and cry out in a deep rolling voice that buried the outcry of five thousand men and awed them to silent attention.

"Betrayal!" cried Ankaria, and every man heard. "The enemy has betrayed us! They have destroyed our city, slaughtered wives and children and parents, smashed our homes with the force of magic. Even now, their wizards make ready to turn the same evil against us, the survivors. But let us swear by Ankaria that they will not prevail. Let us be the avengers! We will be avenged!"

A roar of echoing cries drowned out all other sound for some moments. Ankaria waited until the din had quieted in sheer exhaustion, then went on, "Even now, the armies of the Nine Lords approach, gloating and laughing over their deception. They think to see a field of corpses. Arm, and meet them on the way! Slay them to the last man, and drown their homelands in a tide of blood! We can never turn back. I with my magic, you with your arms, must avenge the dead of the city. Arm! Avenge them!"

Ankaria's words roused them, and the long habit of discipline ordered their rage. The mob fell silent and gathered into its fighting units; the units formed into marching order; and as the scouts raced ahead, the forces of the Empire turned eastward for the last confrontation with their old enemy.

The smoke of the White City rose at their backs, but few turned to look. They had seen all they needed to see, and they thirsted for revenge. In every man's heart was the same purpose: this day to fight to the death and kill to the last man.

Gariel turned from the hooded messenger and said to Panorn, "It's over. We've succeeded."

"So it appears," she said, but her expression was troubled. She asked Morodel, "Is there no more to your message?"

"You are to reward me."

"Isn't it reward enough that the world is free of Ankaria? What more do you want?" Gariel asked.

"Ankaria's power. It was promised to me."

"We made no such promise."

"My master promised. Ankaria said I was to tell you to pass its power on to me. All its power is to be mine," said Morodel eagerly.

"Ankaria's power is not ours to give. It's gone. Whatever your master may have promised, what you ask is impossible," Gariel explained.

"Ankaria's power is mine by right!" Morodel cried. "I was faithful always. It is my reward. I want my reward!"

"You must seek it from your master, not from us," Gariel said.

"You mock me!"

"I have no wish to mock you," Gariel said, his voice gentle. "You are the bearer of good news, and deserve a rich reward, but we cannot give you the reward you ask."

"Then share your own power with me."

"We cannot."

"You speak as if you were powerless! 'We cannot,' and 'We cannot,' and yet I saw you humble Ankaria! You can reward me, but you refuse—you fear to share your power with anyone!" Morodel cried, reddening and on the brink of tears from frustration.

Gariel and Panorn watched him, pitying. Gariel began, "If you ask us—"

"I ask you for nothing! You cheat me and then mock me with soft words—but I will have my reward!"

Morodel thrust his way between them and stalked off toward the shallow open end of the valley. They watched until he turned from sight, and Panorn reached out to take Gariel's hand.

"Poor wretched man," said Panorn. "It's as though Ankaria could not leave without causing one last bit of misery."

"But it's over. Our work is done," Gariel said.

They walked slowly from the valley, thoughtful, not speaking. As they reached the mouth, Gariel was aware of the silence all around them. He looked to Panorn, and saw her smiling. Her voice sounded deep within his mind, sweet and caressing.

We can return to our home and our daughter, and live as others live—or would you prefer to stay in the silence with me?

"A time together in the silence, and then the life of the ordinary world. Everything is different now. Ciantha can grow up without fear."

And what of us? What will we do with all this magic that has been given to us?

He drew her to him and held her close. "We will stay together, and make each other happy. That's all the magic we'll need from now on."

He bowed his head and, with closed eyes, rubbed his cheek against her soft hair. He could still scarcely believe that this was true; he had never known such happiness since those early days with Moarra, but he had come to love Panorn deeply, and the thought of a life with her made his eyes fill with tears of joy. At that moment, his powers and the victory over Ankaria meant nothing; he felt as if his life had been restored.

They emerged from the valley, pausing among the tumbled boulders to survey the land. The sun had set, but the sky was bright with the midsummer twilight.

We can spend the night in that little grove of trees, Panorn said, pointing almost directly ahead.

"Yes," Gariel replied, but he spoke as one preoccupied. When she looked at him, curious, he pointed to the horizon off to their left. "What's that? Do you see, over there?"

I see nothing. The White City lies in that direction, does it not, Gariel?

"Yes . . . the White City . . . and its people."

His voice failed. His eyes were fixed on a monstrous cloud of evil that mantled the White City. It churned in all the colors of corruption and flickered with lurid light; it throbbed and swelled, rolling and folding in upon itself as it mushroomed outward and upward. All the world's evil seemed to hover over the White City, battening upon itself and waxing ever greater. Tendrils crept off to the east, and Gariel, following them, saw a second cloud coming slowly into being on the horizon.

"Ankaria deceived us. All your fears were true, and I was a fool. It remains. It's done some awful deed in the White City, and I fear that's only the beginning," he said in a voice hushed by despair.

We must go at once.

"It will be strong, Panorn. I think it's devoured every living thing in the White City."

We must stop it before it grows stronger. Come, Panorn said, striding forward.

He paused for a moment, rubbing his eyes as if to wipe away the evil they had seen. Looking up, he saw Panorn turn to him, eyes wide and astonished, as a hooded figure struck at her with a bloody dagger. Morodel jerked the blade free and, as Panorn fell, he threw himself at Gariel. His face was distorted with rage, and his mouth worked as he screamed silent imprecations at his intended victim.

Gariel was taken completely by surprise. The fury of Morodel's attack sent him staggering backward, and he fell. Sound burst in upon him, fragmentary and chaotic. Panorn's magic was failing; she was close to death.

Morodel was upon him before he was fully back on his feet. Gariel caught Morodel's wrist in one hand and hooked the other under Morodel's chin. They struggled wildly and finally went down, tumbling over the rocky ground. All the while their harsh breathing and the broken cries of Morodel beat on Gariel's ears.

Morodel was younger, but Gariel still retained the strength he had acquired in his years at the forge. Straining away from Morodel's other hand, which clawed frantically for his eyes, he forced the knife hand over a ledge and threw all his weight on it. He felt the bone give, and Morodel's sharp, brief cry pained his ears. The assassin went limp, and Gariel climbed to his feet and without a further thought for him, ran to Panorn.

She lay on her side, facing him. Only a small spot of blood appeared on her breast, but when Gariel took her up in his arms, he felt the wet warmth that covered her back.

"Panorn, you'll live," he said desperately. "I'll use all my magic to save you. It's no use to hoard it any more. Ankaria's won."

"No," she said softly.

"I'll take you back to the mountains. We'll be safe there with Ciantha, where the spirits can protect us. Another generation will take up the struggle. We've done our best, and failed. We can do no more."

"No!" she cried. With a strength that astonished him she clutched at his cloak. Opening her eyes and fixing him with her intent gaze, she said, "Let me die. Save your power, Gariel. I must die."

"Panorn, I can save you, I know I can. I must save you—I love you too much to let you die like this."

"If you love me, continue the struggle," she said. Her eyes closed, and she strained for breath. Looking at him once more, she whispered, "This is the weapon. The sign. I must die, Gariel, so you can overcome."

"What kind of weapon is death?" he cried. "Let me use my magic to save you, Panorn. I've failed everyone else—let me accomplish one thing for someone I love!"

"Bury me here. Then . . . vanquish Ankaria," she whispered.

She spoke no more. He knelt with her in his arms until the sky was dark. When the moon rose, he took her up and carried her into the valley. There, among eerie shapes and shadows, he dug her grave by moonlight, scooping out a narrow trench and placing her carefully within. He removed the iron torc from around her neck and kissed her for the last time.

THE TIME OF THE ANNIHILATOR 175

Huge flat stones lay on the valley floor, and Gariel covered Panorn's body with a double layer of them, working until midday to drag them into place and fit them tightly together. He used no magic, for Panorn's wish had been that he save it. When the sun was overhead, he stood beside her grave, his body stiff and sore, his fingers scraped raw, and said his farewell.

As he reached the mouth of the valley, he felt the ground tremble underfoot. Turning, he saw the stone towers totter and fall and the overarching rim of the valley crumble and slide downward while clouds of dust rose and hung in the air. Not a sound reached his ears. The Valley of Standing Stones had become the Valley of the Silence. Panorn had joined the legions of light, gone to carry on the struggle elsewhere, in other ways.

Morodel lay dead where Gariel had left him. The face was frozen into a snarling mask. Morodel appeared to have died of sheer rage. Gariel looked down on the corpse coldly, unable to rouse remorse or pity in himself. The man might have been Ankaria's tool in this, or he might have acted out of his own frustrated envy. It did not matter. Whatever the cause, Panorn was dead by this man's hand. It was proper that he die. Gariel stripped the body of food and water, then turned from it and started for the White City.

Each day's journey seemed to take him deeper into the land of the dead. Trees with withered, papery leaves jutted from dry brown meadows. No birds sang, and no creature moved in the fields or woods. When at last Gariel stood in the gap of a fallen wall he heard no sound but the wind that blew across the dry wastes at his back and murmured in the ruins before him. Bodies lay everywhere, but despite the time that had passed since death they were not bloated or discolored. There was scarcely a trace of corruption in the air of the city. No flies buzzed over the dead, no insects swarmed; no carrion eaters circled overhead. The whole city was drained of all life, just as the tumbled corpses around him had been drained, and now lay like husks dried under a desert sun.

At the heart of the White City, where the ruins of the citadel rose jagged above the rubble, Gariel climbed to the highest point and looked around. On all sides he saw desolation so complete that it seemed as though life had forsaken the world forever. The destruction he had hoped to avoid had come about after all; perhaps it had fallen more fiercely because of his efforts, he thought bitterly.

Now, at least, there was no need to restrain his power, for there was nothing left to destroy. Only Ankaria remained, the indestructible, the Annihilator. But Ankaria, though it could not be destroyed, could be overcome. Panorn had believed so, and even had spoken of the weapon and the sign. He did not understand, but that did not matter. Ankaria must be fought, whatever the cost.

"Ankaria!" he cried, and his voice echoed in the silent ruins. "Ankaria, come and face me now!" The echoes died, and all was still. "Face me while you're strong, Ankaria. I'll hunt and find you. You won't escape. Face me now, Ankaria, and destroy me if you can!" he cried again.

No answer came. The silence was worse, to him, than mocking laughter, for it made him think of Panorn, and remember all he had lost.

In the morning, Gariel left, heading eastward. The next day he came upon a sight that sickened him. A battle of unparalleled savagery had taken place on a field between two low hills. Thousands of men lay slain. This time, the scavengers had gathered. Few bodies were intact.

He walked amid the stench of carrion, brushing away the swarming flies, as sick with the despair in his soul as with the revulsion of his senses. This was the triumph of the Annihilator: a world where men did its work eagerly, and called that work brave and glorious.

As he passed a charred pile of stores, Gariel heard a voice cry out. It came again, and he traced it to a man who sat with his back against a bale, sword in hand, legs straight out before him. His legs were transfixed by a lance that had pierced both thighs a handbreadth above the knees and broken off short in his right leg.

At sight of him the man bared his teeth and brandished his sword, snarling like a wild beast. Gariel raised his open hands.

"I'm not the enemy. I'm a healer," he said. "Let me help you."

"Healer?"

"Yes. I've just come here. I think you're the only one left alive, and I want to help."

"Get me water," the man said in a rasping voice.

Gariel brought him water. As the soldier drank deeply, Gariel searched about for healing materials. He found a kit nearby, and returned to the injured soldier.

"Who sent you?" the man asked as Gariel examined his wounds.

"No one. I came to see if I could help."

"Which side are you on?"

"I'm not on any side. I'm a healer."

The soldier raised his sword. "If I thought you were one of them, I'd kill you."

"Put the sword down," Gariel said firmly, not raising his eyes. "I told you, I'm not your enemy."

"I've been betrayed once. I won't be betrayed again."

"How were you betrayed?"

"We came here in peace. Our holy men told us to fight no more, and we obeyed. No fighting for a year, and then we came here to celebrate the peace and lay down our weapons. They attacked us without warning—came over the crest of those hills screaming for our blood."

"That's strange," Gariel said thoughtfully.

"Nothing strange about it. They're treacherous, lying vermin, all of them, and their leaders, too."

"But if you were coming to lay down your weapons, they could have waited a little while and then killed you without a battle that cost them as dearly as it did you. Doesn't that make sense?"

The wounded man stared at Gariel blankly. He took a deep drink of water, shook his head, and said, as if the truth had come to him at last, "They couldn't wait, that's what. They hate us so much they couldn't wait one more day."

"Maybe they were betrayed, too."

"Not by us!" the man snarled, taking up his sword and drawing it back in a threatening gesture.

"Their city was destroyed before their eyes."

"Good!"

"They must have believed that you were responsible."

"Never us. We came in peace."

"Then perhaps we were all betrayed. You and I, and all these dead . . . and everyone else."

The man was silent. Then he said, "Talk sense, healer. Who could betray both sides? Why would anyone want to?"

By this time, Gariel had cut away the clothing around the wounds. He laid out the ointments and wrappings he had found, and ignoring the question, said, "I have to get that lance out. It's going to hurt."

"It's hurt for four days. Do it quickly."

Gariel handed him a wad of clean dressing. "Bite down on this. Here, lean back," he said, reaching up to touch the man's forehead and whisper the words of oblivion. When the man's eyes had gone vacant, he took a firm grip on the lancehead and pulled it free. The soldier gave a moan and his head slumped forward.

Gariel cleaned the wound as best he could and dressed it carefully. He carried the unconscious man to a clearing beyond the site of carnage, where he made a shelter out of cloaks and lances. Lighting a fire to keep the scavengers off, he returned to the field to search for other survivors. He found none.

The soldier slept through that day and night. Gariel built a little shelter for himself near at hand, where he could rest and keep watch. He slept in short snatches, and spent most of his time thinking about the man's story.

It was clear that Ankaria had planned the deception from the moment the oath was proposed. In his eagerness and his vanity Gariel had been an easy dupe, and even helped persuade Panorn to put aside her suspicions and agree to the oath. He thought of the encounter in Ankaria's chamber and burnt with shame. Fool, to believe that he could so easily overcome a being of Ankaria's age and wisdom. Fool, to swear a hasty oath and never suspect that a thing like Ankaria would know a thousand ways to bend any oath to its purpose. Fool, to ignore Panorn's doubts and lead her to her death. Fool, to be deceived by the appearance of Bellenzor and ignore the monstrous power that couched within the familiar form. Fool, fool in so many ways, and at such cost to the world.

And now he, this fool, this failed savior of the world, stood alone between Ankaria and this generation, and generations yet unborn, until the descendants of Ciantha were ready to take up the struggle. Gariel sighed, and rubbed his weary eyes, and looked hopelessly into the dying fire.

How was he to fight such an enemy? Ankaria had fed deeply and was stronger than ever. If ever it had feared him, it did not fear him now; and yet this challenge had been ignored.

Perhaps Ankaria would rest for a time, then erupt into some new destructive fury. It might even now be ravaging some far land. Yet it seemed to be tied in some way to this part of the earth. It would return, and Gariel could only wait, and be ready.

The soldier stirred and groaned in his sleep, taking Gariel's thoughts back to the present. This, Gariel thought, was his way to fight the Annihilator: to save with his healing; to protect and defend with his magic; to thwart the enemy at every opportunity, until Ankaria could ignore him no longer.

PART THREE

18

The Messengers

In the years that followed, Gariel crossed and recrossed the land. Wherever he went, he encountered fear and suffering.

The power of the White City was gone, and the Alliance of the Nine Lords was broken. All was in turmoil, and once again little bands of lawless men spread death and terror where they passed. It was a world at war with itself, where life was brief and violent and filled with mistrust.

With his magic, his skills, and the strength of his hands, Gariel brought hope. He healed the survivors and cleansed their minds of fearful memories and the hunger for vengeance. He helped to rebuild and fortify settlements, and drew families together into communities less vulnerable than isolated farmsteads. Whenever he learned of a raiding band he sought it out and burst into the minds of the harriers, scattering the men in blind terror.

Sometimes, when he left a strong and united village, or listened to people plan for the future, Gariel believed that he was making headway against Ankaria, turning back the chaos and stemming the tide of blood. But before long he would see the cloud of evil rising before him, and find some charred and blood-spattered croft, or the hacked bodies of travelers flung by the wayside, and know that at best he was only matching Ankaria's efforts with his own countermeasures. He persisted, hoping to bring Ankaria to move against him, but he found no Ankaria, only its eager servants busy everywhere in destruction.

In every place he stopped, Gariel spent some time at the forge; for this, and for the color of his robes and his hair and eyes, people came to speak of him as their Iron Mage. He smiled at the title, but he accepted it, for it pleased and encouraged the people who spoke it.

Gariel worked on without respite as the years passed. His magic was undiminished, and the strength of his body was scarcely less than it had been in his younger days, but he felt himself growing weary. All his efforts seemed to be fruitless; the situation never changed; when he forced back the darkness in one place, it crept forward in another. For every life saved, another was lost. His spirit and his will began to feel the toll.

In the heart of the great forest, he found Banseele in a strongly fortified walled village with upwards of threescore adult inhabitants and nearly a score of children. Here, for the first time, he met a people filled with confidence. He was welcomed among them not merely for what he offered, but as a friend.

Two of Banseele's old companions were still with him, and Gariel sat up late into the night with the trio, telling of what had befallen him since they parted. They listened with scarcely a word of comment or question, except to express their sorrow at the death of Panorn. When Gariel was done, Banseele heaved a sigh and glanced at his companions.

"It's as we feared, then. The war is over, but the fighting goes on," he said glumly.

"Has there been much trouble here?" Gariel asked.

"It was quiet at first. We met others on our way here—women and men—and they joined us. We built a good place here, and people came, year by year. First raid was three years ago. We drove them off, but they killed Jenicol and four more."

"We got eight of them," said one of the others.

"So we did. I know you disapprove, Master, but our blood was up," Banseele said. Gariel nodded but said nothing, and Banseele went on. "For a time there, we thought it was all behind us, and we could go back to living as people used to

THE TIME OF THE ANNIHILATOR

live before the war began. Then we found out that nothing had really changed at all. We built a good solid wall, and there's been none of us killed since. Raiders come from time to time, but they don't take us by surprise any more." Banseele paused for a moment, then said heartily, "I'm glad you're alive, Master, and sorry the Mistress Panorn is dead. You're welcome to stay here."

"I'd like that, Banseele. I'm tired of wandering," said Gariel.

"We have a healer woman. She'd be glad of your help."

"Good. Do you have a forge?"

"We do, Master, but the smith is an old man. It's hard for him to get all the work done."

"Then I'll be your smith, too."

"Stay in my house tonight. We'll go to the forge in the morning," Banseele said.

Gariel's wanderings ended for a time. The people of the village were pleased to learn that the legendary Iron Mage had come to them, and their welcome made Gariel all the more willing to remain.

He told himself that he could do as much good by staying in the village as he could do by continuing his travels. Refugees from the surrounding violence and turmoil often came here, and his help would be needed; lives would surely be saved.

Late in the autumn, a family arrived with word of raiders approaching from the west, and a solitary man came in the spring with news of another band. On both occasions Gariel went in search of the raiders and sent them off in terrified flight. He considered these successes a vindication of his decision.

He healed, and passed his healing knowledge on to others. He stood long at the forge, making tools and implements of every kind, from fine needles for stitching wounds to massive straps to bind the log palisades more firmly. These skills, too, he taught to others.

At the end of his second year in the village, Gariel was called from the forge one day to care for a man and woman who had come seeking sanctuary. Semerel, the healing woman of the village, met him on his way.

"The woman is strong enough, Master, but the man is broken. He shakes from head to foot and babbles nonsense. I don't know how she brought him all this way," Semerel said.

"Have they come far?"

"All the way from the sea."

"And the man looks bad, you say."

"He looks to be dying, Master. No wounds on him at all, but something's taken his life from him. I hoped you might be able to give him ease. I've seen you do it with others."

"I'll help him if I can, Semerel."

The newcomers were in a shed near the village gate, the man lying on a straw pallet, the woman seated on the ground at his side. She rose when the healers entered, and threw herself on her knees before Gariel.

"Don't kneel to me," he said, raising her to her feet. "I've come to help, if I can."

"Save him, please, Master. They say the Iron Mage can bring a man back from death. Save my Tembrash, Master," she said, clinging to his hands.

"I have no power over death. What I can do, I'll do."

The man lay on his back, staring upward with terror in his eyes. There was little left of him; Gariel felt that a puff of wind would blow him away like a dry, dead leaf. His hands trembled, and spasms shook his head and body. His skin was pale, and his hair was white. He mumbled softly, and Gariel bent over him to try to distinguish the words. He heard "stalking towers," and "eyes out of darkness," and then Tembrash, aware of his nearness, cried out and shrank into the corner of the shed, whimpering like a child. Gariel touched his forehead, bringing oblivion, and the man sighed and lay still. His limbs and body ceased to shake, and he breathed like an ordinary sleeper.

Gariel arose and led the woman outside. "He'll sleep, and he won't remember this when he awakens. He'll know that he was sick and troubled, but it will all seem long ago."

"Bless the Iron Mage!" the woman cried.

"I can't undo what's happened to him. He's an old man, and he's had a bad time."

"My Tembrash is no old man, Master. He's not two years older than I," the woman said.

Gariel looked at her in astonishment. Under the dust and fatigue of long flight, her skin was unwrinkled. Her hair was thick, a deep brown with not a trace of gray. She could not have been past twenty; yet the man sleeping on the pallet was an aged, withered patriarch.

"What happened to him?"

"I don't know, Master. We were separated along the way, and he came back to me the way he is now, shaking and talking nonsense and afraid of every shadow."

"You must tell me everything you can," Gariel said. "Tembrash will sleep soundly for a long time. You need rest, too. When you've slept, and eaten, I'll talk with you."

He left her in Semerel's care and returned to the forge, but he did little work the rest of that day. He was puzzled and disturbed by the plight of Tembrash. Only magic could have such an effect on a man, and magic of this nature and force was wielded only by Ankaria.

The woman's name was Cazron. Semerel brought her to the forge in the evening. Rested and bathed, wearing clean clothing, Cazron appeared even younger than she had when he last saw her. She told her story plainly and directly, and Gariel did not interrupt.

She and Tembrash had left their home far to the north to find safety from the monstrous things that roamed the hills around them, gray giants that moved like animated stone. Traveling with eight other families, all armed and carrying only the necessities, they crossed the broad plain that lay between the mountains and the coastal hills. For days they saw no sign of life, but one stormy night there was an alarm, and they became separated. Tembrash and three others fled east, toward the sea, while all the rest continued south. Cazron remained behind at the appointed rendezvous while the others went on. She waited nine days, and at last Tembrash appeared, looking as Gariel had seen him. He was alone. Neither then nor thereafter did he speak of the others.

"He never stopped talking to himself, Master, but I could make no sense of it," Cazron said. "He talked of towers that hunted for him, and walls that crawled and had eyes, and a darkness that burned. I was afraid. He was very weak, but I helped him along, and we got away from that place."

"Where did he see these things?" Gariel asked.

"I don't know, Master."

"Did he give no indication?"

"He spoke of the sea, that's all. Someplace near the sea.

'Sea on three sides and twisting stone in the center,' he said once, but I don't know what that means."

"Nor do I, Cazron," Gariel confessed. "Did you see any more sign of the ones who went ahead?"

"We found their bodies by the way, all cut to pieces," she said matter-of-factly. "Whoever did it, they didn't even take their goods—though there was little to take. They just killed them."

Her words, and the scene they described, were familiar to Gariel. Killing for the sake of killing seemed never to have ended.

"You're safe here, Cazron," he assured her. "Tembrash will never get his old strength back, but he'll recover and grow stronger."

"Thank you, Master, and bless you," she said.

Cazron returned to the shed where Tembrash rested, and Gariel climbed to the loft above the forge and sprawled on his pallet. This night he did not sleep until very late. He lay long awake, staring into the darkness, pondering Cazron's story.

Tembrash and his unfortunate companions had stumbled upon the stronghold of Ankaria: of this Gariel was certain. Somewhere on those stony outcroppings beyond the hills Ankaria had raised an obscene and terrifying keep in which to dwell, and the mere sight of it had blasted Tembrash's mind and body.

Now Gariel had an idea of his enemy's whereabouts. If Ankaria would not hear his challenge, he could go to Ankaria's stronghold and hurl the challenge in the creature's face, defy it and goad it into action. His first thought was that one way or another, the long agony would be ended, and the world would be free of the shadow of the Annihilator. It might mean his own death, but Gariel was reconciled to that.

As he dwelt on the prospect of their meeting, his old concern revived—in a clash between such powers as his and Ankaria's, what might become of the world? If it were left lifeless, then his saving it was no different from Ankaria's devouring it; and yet there could be no peaceful resolution. Ankaria's oath and its consequences had made that clear.

Ankaria must be faced, fought, and overcome by the strength of Gariel's magic. There was no evading this. And yet their confrontation would shake the world.

He thought of the people of Banseele's village, good people who had become almost a family to him. Bad as the world was, they survived in it, and though all here had their grim memories, there was hope, and even happiness, in the village. Gariel could not bring himself to accept the risk of their destruction.

The village itself was like a warm, brightly-lit shelter in the middle of a cold wasteland, welcoming all, comforting and offering safety. It was a bulwark against the power of the Annihilator, and it occurred to Gariel that other such outposts of mankind might well exist. To chance destroying them would be wrong.

Gariel had already waited long, and each day he waited more blood was shed and Ankaria's strength grew. Yet the strength of mankind was growing, too. The raiders were being turned back and lives were being saved. In time, Ankaria's strength was sure to wane, and if Gariel waited, the creature might then be overcome with little harm to the world.

The problem seemed insoluble. Gariel struggled with it through the night and fell into troubled sleep without a resolution. To act without delay or to await the proper moment seemed equally dangerous to those he cared for and hoped to save.

In the end, he waited. He questioned each new arrival for word of the hideous structure by the sea, but no new information came. He began to think that Tembrash had spoken out of delusion. The man's mind and body might have been broken by some natural event—perhaps the death of his companions—and not by Ankaria.

The simplest course was to travel to the seacoast and look for himself, Gariel knew, but that would leave the village without his protection for too long. He was needed here. And so he continued to wait.

The fall and winter passed without bringing any newcomers to the village. In the spring, Tembrash had recovered enough strength to be able to work in the fields. Gariel looked upon his recovery as a strong indication that the man's sufferings had been caused by some natural event, and not by magic. He thought less and less often of that twisted fortress by the sea, and of a final confrontation with Ankaria. The time for that was still in the future.

* * *

On an afternoon in early summer, Gariel looked up from his bench to see a slight figure in the entrance to the forge. He thought it was a child, but as the visitor entered and threw back the hood of her dusty traveling cloak, he saw that it was a young girl. Her hair was a deep dark red, her eyes were green, and she possessed a serene beauty more befitting an empress than a slender girl in worn and dusty garments of common stuff. Gariel blinked at the pale brightness that hovered about her. It was more than the afterimage of the bright sun at her back; the very air seemed to glow with her presence.

"Are you the healer they call the Iron Mage?" she asked.

"I am."

"My husband is badly injured. Will you help him?"

"Take me to him," Gariel said, rising. "Are you newly arrived in the village?"

"Yes. We've come a long way. We lived in the mountains at the edge of the world."

"That's a hard journey."

"All went well until yesterday. A band of men attacked us and our friends. We fought, and we drove them off. Colberane is very strong," she said proudly. "He'd never let anything happen to me or the children. But Colberane was hurt, and two of our companions were killed."

Her voice troubled him by its familiarity. He had never seen this girl before, yet he felt that he had heard her voice, or one very like it. In his wandering, he had heard many voices, but hers was distinctive; yet he could not place it.

"How many were in your band?" he asked, concerned less with the information than with her telling.

"Twelve of us, and four children. The others were all from settlements along the seacoast. Only Col and I were from the mountains." She glanced up at him shyly. "It felt strange to be with so many people. I grew up with Col and his parents and no one else. It was a lonely life, but we were happy. I would have stayed there, if we could, but Col decided we'd be safer among other people."

"Did his parents come with you?"

"They're dead. That's why we left the mountains."

Just ahead was the gate. Clustered around it, a group of men, women, and children sat or reclined in the shade of the

THE TIME OF THE ANNIHILATOR

wall in postures that attested their weariness, while villagers cared for them. One of the villagers, seeing Gariel and the girl, pointed to the shed.

"The injured are inside," she said.

The shed by the gate had become the village infirmary. Gariel found two men lying on pallets. One sat up, propping himself on an elbow, and said, "See to Colberane first, healer. I can wait."

Without replying, Gariel knelt beside the still figure on the other pallet. Colberane was not much older than his wife, but he was already taller and broader than Gariel. Even now, as he lay injured and unconscious, he radiated strength and vitality. As Gariel examined the man's wounds, he marveled. His back and shoulder were deeply gashed, and he had lost much blood. One forearm was swollen and discolored. A flap of skin hung loose from his ribs. An ordinary man would have been rendered helpless by such wounds, but Colberane, though weakened, was breathing regularly and seemed in no serious danger.

"He drove them off almost single-handed," the other man said.

"How many were there?" Gariel asked as he set to work.

"Seven, I think. Maybe eight. It's hard to tell . . . they kept coming. A dirty, ragged lot they were. We felt sorry for them at first. Even offered them food. But they attacked anyway. If it hadn't been for Col, they would have killed us all."

"He's going to be all right. You get some rest. I'll take care of you as soon as I'm done with him."

"I've only got a few bruises. Do your best for Col, healer."

Gariel attended to Colberane's wounds and left him sleeping. When he had seen to the other man, he left the shed and sought out the red-haired girl, to reassure her. She was nowhere to be found. He inquired, and a village woman told him that Cazron had taken the woman and her two small children to her home.

"Poor child, she didn't want to go until she knew her husband was safe," the woman said. "Cazron told her how you saved old Tembrash, and she felt better. She barely made it to Cazron's door before she just collapsed."

"Is she hurt?"

"No, nothing like that. Just exhausted."

Gariel returned to the forge deep in thought. He felt concern for this strange girl, an instinctive protectiveness. He had aided scores of people since coming to Banseele's village, in his life he had given help to hundreds, but none had ever affected him so deeply. It was odd, he thought.

The next day, she came to the forge in the morning to thank him. When she entered, she seemed to bring the sunlight with her. Gariel wondered at this. He had grown accustomed to seeing men and women enveloped in the misty aura of their weaknesses and wrongdoings, and this girl seemed to be clad in light. Then she spoke, and recognition came upon him: Her voice was a softer, more childlike version of Panorn's.

"No need to thank me, child. Tell me your name," he said.

"Ciantha."

"That's not a common name."

"No. I don't know where it comes from. I asked Col's parents, but they couldn't tell me."

"Did you know your own parents?"

"They went away when I was very small. Roak—Col's father—told me that they were summoned to do some work of great importance, but great danger, too, and they left me where I'd be safe."

"You're safe now, Ciantha."

"I've always felt safe . . . as if someone strong was near me, ready to protect me. I don't mean Col, I mean someone I can't see." She looked aside and said softly, "You must think I'm childish to say that, but it's how I feel."

"Perhaps it's true. You've escaped great dangers."

"Do you ever have the feeling that you're protected?"

"Sometimes."

She smiled at him and took her leave. Gariel glimpsed a brightness hovering near her. It vanished as she stepped outside into the morning sun, but he had seen enough to know that the guardians, that legion of light, were with her.

His heart was light that day. His daughter was safe and happy, and he could protect and aid her without her knowledge. It was all he had hoped for since the death of Panorn. He knew now that his decision to remain in the village had been the right one.

That evening he visited Colberane and found him weak but conscious. His injuries were healing well, and he had a prodigious hunger, but his mood was black.

"Cheer up, lad," Gariel said. "You're going to recover and be as strong as ever. It won't be long."

"I'll need all my strength to fight again. I'll be fighting all my life to keep Ciantha and our children from harm," he said.

"They're out of danger here."

Colberane looked at him coldly, scorning such comfort. "No place is free from danger. Something terrible is loose in the world, healer, and it's everywhere."

"What do you mean?"

"Something is working at people, making them cruel and destructive. I've seen it. Those men who attacked us were just ordinary men, like ourselves. They could see that we had nothing worth stealing. We even offered to share our food with them, but that's not what they wanted. They wanted to shed our blood. No—it's not that they *wanted* to. They *had* to. Something drove them."

"Why do you say that? Perhaps they were simply desperate starving men, pushed past reason by their suffering."

"I've seen such people, healer. These men were possessed by a demon."

"How can you be so sure?"

Col turned on him furiously. "Because I felt it myself! I felt it digging into me, making me hate. If Ciantha hadn't been with me, I think I would have surrendered to it. The others felt it, too, I could tell. But Ciantha kept it at bay."

"When did this happen?"

"Many times. It was worst when we were crossing the plain. It seemed to come over us like the sea wind." Colberane shook his head and covered his eyes. "It was terrible . . . as if something foul had suddenly become beautiful and irresistible, and yet retained all its foulness. I knew, and still I wanted to give in to it."

"But you didn't, and your companions didn't, either."

"I think it was Ciantha who gave us strength. There's something about her. I don't understand it, but I feel it."

Gariel made no response. After a brief silence, he rose, saying, "You need rest, Colberane. Ciantha will visit you tomorrow. Don't trouble yourself about her and your children, please. They're safe here."

"Thanks, healer. I meant what I said. I'm not raving."

"I know you're not. Something terrible is moving in the

world, and in men. It must be driven out."

Gariel returned to the forge, where he worked through the night. He had much to do, and he feared that time was running out.

19

To a Place of Crawling Stone

Just before dawn of a midsummer day, Gariel left the village of Banseele. He carried a staff shod, crested, and banded with the iron that had once circled Panorn's neck as a torc. Around his own neck hung the iron amulet bearing the green stone of Valimagdon. A light traveling cloak lay over his shoulders, and on his back was a pack holding food and water sufficient for the journey to the sea.

He carried no weapon, trusting to his magic to protect and shelter him on the way. He had no fear that Ankaria might sense the magic and learn of his coming and be prepared, for he was certain that whatever cautionary measures he might take would be of small use. In a short time, he would face the full might of Ankaria, and oppose it with his own. The world could not be spared the risk of this clash; to delay was to surrender.

He left the forest and traveled on the broad plain that lay between the mountains and the low hills of the seacoast. After a time he could sense something in the air, like the threat of an approaching storm. He climbed the gentle slope of a hill and continued along the crest, and soon he saw, far ahead, lying over the dark sea, a darker pall.

The sky was lowering from horizon to horizon, but in this

place it was murky, as if the air had congealed and darkened over a neck of land that reached out into the sea. As he moved closer he could see the thick cloud and discern the sluggish irregular rise and fall of its upper outline and the dark flashes that darted down to lance the earth. Though the skies were ominous, the sea was calm. It lapped gently at the shore with scarcely a sound but the clatter of tumbled pebbles. All the way to the horizon, not a wave could be seen to ruffle the smooth leaden surface. No breeze stirred, though the air was charged with eager energy. The world seemed poised, waiting.

Gariel stopped at the point where the hills left their smooth coastal path to reach out to sea. Here they formed a narrow promontory that curved southward, dipping almost to water level before rising to terminate in a broad flattened mound. On that mound, like a spiny growth rising out of the dead land, under a shroud of living, flickering darkness, stood the castle of the Annihilator.

Its tall towers sprang upward and outward at impossible angles, bent and twisted in upon themselves like a tangle of vipers. They seemed to move before Gariel's eyes. He recalled the tormented ravings of the unfortunate Tembrash, who had looked upon this sight unprepared and unprotected and paid for his error with nightmare and madness.

Gariel felt that the place was aware of him; as Tembrash had said, the walls seemed to see him, and reach out for him, the inanimate stone infused with malevolent appetite. As he came closer, Gariel found that this was no illusion fostered by the gloom; the stone truly crawled, and flowed, and moved with life. The walls observed him with stony eyes, and the towers bent slowly in his direction, like curious angular serpents.

Gariel walked on and was not attacked. The groping towers twitched back from his passing, and a wall opened like a mouth to admit him. The transition from exterior to interior was marked by no noticeable increase in darkness. The shadow of Ankaria was everywhere within and without. Gariel raised his iron-tipped staff and spoke a phrase. The curved crest of the staff began to glow with a cool and brilliant light.

He was in a bare hall. The floor flowed upward into the walls and they in turn into the many-vaulted ceiling. All was still, but always at the corner of his vision was a fitful motion that froze as he turned to view it directly.

The wall on his left suddenly swelled and flowed into the form of a hand that clutched at him. He struck out with his staff and the hand burst apart; the fragments clattered to the floor, where they were absorbed like snowflakes fallen on water. From the far wall burst a snaky coiling thing, eyeless and featureless but for the toothed maw that opened, cavelike, at its end. Gariel swung the staff again, and again the thing shattered like a shaft of glass and fell in a rain of vanishing bits of stone.

"Ankaria! Come forth, Ankaria!" Gariel cried.

No echo came back. The enclosing stone swallowed his voice as it had absorbed the fragments of his assailants.

Ankaria knew of his presence, there could be no doubt of that. Gariel paused for a moment, and before he could issue his challenge a second time, he heard a soft voice behind him say, "I am here."

Gariel turned and saw not his brother's form but a creature of living gold. It stood naked in the glow of light reflected from itself, an androgynous human form of consummate splendor.

"It is I, Ankaria," it assured him. "Bodies of flesh do not endure my presence long, so I have created my own perfect body."

"You've created a monstrosity."

The golden creature laughed, and its laughter was sweet to hear, as its voice had been sweet. "Few but yourself would say so. Men may delight in the brief pleasures of the body, but they kill for gold."

"Take what form you like," Gariel said contemptuously. "It doesn't matter. I've come to do what I should have done when I found you in the White City."

"I am stronger than I was then, Mage."

"Not strong enough to save yourself."

"I am strong enough to destroy the whole world and all in it, rather than submit to losing it."

"I think not."

"But will you risk a clash with such power?" the golden creature said in its honeyed voice. "Are you right to risk it? Such questions trouble you, do they not?"

"There's no doubt in my mind, Ankaria, not any more.

You'll willingly consume the whole world to feed yourself. If I save a single life from you, it's worthwhile."

"You might still save many and destroy none. You might do great good with the power you are prepared to expend in trying to destroy me," said Ankaria.

"You can't tempt me."

"Hear me speak," it said, raising golden hands in a graceful gesture. "It is foolish for you to oppose me. We will squander our power in destroying one another, and the world that you hope to save, and I to possess, will be left barren. Let us avoid this, Mage. Hear my offer: I will give you life, the great gift, the only gift. Generations of men have prayed to me for what I freely offer you."

"And why do you offer it?"

"Because I wish to live unhindered. Think, Mage. I can give you life for as long as the stars burn. You will never grow older, never feel sickness, or weakness, or weariness. You will go from strength to strength, on to ever greater knowledge. In time you will know all things. You will learn—as I did—to change your outward form and move from body to body at will. Nothing will limit your power."

"Nothing but subservience to you."

"You need not serve me. I ask no worship, only that you swear never to oppose me. Be as powerful as I, be ten times more powerful—be a god! It does not matter, if only you swear never to use that power against me. Is that so much to ask?"

"I must oppose you. I will always be your enemy," Gariel said.

The golden creature returned his cold gaze sadly. "Why do you hate me and fear me so? You blame me for all the evil and suffering in the world, yet now I offer you the chance to do good, and you scorn me. Think of the good you can accomplish in a hundred lifetimes—in a thousand! Clash with me and you will surely die, and cause great harm to the world, and all for nothing. If you succeed—you will not, but even if you did—if you drive me from the world, another will call me back some day, and I will return in anger, with my strength increased. Accept what I offer, if you love the world and the race of men."

"You deceived me once. You will not deceive me again."

"You deceived yourself, by your eagerness and vanity, and

your pity for the figure you saw. I seized the opportunity you offered. I kept the oath to the letter, Mage."

"You violated the spirit of it."

The lips of the golden figure pursed in disapproval. "A quibble, Mage. I outwitted you. Admit it, and accept my generosity."

"You offer life, but you can give only death. It's your nature, and you can't do otherwise."

"I can give life as freely as I take it."

Gariel shook his head patiently, as if at a child's boast. "You killed Moarra and our children—not with your own hand, but you were the cause. When I married again, you deceived your servant so he slew Panorn. You destroyed all living things in the White City. You are death and destruction, Ankaria: truly the Annihilator. Your deeds mock your promises."

"Live a thousand lifetimes, ten thousand—live for ten million lifetimes!" the golden figure purred. "Heal the sick, and ease the world's pain. Be teacher, guide, comforter. Become a god to these pitiful creatures you find so important. I will never interfere. As the lifetimes are added one to another, what will you remember of the single one that stands at the beginning? Will you remember a woman? A child? A home?" The golden figure laughed melodiously, its eyes eager and bright. "None of these things are important, Mage. Nothing else matters—only life. Choose life!"

Ankaria's final words made all things clear to Gariel. In an instant, as if the sun had blazed in darkest night, he recognized what Panorn had tried to tell him with her dying words, and Valimagdon long before her, and he understood. He had learned the Sign of Denial at last—from Ankaria.

"I choose something more important than life, Ankaria. I would give up a million million lifetimes to drive you from the earth forever," he said firmly.

"No! You speak like a fool. Only life matters. To live on, and on—there is nothing else."

"I live for one reason, Ankaria—to stop you."

"You will die in the attempt."

Gariel laughed, a loud triumphant laugh that even the walls of this palace could not damp. "But that doesn't matter to me. If I must die in order to stop you, then I'm willing to die. There's something more important to me than life, and that makes me stronger. You've lost, Ankaria!"

The golden figure flung up its hands, and all around Gariel the abiding stone flowed into life and closed about him. He drove it back with his staff. The deadly blast of Ankaria's withering magic beat against him unavailing as he sent the things of living stone writhing in flight to escape the destruction of his iron touch. As they fell back, Gariel turned his full power against their master, and the golden figure was shaken; but only for an instant. Recovering, it sent the stone hurtling in a great curling wave to crash down and bury the enemy.

Gariel burst into incandescence. Enchanted fire turned enchanted stone to glowing liquid, and Gariel sent it like a tide against Ankaria's glittering gold flesh.

Suddenly all was gone, and they stood on the bare rock under the crackling, roiling canopy of darkness. The man and the effigy were scarcely a body's length apart, eyes locked, waiting.

"You see that I have not lost, Mage," the golden figure said in a calm and confident manner.

"The struggle is only beginning," Gariel replied.

"That is true. And already the world feels its effects," said Ankaria, gesturing toward the sea that all but surrounded them.

Gariel looked, and saw the sea rising. Waves crested with white were rolling into shore and breaking high up the strand.

"It will be much worse if we go on," Ankaria said. "Think again of what I offer. I give you a chance to do good far outweighing any evil I might have done."

Gariel smiled. "You offer to make me a god—if only I agree to be your pawn."

"You are a pawn already, and what is your reward but a life of suffering, and death at my hands?"

"I am no pawn. I come here of my own free will."

"Vain creature!" Ankaria cried in sudden fury. "You are insignificant. You are less than nothing. Could a mere human have withstood my power even for an instant? You are a vessel. The power working in you and through you is the power of my ancient enemy. It was there when I first lived . . . as if it had been waiting. I've forgotten everything else of those times, but I remember that . . . the feeling of the other . . . always there to check me, and thwart me . . . letting me come within sight of my goal, and then snatching victory from me . . . again and again. It helps those who oppose me, giving them its strength and its wisdom, and yet it never faces me. I have never seen it, for always it operates from behind a human mask."

"I'm wearing no mask. I'm a man, and that's reason enough to be your enemy. It's you who wear the mask, Ankaria, to hide your loathsomeness."

The golden figure stepped back as Gariel spoke, placing its hands on a jagged rock jutting like an upthrust column from the ground. It spoke words that growled like wrenched boulders, and when it ceased to speak, the ground quivered and bulged, and a shape dragged itself forth. It was a thing the color of earth and stone, in a shape unlike any Gariel had ever seen. Its legs were short and thick, its arms long, bowed in front of its massive chest. Its back was higher than the flattened hanging head that was no more than an eyeless yawning cavity. As the creature stirred and stretched a massive arm toward Gariel, who retreated from it, Ankaria repeated the spell, and the ground humped a second time, and another such thing broke free. Again Ankaria spoke the words, and as Gariel stepped back he heard the ground erupt behind him and a third creature emerged.

Gariel struck the nearest as it groped for him, and the iron of his staff rang against its stony flesh. The thing flinched and withdrew, but only for an instant, and Gariel was unable to press on and drive it into the sea because he had to turn his attention at once to the others; and while he fought them, Ankaria called forth still others. When Gariel was surrounded by nine of the things, like moving menhirs tightening a deadly circle around him, Ankaria once again turned its withering power against him. Gariel thrust at three of the shambling monstrosities in quick succession and sent a counterspell against Ankaria, but the other creatures beset him, and the spell faltered. Ankaria pressed its attack.

Gariel could not escape, nor could he fight through to confront Ankaria. The stone monsters clawed at him, massive arms flailing blindly, and he could do no more than thrust them back and hold them at bay. Ankaria's power was pouring into them, but their untiring onslaught was draining Gariel. He was weakening, and he knew that unless he broke free of these things, he was lost.

He spoke a spell to shield himself. The stone creatures, no

longer feeling the power of his staff, lurched forward and battered at him on all sides. Ankaria hurled its own power against the barrier. Gariel felt it weakening, but channeled all his reserves of magic into it, to hold out the enemy while he made his last attempt.

Raising the ironbound staff in one hand and the amulet in the other, he cried, "You who gave me the sign and the weapon, save me! I've given all to this struggle, and I'm not strong enough. Help me, now, or all is lost!"

The barrier between him and the powers of Ankaria held, but Gariel was near the end of his strength. He searched his memory for one last spell, some way of getting to Ankaria, or escaping to face it another day, and in his concentration he did not see the stone things hesitate and turn their blank faces upward.

The first thing he noticed was that they were no longer attacking. Then, to his amazement and joy, they fell back and began to lurch about in confusion. Gariel heard a roar, a sound like the tearing of heavy cloth. It grew louder and nearer, filling the air and shaking the earth, and suddenly, bursting through the darkness overhead, an iron rain fell on his assailants, battering them with fist-sized chunks of smoking metal, cracking and shattering and pulverizing the frenzied things until the surface of the ground was covered with broken stone under a blanket of dust.

Ankaria stood its ground. "Your power is almost gone," it said in a soft, weary voice. "Mine, too, is much depleted. But you are in the body of a man, and I am living metal. I am the stronger now."

It raised its hands in a gesture almost of supplication, and as Gariel stood confused, lulled by its voice and his own exhaustion, Ankaria sprang forward and clasped its hands in a death grip on his throat.

Gariel seized the forearms. They were flexible as flesh, but cold and strong as metal. The fingers dug relentlessly into his throat, piercing the skin. Smiling, Ankaria lifted him off his feet and drew him closer to its golden face so it might savor his death more fully.

With his last strength, Gariel reached for the amulet and pressed it to Ankaria's breast. An unearthly sound, half rending metal and half human scream, shrilled in his ears; light dazzled him, and he felt himself flung aside.

He lay for a time on the broken stones, gasping and trying to swallow. His head rang and his eyes burned. Blood from his lacerated neck congealed in his beard. He ached from head to foot and felt sick with exhaustion, as if every drop of life but one had been drained from him. But he was alive.

He raised his head and saw the glint of sunlight on gold. Ankaria lay almost within reach, and did not move. Gariel dragged himself to his feet and leaning on his staff, looked down on the golden effigy. It lay like a broken doll, limbs askew and head twisted at a crazy angle. Empty eyes of blue stone stared upward into the sun that glittered on its golden flesh. On its breast was a single mark: a small starburst of dull black, the size of a man's hand.

Gariel touched the amulet at his breast. The iron was warm against his fingertips. He raised it, and found that the green stone was cracked and clouded over, and the surface that had touched Ankaria was blackened. Valimagdon had saved him in his time of need.

Gariel sank down and leaned back against a sloping rock, letting the memories flood back, recalling the visit to the land of the dead, and the sign of the iron from the heavens, and the cryptic prophecy that he and Panorn had worked so hard to decipher. She had grasped its meaning in her dying moments; he had learned it from the lips of the enemy.

Ankaria was gone, overthrown and driven from the earth. Nothing remained of it but a twisted golden statue in the midst of rubble. Here was victory at last, come to a weary man alone on a rock in the sea. Whether it was the final victory or not no one could say. Ankaria had been defeated before, exiled and imprisoned by strong enchantment, and men had brought it back, deluded by their vanity and greed into believing that it would be grateful, and would serve them. He thought of Bellenzor, and remembered that wretched sorcerer among the dead who had brought Ankaria upon his people and been punished with an eternity of pain and remorse, and he wept for his lost brother.

There were many to weep for, but there was cause for rejoicing, as well. Lives had been lost, but life went on. Ankaria was gone. For a time, the world was safe.

Gariel rose. Overhead, the sun was bright in a clear blue sky. The air was cool and sweet, and the wind was rising. He made his way back along the neck of land, now washed by the sea in several places, and when he reached the hills, he turned to look back.

The sea was higher than he had ever known it to rise. Waves were breaking close beneath him. He felt the spray against his face and hands. In some places, waves were breaking over the hilltops, leaving pools of sea water on the plain behind them.

Gariel cried out as the earth heaved beneath his feet, reliving for an instant the fear of Ankaria's stone monsters; but this was no enchantment, it was the mortal aftermath. His struggle with Ankaria had shaken the world.

A wave higher than the rest broke against the mound where the golden image lay, and another broke close behind it. Stone split and slid into the sea, and Gariel saw the glint of gold among the fallen stone. The connecting strip of land was no longer to be seen, only here and there an outcropping of rocks, and the seas rising and crashing over them. The high waves reached shore, breaking hard against the hillsides, cascading over them onto the plain. The first wave drenched Gariel; the second nearly knocked him from his feet. Clutching tightly to his staff with one hand, he wiped the salt spray from his eyes with the other.

The mound was now an island. Gariel saw a giant wave crash over it and race for the shore. He scrambled down the hillside and headed inland. When he stopped to look back, he saw that the hill on which he had stood was no longer there. The pounding sea had breached the coastal hills in several places, and the plain was flooding.

20

Parting Gifts

The sea was victor in the end. After Gariel's battle with the Annihilator it surged against the shore, overrunning the low range of hills that had held it back for so long and penetrating deep inland. It swept over the peninsula that joined Ankaria's mound to the mainland, and it battered the mound itself into an islet in the shape of a crooked hand, surrounded by jagged rocks and murderous currents. All up and down the long coast the sea hammered the shore, making deep broad bays where once there had been only shallow coves and inlets. Far to the north, it carried away much of the peninsula that led to the land of the Crystal Hills. Travel to that far land became ever more perilous as the gaps widened and the icy northern waters rushed through to add their force to the eddying flow and counterflow around the new-formed islands. It undercut high cliffs and widened narrow channels, turning quiet streams into impassable torrents. On the far side of the mountains, the surging sea divided the headland from the main by a great fissure with a deadly tidal bore in its depths.

The people of the region, knowing nothing of the cause of these things, were filled with dread, and some spoke of the end of the world. But at last the waters ceased their assault and encroached no further. The plain was flooded to the foot of the mountains, and the once smooth sea was now an archipelago of barren islets and sharp rocks swept with ever-changing currents no craft could hope to navigate.

Inland, the effects were less cataclysmic. Violent storms had struck the forests in late summer and there had been flooding in the lowlands, but Banseele's village had escaped all harm. When Gariel returned in the autumn, he came to a countryside almost untouched by the recent upheavals, and he knew that he had won the victory most important to him. His friends and the people closest to his heart had been spared.

The guards gave him a hearty welcome and sent a boy to inform Banseele, who was off to the north of the village, supervising the clearing of new land. Gariel walked alone to the forge, stopping to exchange a few words with old neighbors on his way. The mood of the village was hopeful, and spirits were high among all he met.

As he neared the forge, he heard the ring of a hammer. Smoke was rising from the chimney. He entered and looked on silently for a moment until Colberane noticed him in the doorway.

"You're back!" the young man cried, laying down the hammer. "We all wondered where you'd gone—and when the rains came, and the flooding, and the tremors in the earth—but you're safe!"

"I had something to do. Now it's done. You've made a good recovery, Col. How does your arm feel? Any stiffness?"

"It's as good as ever."

"And the shoulder? Let me see how it healed."

Colberane turned to display a thick white scar that ran over his shoulder and ended in a knot of white flesh at the base of his shoulder-blade. The deep wound had healed completely.

"I've been working at the forge," Colberane said, without turning. "I hope you don't mind. There was a lot to be done, and the work was good for me."

"I'm glad you were able to help. If I'd thought of it, I would have suggested just that."

"Ciantha and the children and I have been staying here. Now that you're back, we'll find a place."

"No need for that. There's work enough here for two men, and plenty of room for all of us."

"I'm not a good smith. There's a lot I don't know."

"I'll teach you all you need to know. Raise your arm, now, so I can see your ribs," Gariel said. He inspected the thin scar, then stepped back and said. "You've healed well. You must have had good care."

"Ciantha looked after me. She helped with others, too. She doesn't know anything about healing, really, but she seems to do good for people. Sometimes I think she has a magic about her."

Gariel smiled. "Maybe I can teach her what I know of healing. The two of you can do a lot of good here. Do you plan to stay?"

"We've talked about it often. I think we will."

Gariel's loft had been kept ready for him, and he went up to rest after his long journey. That evening, after a long, relaxed dinner, he told Ciantha and Colberane something of his travels. He left out much, and made no mention of Ankaria.

"Something changed while you were gone," Ciantha said when he reached the end of his account. "Don't you feel it? It's almost as though the world has recovered from a long sickness—as though some poison has been drawn from us."

"I feel it, too, Ciantha," Gariel replied softly. Their eyes met, and though no more was said, he felt that she knew why he had left them, and what he had done.

Colberane was a good pupil. He was immensely strong, and quick to learn. With the village growing and expanding, he had all the work he could handle, and often more than he wished. Within a few years, he was doing most of the work of the forge and training a strong youth of the village to assist him. Gariel, freed of these labors, gave his time to healing and passing on his knowledge of the healing arts to Ciantha.

It was some years before Gariel left the village again. His powers and his bodily strength had been much depleted in the clash with Ankaria, and he wanted time to recover. Time, and the simple round of everyday life, and the daily presence of Ciantha were all the medicine he required.

He never acknowledged his true relation to her, for he felt that to do so would be to mark her and set her apart from her husband and children. He still recalled Panorn's words that had sounded within him just before they left their sanctuary in the far north: Ciantha was to live as an ordinary woman among ordinary people. Knowledge of her true parentage would make such a life impossible, so he must conceal it. He contented himself with being a benefactor to her and those she loved.

When the older boy, Ordred, had begun to assist his father at the forge and the younger, Staver, was learning the rudiments of healing from his mother, Gariel felt that his strength was sufficient for a journey. He had heard many travelers' tales over the years, and he longed to see for himself how the world fared now that Ankaria was gone. As important in his mind as the things he had heard was the fact that certain places were never mentioned and indeed seemed to be shunned.

In addition to his curiosity, he had a less clearly definable sensation of something still undone. He had no idea what it might be, but he felt that some work of great import remained to him, and he must seek it out, and do it while his strength endured.

He left on a fine spring morning. His parting this time was a public event, for he had gained great respect and love among the villagers. They were sad to see their Iron Mage depart, but he consoled them with his promise to return.

Ciantha and Colberane walked with him past the outlying fields and farmsteads, to the edge of the cleared land. In the shadow of the forest, they took their leave.

"You must return. The village needs you," Colberane said.

"I've promised to return, and I will. But the village has small need of me now, Col. I'll return because it's my home, and my friends are here."

"You're our mage. We'll always need you," Ciantha said.

Gariel embraced them both, then turned and took the forest trail. He did not look back.

The world had changed during his stay in the village. Evil no longer hung over it in ominous clouds of clotted darkness. Farms and hamlets welcomed him; settlements stood with open gates unguarded; solitary travelers along the roads hailed him without fear. Children who had never known the terror of marauders greeted him as an honored guest. Everywhere he traveled he heard the same message: Peace had returned; the world was healing and rebuilding after a long age of pain.

No one knew precisely how or why the change had come. Gariel heard much speculation on the subject. Some of it was amusing, some absurd; none was even remotely near the truth.

On one point all were agreed: The turning point had come in the time of the great storms, when the waters rose and the earth shook. Gariel listened to the explanations and added nothing of his own.

After leaving the outermost settlement, he traveled alone for many days until he came to a plain. It reached to the horizon in unbroken flatness save for a low hillock at its center. Toward this Gariel directed his footsteps, walking on a broad roadway of crushed stone, through which blades of grass had thrust their way.

The fields were green around him, and the high grass swayed in the breeze. The day was warm, and he stopped to rest in the scanty shade of a young tree—there were no old forest giants here to shield him from the summer sun—and he listened, remembering his last crossing. Life had returned to the plain.

New life was everywhere around him, but it abounded in the low rise at the center, where dust had blown over the ruins of the White City, softening their jagged outline. Seeds had taken root, and sun and rain had nurtured them, and the shattered stone was carpeted with soft green. Insects buzzed in the air, and small burrowing creatures darted for cover at Gariel's approach. No humans were near, and he sensed that men would not return to the site of the White City. The Empire and the Alliance had failed. Their time had passed, and a new and simpler life had prevailed.

Gariel stayed among the ruins for some days, remembering the youth he had passed here: his studies, his love for Moarra, their flight. It seemed so much more than a lifetime ago. He thought of Bellenzor, but he did not weep for his brother as he once had done. He was no longer so certain of Bellenzor's damnation. What Bellenzor had done, he had done out of love for the city and the people in his care; if Ankaria had turned that love to destructive ends, Bellenzor's intent was no less good.

Bellenzor had suffered greatly for his error, Gariel reflected. And in the end, it was not for him to judge his brother; his own misjudgment had caused harm enough.

He left the ruins and traveled to the valley where Panorn lay. Over the years, the valley walls had eroded and fallen in, and he could not say precisely where he had placed her body, but her magic still lingered. All was silent in its confines.

He made his way to the center, noiselessly crunching the loose rubble underfoot. There, he raised his hands and said in a voice swallowed by the magic still lying over the place, "Panorn, you taught me what I had to know. Life is sweet, and long life is good, but we must be willing to sacrifice our lives for the right cause, or it has no meaning. Ankaria can never understand that, and so we defeated him. You were with me at the end."

He watched as a bit of the rim crumbled and slid in a silent plume of dust down the sloping valley wall. "Goodbye, Panorn," he said, and turned to go. Except for the journey back to the village, he planned to travel no more.

The village became a busy place, with an inn and a market, and there was much coming and going. Many of the visitors came to speak with the Iron Mage, seeking his help and his advice, and Gariel helped them when he could, healing and counseling and, when necessary, cleansing troubled memories from their minds. He worked magic very seldom, for the feeling of a final task awaiting still lingered, and he believed that his powers might yet be called upon.

Banseele died one day, quite suddenly, in the midst of his work. The villagers asked Gariel to be their leader, but he declined. They turned then to Colberane, and their choice proved a happy one. The village continued to grow and prosper.

Over the years, Gariel had cultivated a sizeable garden behind the forge, where he grew medicinal herbs. As he walked in his garden one evening, his mind far away, he noticed a figure in the shadows of the arbor at the end of the path. He approached, and a young man stepped into the fading light.

"I must speak with you, Mage," he said.

"Ord, you can speak with me any time," Gariel said as he recognized Ciantha's oldest son.

"This is important. I don't want anyone else to know."

"We'll sit here in the arbor. No one will disturb us."

Once inside, Ordred looked about cautiously, then leaned close to Gariel and blurted, "I want to leave the village. I'm nearly twenty, and I want to make a life of my own."

"You could have a good life here, Ord. Everyone respects your family."

"But no one sees *me*, Mage! If I'm respected by the people

THE TIME OF THE ANNIHILATOR

here, it's only because of my mother and father. I don't want to be liked—or disliked, either—for what other people do, I want people to see me as myself."

Gariel nodded sympathetically. He had heard similar words from many of the young people of the village, and he understood. "Surely someone here likes you as yourself, Ord," he said.

"Mirla loves me. We're leaving together."

Mirla was the youngest daughter of the finest carpenter in the village. A tall and slender girl with pale hair as gold and curling as the shavings in her father's shop, Mirla was a rare beauty, and wise. Gariel had seen Ord glance at her a few times, and speak very shyly to her once. He was surprised by the news.

"Is it Mirla's idea to leave the village?"

"Hers and mine. And others', too. Her brother wants to go—he's a good carpenter. There's ten of us, so far. We want to start our own settlement in the forest beyond the mountains. It's not as though we were going off forever. We'd be back to visit, and to trade. I think others would join us, once they learned what we'd done."

"I suppose they would."

"Then will you speak to my parents? They think I'm going to stay here for the rest of my life, like Staver and little Ciantha. I don't know how to tell them without hurting them, but they'll listen to you, and understand."

"Are you so sure the others will stay?"

"Oh, yes. Well, Staver certainly will. Some people say he's already a better healer than . . . than my mother."

Gariel laughed softly. "Better than the Iron Mage, you mean, don't you?"

"There are a few silly people who say that, but no one pays attention to them. Staver might be as good as you are some day, if he works very hard, but no one will ever be better."

"Staver might surprise you. He has a great gift for healing."

"I think what he really wants to be is a mage, like you. He's never said so, but . . . well, sometimes he makes me think of you. He acts a little bit like you."

"If Staver wants to be a mage, I'll teach him all I know. I'll speak to little Ciantha, too, and see if I can help her in any way."

Ord smiled and shook his head. "She doesn't need any help from anyone. She's the prettiest girl in the village, and the smartest, next to Mirla. If there were any kings or lords left, they'd be coming here to pay tribute to her."

"Then I'll warn her against flatterers. And I'll speak to your parents about your plans, too," said Gariel.

As things turned out, it was no nobly-born suitor who won Ciantha, but a very intense, energetic young man who stopped in the village on his way north. He was a farmer's son, and his name was Forraker. He was full of ideas—which no one quite understood—for locating metals, and extracting them from the ground in new ways, and refining them to greater purity than anyone had ever done before, and his ideas brought him to the attention of Colberane. He was a frequent visitor to the forge during the winter, and in the spring, when Ordred married Mirla, young Ciantha married Forraker.

Ordred was the first to leave the village. His band numbered fourteen now, seven couples of about his own age, eager to start west as soon as the roads were dry. The day before he left, Gariel gave him a sword he had forged himself, using iron stripped from his staff to form the simple crosspiece, a slender bar, square in cross-section, with an orb at either end. The blade was wave-patterned and very strong. He gave it to Ord with the hope that it would never be used in anger, and would become a prize passed down through the generations of his family.

Twenty days later, Ciantha and Forraker left for the land of the Crystal Hills, joining a small party headed in that direction. Forraker was confident. He explained that the sea was receding from the plain as the tides wore away the submerged hills, and passage to the north was now easier than ever. Bridges had been built to link the Crystal Hills with the mainland, and he intended to study them with an eye to improvements; since he planned to extract considerable quantities of ore, and produce refined metals of the finest quality, he wanted to be sure of dependable access for interested traders.

Gariel presented Ciantha with a cloakpin, small and delicate and very beautiful. He had made this, too, from the iron on his staff, inlaying a close design in gold and silver wire, and setting it with garnets. She wore the pin at her breast when she left the village.

THE TIME OF THE ANNIHILATOR

From this time on, Gariel spent part of each day with Staver, the younger son of Ciantha and Colberane, instructing him in magic lore. Staver worked hard and learned quickly, and at the end of two years Gariel found that he had no more to teach. His own training had been brief; the power he possessed came not from study but as a gift. Yet there was much to be learned from the ancient books and scrolls, and he knew where a treasury of magic knowledge awaited them. He had one more journey yet to make.

He and Staver visited settlements where the arrival of the Iron Mage was cause for feasting and celebration. Gariel worked no magic in these places. It seemed superfluous; his presence alone was enough to heal and encourage all who saw him.

They traveled at an unhurried pace and came at last to the edge of the plain. Gariel pointed to the low hummock at the center and said, "That's where the White City stood before it was destroyed by sorcery."

"Is that where we're going?"

"It is. There's knowledge under those ruins that exists nowhere else in the world."

Staver turned to him, puzzled. "But after all this time... can anything be left?"

Gariel nodded, smiling. "Those old books and scrolls are guarded by spells that could withstand anything Ankaria did to them."

"Who's Ankaria?"

"A power that once did great evil in the world. It's gone now, I hope never to return. But it may, one day, if men summon it." Gariel stood looking at the low rise for a time, silent, remembering it as it once was. Then, with a sigh, he said, "Come, let's be on our way. We can reach the hill before dark."

They made their camp near the ruins of the citadel. The next day, they began to dig. The work was hard, and their progress slow, but after many days they broke through to a sheltered place where scrolls, tablets, and books lay in jumbled heaps, with other items that Staver did not recognize.

"This used to be the tallest tower in the city," Gariel said. "I was hardly more than a boy when I entered it for the first time."

"Do they all hold knowledge of magic?" Staver asked, looking around in the faint shafts of light from above.

"They do, but you don't need to learn everything. We'll stay here for a time, so you can acquaint yourself with them. There's about a dozen you'll have to take back with you. The rest will be safe here until you need them."

The tower, though buried, was intact. When Ankaria's destruction had come upon the city, it had sunk into the ground, protected by a spell cast by one of the Thirty-three. Gariel and Staver rummaged through the storied darkness, finding lamps and oil and even a number of intact wine jars. Streams on the plain provided them with water. Fish, birds, and small game abounded; fruits and berries grew near at hand. On hot or rainy nights, they slept in the room of books, where the temperature was always comfortable and the rain could not reach.

With Staver's help, Gariel moved three massive, heavy volumes onto the wide work table. "These are the ones to start with," he said. "Study these until you have them by heart, then you can bring the others home to work on. But until you know everything that's in these three, you won't understand what's in the others."

"Will it take long?" Staver asked.

"You've got a good mind, Staver. If you work hard, you'll be ready to go home before the snows. But you may have to spend a good many years on the books you bring to the village."

"Couldn't we bring these home? We could go back sooner if we did."

"No. For one thing, they're too big and heavy."

"We could use magic."

Gariel looked at him severely, and did not respond to the suggestion for a time. At last he said, in the manner of one expounding an inviolable rule, "A good wizard doesn't use magic to save himself a bit of sweat. Magic is precious. Don't ever forget that. Light the lamps and get to work."

Staver applied himself to the three huge volumes while Gariel busily searched among the rest. At first, Staver came to the mage with a question at nearly every word, and Gariel patiently explicated the embrangled phrases in their crabbed, ancient script. As Staver struggled on, bent over the giant pages until his back ached and his eyes burned, he had fewer questions each day. Gariel observed his pupil unobtrusively. He could almost see the youth's confusion dissipate as terms and symbols grew familiar and connections formed in his mind. He watched

Staver turn clumsily back in the oversized pages, or jump up impatiently to refer to one of the other huge volumes, in order to check some uncertain point, and then return to the lines under scrutiny with new assurance. Gariel was pleased, but he said nothing.

One day he laid two small volumes by Staver's hand, saying, "That's a difficult passage you're working on. These may help clarify it."

Staver, totally absorbed in his inquiry, opened one of the books. His interest was caught at once. He read on for a time, skipping pages, turning back, then rushing ahead, and at last he cried happily, "That's right! It seems to contradict the fifth law, but if you read it with the proper pauses ... it's the pauses, of course, it's the pauses!" He looked up, beaming, at Gariel. "I thought it had to be that way, but I wasn't.... Thank you, Mage."

"I spent one whole winter on that page, and I still wasn't completely sure of what it meant. You're making good progress," Gariel said.

"It's fascinating. I could stay here for the rest of my life, and never stop learning."

"You'll have to leave soon, Staver. I've found the books you'll need to bring to the village."

"There's plenty of time before the snows begin."

"And there's plenty still to learn from the three volumes in front of you, and if you work very hard, you might just make it."

Staver bent to his study again, but in a short time he looked up and said, "You always say, 'When *you* leave,' or 'When *you* go,' as if I were going back to the village alone."

"You are. I'm staying here."

"But the village needs you," cried Staver, shocked.

"No, it doesn't. Other people can heal and work metal as well as I ever could."

"You're our mage. No one else can be our mage."

"Why do you think I've been teaching you, Staver?"

Staver rose in his high-backed wooden chair and stared dumfounded at Gariel for a moment before dropping back into his place. At last he said, "I'm too young, Mage. I don't know enough."

"You know enough magic right now to protect the village

from any danger that might threaten. Once you've mastered everything in the books I give you, you'll know more than I do. You can come back here then, and learn more."

"I'll never know as much as you," Staver said.

"You have the gift, Staver. I know. I had it, too, but I turned away from it when I was young. All my power comes from outside me, given to me so I could accomplish a single task. Now I've done the last thing I had to do."

"What will you do here, all alone?"

"I was born in this city. I worked in this very room. It's good to be back, Staver. There's so much to remember that I'll never feel alone."

When the days were becoming ever shorter and the frost lay heavy on the ground in the gray mornings, Staver made ready to return to the village. The bundle over his shoulder held three scrolls and eleven books carefully chosen by Gariel for the young man's further study. At his belt hung a water bottle and a scrip with four days' food, enough to sustain him until he reached the nearest settlement.

Gariel went with him to the place where the main gate of the White City had once stood. The road extended straight before him, a pale track in the open brown land. Master and pupil embraced in farewell, and Gariel held out his staff to the youth. The broad iron bands were gone, but the iron crest and ferrule remained.

"Take this, Staver, and keep it near you. It protected me, and it will protect you if the need arises," he said.

"I mustn't take your last defense," Staver protested.

"I wear an amulet of the same metal. It's all the protection I need."

Staver accepted the staff. "Are you sure you won't return with me? The village will miss you very much."

"They'll have you, Staver."

The youth took a step from him, then turned. "Will you tell me one thing before I go?"

"If I can."

"You mentioned a being named Ankaria that did great evil in the world. You said that men might summon it back some day."

"True."

"Will it return in my lifetime? Is that why you taught me

magic, and gave me your staff?"

"I don't know if Ankaria will ever return. But if it does, there will be someone to oppose it."

"Can you tell me nothing more?"

Gariel reached out to lay his hand on Staver's shoulder. "Master everything in the books you carry, Staver, and then return here. You'll find the answers you seek."

Gariel passed the long winter among the ancient writings, filling page after page with his own detailed account of the struggle against Ankaria. He had stored food and firewood, and oil for his lamps was plentiful. He worked at his own pace, ignoring nights and days, and when he reached the end he wrapped the closely-written sheets of vellum carefully and laid them in the center of the work table for Staver to find on his return.

The account omitted nothing; Staver had to know all. Such knowledge would have been unbearable to the youth who had left, but the mage who was to return would understand.

That night Gariel climbed up and walked among the ruins. The moon was full, and the light on the snow lent a stark beauty to the scene. He looked out over the plain, content. His work was done at last.

He turned and saw Valimagdon, and the sight of his old master did not surprise him. The wizard stood in pale light that enfolded him like a cloak. He smiled on Gariel and raised a hand to salute him.

"You have done your work well, Gariel," he said. "No one has ever achieved more."

"I had help, Master. You helped me, always. Panorn helped me."

"You stood alone before Ankaria."

"Even then, I had help."

Valimagdon extended his hand. "Come, then, and join us. Perhaps one day you will lend your aid to one who does as you have done."

"Then Ankaria will return."

"If Ankaria returns, we will return. Come, Gariel."

All around them, the air was bright. Gariel felt friendship and love like a warm breeze against him, as if he were entering the home of old friends. He reached out to Valimagdon and stepped forward to enter the fellowship of light.

Fantasy from Ace
fanciful and fantastic!

- ☐ 38621-0 **JOURNEY TO APRILIOTH** $2.50
  Eileen Kernaghan
- ☐ 47073-4 **THE LAST CASTLE** $1.95
  Jack Vance
- ☐ 10264-6 **CHANGELING** $2.95
  Roger Zelazny
- ☐ 20405-8 **ELSEWHERE Vol. III** $3.95
  Terri Windling and Mark Alan Arnold (eds.)
- ☐ 44525-X **KING'S BLOOD FOUR** $2.75
  Sheri S. Tepper
- ☐ 56857-2 **NECROMANCER NINE** $2.75
  Sheri S. Tepper
- ☐ 90208-1 **WIZARD'S ELEVEN** $2.50
  Sheri S. Tepper

Prices may be slightly higher in Canada.

ACE SCIENCE FICTION
Book Mailing Service
P.O. Box 690, Rockville Centre, NY 11571

Please send me the titles checked above. I enclose _____. Include 75¢ for postage and handling if one book is ordered; 25¢ per book for two or more not to exceed $1.75. California, Illinois, New York and Tennessee residents please add sales tax.

NAME _____

ADDRESS _____

CITY _____ STATE/ZIP _____

(allow six weeks for delivery)

SF 1